SUMMERDALE

by

David Jay Collins

To Anthony ~

Happy Birthday!

ISBN: 978-0-9975350-0-6 digital
978-0-9975350-2-0 print

Cover artwork (digital and print) and print book design by TD Collins.
Follow David at davidjaycollins.com

TABLE OF CONTENTS

ACKNOWLEDGEMENTS

It is with deep gratitude that I thank the readers who offered me their indispensable comments on the original manuscript: John Edward Campbell, Dan Fulwiler, Kylon Hooks, and Chris Rinere.

Thank you to my editor, Windy Goodloe, who has been a true partner in bringing the first *Summerdale* novel to life. Many thanks to TD Collins, my incredibly talented graphic designer who created a book cover that captures the entire story within a single, striking image.

I thank my parents, Robert and Pamela, for their tremendous love and encouragement on this and every creative project. Thank you to my dear family and friends who strengthen my resolve and inspire me when I need it most. Jacqueline Teresa Jackson, my beloved Twin, I love you always.

And finally, I would like to express my appreciation for the warm welcome I've received in Andersonville, the dynamic Chicago neighborhood where *Summerdale* is set. Thank you to the dedicated, indefatigable staff of the Andersonville Chamber of Commerce, the amazing small businesses on and around Clark Street, especially Women and Children First, and the many local residents who've shown tremendous interest in the premise of *Summerdale*.

CHAPTER ONE

The old house appeared to Eric just as leafy, low branches parted for him at Summerdale & Wayne.

The house unveiled itself to Eric suddenly: a fine American Four-square with wide red bricks and stained glass windows on the first floor and white wooden clapboards on the second. A wide dormer window peeked out of the triangular, pointed roof topped by a Hercules weathervane. The stairs from the porch toppled down to the sidewalk, for the house appeared to Eric upon a hill, with overgrown ivy crawling down the stairs.

As Eric squinted to read a historical plaque, a hand appeared in a picture window and dropped a FOR RENT sign in front of white curtains. And the hand was gone.

The curtains were still shaking when the front door opened.

Eric stood at the intersection of Summerdale & Wayne, an intersection he didn't know, and stared at a house that had appeared to him suddenly. He had been walking around Andersonville, contemplating his next move, and had passed by FOR RENT signs in many apartment buildings. But this house was different; it was familiar, as if he knew its inside from its outside.

The front door, embellished with fine wood details and leaded glass, stayed open. Each beveled pane shined like a diamond. This, too, Eric could see from the sidewalk. An old man walked onto the porch. He smiled down at Eric. "Why don't you come in and have a look?"

Eric sprang from his trance. "Sorry, I was just noticing your house. I studied architecture a little in college." He drew his eyes up and down the street. "It's a nice Foursquare. It's different from all the others on the street."

"*Quite* different!" the old man shouted. "You're looking for a new place, aren't you?"

"Actually, I am..." Eric furrowed his thick brows. "How'd you know that?"

"I've been doing this a long time." He darted his eyes to the picture window. "That old FOR RENT sign doesn't last five minutes anymore. Come on inside. Get out of this morning heat."

Shrugging his wide shoulders, he bounded up the stairs to the porch and held out his hand. "I'm Eric."

The man put down his curled-up newspaper on a wicker table and shook. "Name's McGreevy."

"Nice to meet you, Mr. McGreevy."

"Come on in, Eric. Let's go see your room."

As Eric entered, he glanced at the historical plaque and looked curiously at the date. *That year can't be right*, he thought to himself. *Foursquares didn't exist in 1837.*

Mr. McGreevy closed the front door. "Just through here."

Eric followed the landlord through a parlor with dark wood paneling and built-in glass cabinets. A cream-tiled fireplace with white columns held a mottled mirror within it. Eric's reflection swiveled as he walked past. Paintings of pastoral landscapes hung on cords of many colors, hooked on high rails.

McGreevy stopped. "Oh! I just finished sealing the front stairs, so let's use the back." He chuckled, "It's always *something* with a house this old..."

Eric paused, admiring a cherry newel post and carved handrail descending from the darkness. A hall tree with hooks and a mirror had been built into the paneling, with a drawer and curved rods for umbrellas beneath.

And then Eric stopped and set one foot back toward the door.

McGreevy turned, sensing his reluctance. "It's fine, Eric! Look, with arms like yours, *I'm* the one who should be scared..."

Eric laughed. "All right."

He followed McGreevy up a switchback staircase off the kitchen, looking onto a lush backyard through dusty windows on every landing. Finally, on the third floor, they stopped.

"Whew! No elevators when this house was built," McGreevy said with a laugh. "And this, Eric, will be your room," he said, opening a simple wood-paneled door.

Eric stepped inside. His eyes widened. "This's an apartment!" he shouted, looking over drawers built into the wall, speakers built into the ceiling, three large windows looking onto leafy Wayne Avenue, and shiny, dark hardwood floors. A king-size, four-poster bed. A mini-fridge beneath a microwave. A big-screen TV over a fireplace. Couches, tables. He turned to McGreevy and smiled. Sold.

The old man pointed. "Have a look in the bathroom."

Eric darted across the freshly waxed floor to admire the marble double sink, claw-foot bathtub, and glass-enclosed shower system that he had seen only in upscale health clubs. "A *RainArray?*" Eric asked as he opened the heavy door. His words echoed as he pawed the pivoted sprays and digital control panel. "How do you have a RainArray?"

McGreevy laughed. "I try to keep up with what you young people want."

Eric closed the glass door gently and shook his head. "I wasn't expecting all this. I thought it was going to be a little bedroom with one light hanging down from the ceiling." He walked to the claw-foot tub and turned on the faucet. He turned it off once the hot water burned his fingers.

"So," Eric started, drying his hand on his shorts. "What's this cost?"

"Let's go back down to the kitchen and talk terms. But you like it?" McGreevy raised an eyebrow. "Everything you ever wanted?"

Eric chuckled. "It's like you read my mind."

Later that morning, Eric began moving in.

Upon his return, the kitchen of Summerdale was larger than he remembered—a bright, spacious room girded by heavy late-Victorian shelving and cabinetry that struck Eric as impossibly intact. The kitchen smelled of cinnamon and coffee, and Eric inhaled the sweet fragrance as he looked around the welcoming room.

The kitchen walls were a shade darker than lime; cabinets with wide-paneled doors and shiny brass pulls hovered over light countertops. Above a ceramic double sink, a greenhouse window held terra-cotta pots and foam cups with overgrown herbs and leggy violets; on every shelf a carpet of freed roots interlaced like veins.

Green and white floor tiles reflected light from pendants hanging from the pressed tin ceiling. A standard coffeemaker, a vintage refrigerator with a silver door-lock handle, an antique kitchen table at which they both sat.

"House rules are simple," McGreevy started, filling Eric's mug from a carafe and topping off his own; the coffee was hot but not steaming. He slid a plastic bag to Eric. "There's other tenants here, so we like it quiet. Shirt and shoes in the common areas. This is a key for the main doors and a key for your room upstairs. The room key is yours, and no one else has a copy. You're welcome to use the parlor as you like and, of course, the kitchen. Ummm..." McGreevy turned, scoping the cabinets. He pointed to a pair as he sipped. "I think those are free."

Eric swigged his coffee and jumped to where McGreevy pointed. "These right here?" He opened both doors.

"If they're empty, they're yours."

He looked inside. "This is more space than at my old apartment. I gave notice this morning. I was month-to-month, so I'll take the next few weeks to finish moving. And thanks again for taking a check for the deposit," he said, inspecting the shelves above and the drawers below. He wiped his finger across a high shelf, checking for dust. There was none. "That was really nice of you."

McGreevy sipped. "I'm a good judge of character."

Eric closed the cabinet doors and sat down. He blew over the mug and sipped. "Those are perfect. I'll fill 'em up today with food. I'm going to the Jewel after the gym and back down to my apartment for more clothes."

McGreevy shook his head. "Isn't moving enough of a workout? Here. Have some more coffee..."

"Thanks!" Eric ran his index finger along the scrolled edge of the table and admired the thick, carved legs beneath.

McGreevy smiled as he topped him off. "I see you have a good eye for design. It's original to the house, believe it or not. Cabinets, too. Beautiful old piece, this table. If you want cream, you'll have to grab it from the fridge."

"Black for me. And you like your coffee black, too?" he asked, sipping his mug, which said *Trouble's a-brewin'!*

"It's the *only* way."

"You know what, Mr. McGreevy? Everything here seems perfect."

Eric's new landlord leaned back. "Everything at Summerdale House is perfect."

"How long have you lived here?" Eric asked, sipping and studying the gentleman sitting across from him. He was elderly but sturdy; Eric estimated Mr. McGreevy at a solid, six-foot frame. White hair. Wrinkles. Gray eyes, both deep-set and kind. A bit of stubble. He kept a pair of tortoiseshell glasses in the pocket of his flannel shirt, whose rolled-up sleeves revealed striated forearms. Eric wondered what kind of work Mr. McGreevy had done earlier in his life to forge muscle so permanently into his flesh. Eric had built his forearms with hard workouts. McGreevy, Eric guessed, had built his through hard work.

"How long have I lived here?" he asked, looking at the ceiling. "Well, a very long time, I'll say that. Summerdale has been in my family for generations. My family had a butcher business over on Clark Street.

First floor of a wooden two-story building and the family lived above."

"Wooden?" Eric asked, surprised. "That must have been a long time ago."

"All gone now, those old buildings. Fire codes and whatnot. But butchering is still in my blood. That's what this table was built for, actually. Butchering..." McGreevy pressed hard into the scrollwork. He showed Eric the swirl as it evaporated off his palm and snapped his hand closed, like a magician pulling a trick. "So tell me more about you, Eric. I know you mentioned when you were signing your lease that you're not happy with your job in the Loop." He gave Eric a wink as he sipped.

Eric popped his brows. "Did I? I must have, I guess. It's kind of a blur, everything from this morning," Eric said, rolling his eyes. He sipped. "I still can't get over the shower system. So work. It's just something to pay the bills. It pays OK." He looked out the greenhouse window and took a breath. "I always feel like I should be doing something better, something more. I'll be thirty-five soon, and I don't think I've accomplished anything yet..."

"Well, that can't be true. You mean you haven't done anything *remarkable* yet?"

"Yeah," Eric said, pushing back from the table and swinging out his arms. "Remarkable. Worthy of my gravestone! Like, when people remember me, they'll think of...*this*. This *thing*, whatever it is, I haven't done yet that will be amazing. I feel like I just punch in and out and go on vacation with the same guys over and over. Like, what am I *doing*? What do I have to show for my time here?"

"Here in Chicago?"

"Here in life! From growing up out in Lombard 'til now. What do I have to show for any of it? High school, college, everything since."

McGreevy waved one hand dismissively and raised his mug with the other. "That's an awful lot of pressure to put on yourself, Eric." He sipped. "And you're still young. There's a lot you can accomplish if you don't get..." He paused and sipped again. "If you don't get caught up in the *nonsense* of life."

A quick smile faded. "That's a good way to put it, Mr. McGreevy. I guess that's why I wanted to move out of Lakeview. Just needed to get more serious about my life and not drink so much."

"Lakeview's a very nice neighborhood."

"It is! I mean, everything's right there. You walk out your door, and *it's all right there*. But I've been living there since I graduated and now my mid-thirties are coming and..."

"Now that your mid-thirties are coming, you feel more comfortable around guys in their forties and fifties. So you moved to Andersonville."

Eric laughed. "I'm not saying any of this right! I just feel like I've aged out of Boystown. Everyone there is so young or straight."

McGreevy gently knocked the table. "Well, you'll be a fresh face up here. Which brings me to another rule—no guests. At all."

"That's fine." Eric said, sipping.

He winked. "It's not judgment, Eric. It's security. A rooming house runs a little different than an apartment building, and I want all my boys to know that Summerdale is the safest place they'll ever be."

"I get it." Eric nodded his head. "I even deleted all my dating apps, so I can really focus. Fresh start. Got it. No guests."

"A little more?" McGreevy asked as he topped off his own mug.

Eric spread his fingers over the mug to decline.

"I know what you do for work, Eric, but what else do you do, if you don't mind me asking? You obviously go to the gym."

"Well, that's one of the reasons I'm up here, I think." He leaned the chair back and flexed his shoulders, broadening them. "You know, what the hell!" He leaned forward and dropped the chair. "I feel like I can share this with you. So, I've entered a bodybuilding contest in November."

"Really? You?" McGreevy said, mocking surprise. "I'd have never guessed..."

Eric laughed along. "You probably think that's silly."

McGreevy tucked in his neck and raised an eyebrow. "Not my place to say if something's silly or not. There's no judgment here, Eric. But this must be a journey you have your heart set on." He paused and sipped. "Or you wouldn't have found Summerdale."

Eric's eyes met his landlord's. "This is a journey I have my heart set on. And it has been, Mr. McGreevy, for quite some time." Playfully, he threw his arms up and flexed, which drew out his nipples from the narrow front of his cutoff T-shirt. After a self-satisfied head nod, Eric set his hands back in his lap. His nipples retreated. "This is something I've always wanted to do, but I've been afraid of it. Kinda like, I'm more in love with the *idea* of it than actually doing it. But now I'm going to do it." He nodded. "You know what, I've posted about this, but you really are the first one I'm telling."

McGreevy smacked the table with an open hand. "What's stopped you until now?"

"None of my friends support me, I guess. Not really, not the way I need. To them, the gym is just a background slide for Instagram.

They're into drinking and posting pics of themselves at brunch. And no one wants anything more."

"I see. So you're growing apart?"

"We are. But if I'm serious about contest prep, I can't be out drinking every night and going to hangover brunches every weekend. So when I was walking around this morning and found this house a few blocks from that new bodybuilding gym on Ashland, everything clicked. It's crazy how it just fell into place. This is my home."

McGreevy tilted his head and smiled. "I'm glad you feel that way already."

"I do." He looked out the greenhouse window again. "Some bodybuilders live out of their cars, just to be near their gym. They put everything they have into training and competing."

"Out of their *cars?*" McGreevy yelped. He laughed and sipped.

"That won't be me. But I'm going to sell my car after I finish moving in. I'll save on parking downtown, and I'll start taking the Red Line tomorrow. Finally use that card I pay for every month and never use. But even with that, PT and supps are going to be killer."

"PT?" McGreevy asked, sipping. "Oh, is that personal training?"

"Personal training, yes. That's going to be hundreds a week, plus supplements."

"So, if I may ask, Eric, why the rush?"

Eric sipped and smirked. "Because I've made it public. I need to finish what I start, do what I say I'm going to do. It's become a joke with my friends, anytime I mention bodybuilding. So this is my new home, and that big new gym on Ashland is my second home. I went over and signed up this morning after I moved in the second load."

"Well then, Eric," McGreevy said, raising his mug to toast, "it just makes sense that you found Summerdale when you did."

Eric clinked his mug to McGreevy's. "Cheers. I love when everything falls into place."

"Cheers, Eric. So do we."

In the full-length mirror in his bedroom, Eric looked at himself naked. He tensed and angled his muscles, dipping the incoming sunlight into his quads, then into the slight separation between his upper and lower pecs. He ran a hand over his legs and felt stubble. *Shave down today,* he told himself, *and try out the RainArray!*

He walked into the bathroom and opened the vanity. *Plenty of razors.* As he closed the cabinet, he caught his nude reflection in the glass shower door. The RainArray dials and nozzles faded away and his distorted reflection magnified. In the glass door, he looked bigger. Much bigger. His stubbly skin glowed. He stuck out a foot and turned his leg to flex his calf, then ripped off each quad muscle, from his knee to his hip. He stuck out the other foot and repeated.

Hands on hips, he flexed his abs into smooth, hard relief and threw his shoulders back, flaring out his lats. The harder he flexed, the more his muscles grew. Arms came last, and Eric pumped them until his ears throbbed; in the reflection, veins popped across his forehead. He flexed until his skin reddened and tingled. He began sweating.

Eric turned his right arm just so and flexed up the horseshoe of his triceps. He flexed his free arm, working out more volume in the opposite lat. He pivoted on the ball of his foot and blew up his quad into a striated sweep.

As Eric shifted his weight, he caught his true reflection in the vanity mirror above the sink. The skylight threw a chubby shadow over his pudgy stomach; his biceps had no volume and no veins.

And in the shower door, Eric's illusion was gone. He looked his naked body up and down; his physique was nowhere near where he imagined himself by this date, nowhere near the reflection he had just seen in the glass door, nowhere near anywhere, least of all on a stage before judges. He winced at his pale, boxy torso and pulled back the sides of his belly into a midsection sweep. Once he let go, his belly bounced back. And grumbled.

He turned on the water and held the sides of the sink. The aftertaste of Mr. McGreevy's dark roast had turned bitter, so Eric grabbed his toothbrush and toothpaste from a cardboard box and began brushing. He glanced at himself in the shower door. His reflection did not change. No better man appeared.

Spitting, he set his wet toothbrush on the sink and looked in the mirror. *How do I get that size? I would give anything to be that man.*

One more set, Eric told himself, hoisting dumbbells overhead. He watched his form in the mirror as he raised quickly and lowered slowly. And again, and again, and once more. At his shoulders, he paused parallel to the ground, lowered the dumbbells, and dropped them. The floor quivered. He winced in pain, but that shock was the *growth* moment, he told himself. As he managed both dumbbells up to the rack—heave one and heave two—a smaller guy, struggling with a lighter load, looked for an assist. Eric rounded the bench and squatted over him, propping the man's elbows and forcing them up. "C'mon, man, you got this!" Eric shouted. "C'mon! Lift!" The man ground his teeth and pulsed his breath so hard he spit. But he reached a full extension and held it; Eric guided the airborne weight back to the floor. The man was breathless but gave Eric a thankful nod. Eric clasped a quivering, outstretched hand and looked the man in the eye: "Good lift!" And walked away.

Across the floor of new, interlocking rubber mats, already bearing the dings of dumbbells, Eric found a mirror reflecting the afternoon light pouring in from oversize industrial windows high above. He flexed in his cutoff T, which showed most of his chest and all of his shoulders, and worked sunlight into the separation of his delts that looked cut with a butcher's string. But rolls of flab popped over the wide-open sides of his shirt. He frowned. *Why does all my fat settle in the middle?*

Another sneer at his reflection and he headed for the locker room, on the same lower level as the free weights and big racks. The locker room was more crowded than Eric had found it an hour and a half earlier as he waited for an overweight man to step off the scale.

Eric's turn. He kicked off his shoes, and once the readout dropped to zero, Eric stepped on. He threw his shoulders back, blew out his oxygen, and stared straight ahead. This ritual, he told himself, ensured an accurate reading: 237.9 pounds. *Fuck. I need to lose this fat on my stomach. Maybe I should get on the bike again? No, more cardio will just break down my growth. Twelve weeks. I'm nowhere near ready, but I can't get a refund on my entry fees. And I've posted it. I have to do this. In twelve weeks. I can do this.* Eric stepped off the scale and walked to his locker. He took a quick look through the rows, and judging his imperfect body the best, he took off his cutoff and slowly walked to the urinals.

He stared at his shirtless reflection in the glass tiles and noticed a man glancing at his back. He exhaled and rolled out his lats. *Power,* Eric thought. *Twelve weeks. I may kill myself, but I will do this.*

Eric crossed N. Broadway and walked through the propped-open doors of the Berwyn Red Line station with other Monday morning commuters. An announced train approached as he pressed his transit card to the reader, and the turnstile clicked, allowing him to pass. He jogged up worn stairs to the wooden queue and fell into a crowd standing where the doors would open; every platform had a pattern. With his courier bag strapped behind him, Eric caught his reflection in the passing windows of the slowing train: pale, pudgy.

Across the queue, all the doors of the shiny, silver cars opened at once and commuters rushed in for seats. But most stood and grabbed straps. As Eric grabbed his, he saw a man with thick, smooth arms filling two seats. He wore a tight, sleeveless black T-shirt. *Fuck,* Eric thought and turned away. Upon the shelf of his quads, with a veiny forearm on top, the man balanced a blocky orange bag. *Meal prep,* Eric scolded himself, *I gotta start my meal prep.*

As the train moved along, Eric closed his eyes, imagining a future when his own width could take up two seats and no one would try to squeeze in. Stop after stop, after the elevated train descended into the subway tunnel, Eric glanced back at the bodybuilder: cellphone out, earbuds in. When he stood up and waddled off at Lake, he made no effort to pull through the crowd sideways. Standers made room; almost every man looked down as he passed. *Power.* Eric thought as the doors closed. *That man will be me.*

Jackson was next, so Eric moved closer to the exit. He slipped forward his courier bag. The train was emptied of most passengers from Berwyn, but new ones had boarded—same crowd, different bodies. At Jackson, Eric stepped out and walked toward the escalator and up to State Street, the heart of the Loop, Chicago's downtown.

A few blocks away, Eric pushed the revolving doors of his dark-glass office tower and walked to the elevator bank. In the mirrored walls surrounding the elevators, he compared himself to the thick-muscled man on the train. No *Killin' it!* selfie post today.

On the 42nd floor, Eric alighted the elevator and opened a glass door by a keycard in his courier. He passed a large, glowing company logo below a *Best Places to Work 4 Years in a Row!* vinyl banner, awarded by a trade magazine that no one read. The reception desk was empty, save for stacks of rubber-banded mail, dumped delivery boxes, and a vase with dead flowers.

Eric walked down a long row of open cubicles and found his. He turned on both monitors and tapped his keyboard repeatedly to awaken his screens. Walking toward the break room, he looked over rows and rows of cubicles and saw no one else at their desk. No phones were ringing. No low chatter. No foam footballs popping into the air. No one in. *First drone here as usual. I could've done some cardio.*

He opened the break room refrigerator and smashed aside yogurt containers, bottled coffee, and leftover lunch bags to make room for his imaginary stack of meal-prep trays. In they would go, in the top right. He believed in visioning every aspect of his contest prep, including meals he had yet to prep in containers he had yet to buy. Satisfied, he closed the fridge and passed trays of donuts and bagels piled high, which just last week he would have grabbed.

He walked past a wall clock. *It's 7:35. I ate about an hour ago. Get first meal at 9:30, then 12:30, then 3:30 before the train home and back at Ashland to lift by 4, if I can leave work early enough.*

At his desk he sat with his back upright. His monitors were now awake. With an index finger on the screen, he pulled down a desktop calendar and jumped to November. He circled the first Saturday and scribbled *Contest Day* and then flipped backward until he arrived at the day it was: almost exactly twelve weeks away.

"I need *numbers*! Where are your numbers, Eric?" shouted a spindly man, biting into a break room bagel.

"Hang on!" Eric said, turning, shaking bagel bits from his hair. "Got a top customer holding."

"I sent you a fucking email on Wednesday, Eric. Where are your *numbers?*"

Eric's phone rang with the call still on hold. He pushed up the mic on his headset. "I'll get you my numbers as soon as I'm done, Elliott. I'm having a really good morning, and I want today to count for my totals."

The man shook his head and stormed down the cubicle row. "Un-fucking-believable..." he muttered.

Eric turned back to his monitors. He thumbed down his mic and released the held call. "Sorry about the wait. I see your updated manifest right here..."

A young woman in the next cubicle tapped Eric's shoulder and stuck up her middle finger toward Elliott, who was down the row barking at others. Eric laughed and returned to his call.

"I fucking hate him," Megan said with a sweet smile, biting into her organic turkey wrap.

"That middle finger was a nice touch. Doesn't everyone hate Elliott, except Britt?" Eric cocked the side of his mouth as he pushed around the last of his sweet potatoes. "Is it Brett or Britt?"

"He won't be here long enough to find out."

"Ouch. Tell me how you really feel about him."

She stuck up both middle fingers. Eric squinted into the midday sun, then focused on the remains in his container. "Thanks for bringing me a meal today. That was real sweet of you."

"I had a spare, and I was in the mood for this wrap. I prepped more this weekend than I could use. I'm kinda surprised you took me up on it. You usually get one of those horrible subs..."

"Hey, I *love* Subconscious."

As she bit, she glanced at his belly. "It shows."

"You are just *full* of love and light today..."

Megan didn't respond, which was Eric's cue to move on. So he did. "Your meal prep comes out so much better than mine ever did!" He scooped out another forkful. "It's kinda sweet, too. It has a nice flavor. It all works together, even with the green beans. And the chicken's so plump."

"Sweet potatoes are your friend. Keeps everything from drying out."

Eric chuckled. "You mean it keeps everything *moist*?"

"Oh, my God, Eric." She dropped her wrap. "Don't."

"Why do women hate that word?"

She shook her head. "What I hate is dry chicken. So, work-husband," she started, stretching the soft, final vowel, "how does it feel to eat like a builder again? Hey, did you go to Market Days last weekend?"

"No, I would've drunk too much." Eric looked outside their umbrella to the Chicago River, then traced the metal grill of the table with a finger. He cut into his chicken and took a bite. "So I saw this yoked dude on the train this morning." He paused as he chewed.

Megan raised an eyebrow. "Since when do you take the train?"

"I take the train! Sometimes." Eric looked at other office workers at other tables eating lunch, chatting on their phones, texting, walking here and there, taking selfies with the glistening river just behind them. "Made me jealous, to be honest, this guy. So instead of complaining..."

"Like you always do?"

He smiled. "Yes, so instead of complaining, I'm doing something about it. Moved into a new place this weekend. Selling my car. Sent an email to the management office to cancel my garage space here. I feel like things are really falling into place now."

She leaned forward, surprised. "In place for *what?*"

"The Illinois Open Novice."

"Wait. One thing at a time! You *moved?* Where did you move to?"

"Andersonville. I still have my old place for a few more weeks."

"Just out of the blue you moved? You love your place. I didn't even know you were looking."

He nudged her arm. "You're kinda the first one I'm telling. I haven't even told my parents, come to think of it." He smiled and nodded his head. "Novice is the first weekend in November."

"I know, that was my contest last year. That's not much time." She glanced at his belly again. "And you're moving? Can you take all this on at once, Eric?"

"I can."

"Look, I've always believed in Eric Saunders. *You're* the one who's never believed in Eric Saunders." She leaned forward and twisted her mouth. "For sure this time? No backing out? No excuses?"

He curled his lips and nodded. "Yeah. This is it."

Up went his and Megan's hands. She stood so fast that her chair skipped back. Her billowy blouse untucked, and her thick shoulders popped her capped sleeves. "Give it up, work-husband!"

Eric stood and high-fived her back. "Given!" She stuck out a foot to pull back the chair and sat, tucking her blouse back in her pants. "I just fucking lost a button. Are you training yet? Who are you training with?" she asked, pulling back her long, brown hair and fussing with her sleeve. "God, I hate Mondays."

"Just joined a new bodybuilding gym on Ashland. Really industrial, used to be a warehouse or something," he said, sitting, taking another cut of chicken. "I have to find a trainer this week. There's no time to wait."

"I'm still in touch with Dina. She trained me for Figure last year. You met her once with her husband, Joey. He's training hardcore right now. He might be taking new clients." She let go of her sleeve and took a last bite.

"I remember Dina, but I don't remember him."

"He trained a guy last year that won his weight class at Novice." She wiped her mouth with a napkin and crumpled it into her empty plastic container. "I'm proud of you, Eric. You need this. You need a goal." She swung her eyes up to their office building, looming nearby. "And I don't mean your call numbers at this fucking place."

About to joke, Eric stopped, sensing more was coming, so he kept down his words with a swig of his bottled water.

Megan twisted her mouth and pulled back her hair again. "You know, now that you've shared this with me. The move and everything? I can say this now. You've been drifting for a while." She shook out her hands. "I know I'm not one of your drunk-brunch friends and we don't *hang* outside work anymore and, even if you did go to Market Days, you wouldn't have texted me."

"Well, *someone* got married and moved to Oak Park."

She looked away. "You got me there. My life's a little different than when we met here, what was that, six years ago. But I support you one-hundred percent. You know Derek and I will both be there cheering you on in November."

Eric closed his eyes. He threw back his arms and flexed and stuck out his tongue.

She grimaced. "I swear to God, if you ever post that on Insta..."

"I won't!" He laughed. "Promise. I'm not a total d-bag."

Megan clicked her cellphone and checked the time. "So, done with all that delicious blandness?"

He scooped out the last of the green beans and faked a smile as he crunched.

"Really, Eric, sweet potatoes. Stick with me, and I'll share all the secrets of the delicious world of meal prep with you. You know, there really is something different about you today." She looked at her cellphone again and stood. "Even the way you talked back to Elliott. That's the first time you've stood up to him."

"I guess it is!" He stood and clicked the lid on the container. "Act the part."

She shook her head. "Look the part. Then you can act the part. What are you doing tonight after work?"

"You mean after I stop by the health food store to pick up a new meal prep bag and containers?"

"Yes, after that."

"Lifting."

They gathered their garbage and began walking back to their building. "Good. And then?"

"Cooking!"

"That's what I wanted to hear." She turned and laughed. "Because everyone wants to look like a bodybuilder, but *nobody* wants to eat like one."

"Another cup, Eric?"

"Please!"

McGreevy poured out the last of the carafe. "An evening coffee drinker, how refreshing!"

"Well, with the rent check and deposit, I'm a little low on funds right now, so this'll be my pre-workout. Actually, most pre is just caffeine."

McGreevy sipped from a mug that read *So Happy Together* spelled out with marigolds. "Didn't you just go to the gym this morning?"

"Yeah, I did," he said, smiling. "Tonight's cardio, to burn off what I ate today, then lifting again tomorrow morning."

"Is that what all those plastic contraptions are? Those locking lids and whatnot?" McGreevy joked, looking toward the sink filled with new, unwashed containers.

"Sorry, I just dumped them all in," started Eric. "I'll wash them when I get back."

"That's fine. So what'll you do tonight, get on the bike or go running?"

"Probably just the treadmill. Just enough to get my heart rate up and get in the zone."

"The *zone*?"

Eric sipped. "Yeah, it's where I can actually feel the fat burning."

McGreevy shook his head and looked down. "You can feel that?"

"Totally. Like when you're out in the sun and you just feel that you're tanning. Same way for me. It's, like, the zone, the growth phase."

McGreevy stared blankly at Eric. "I guess there's still a lot for me to learn about all this. When I was young, we detassled corn out in McHenry County. *That* burned."

Eric laughed as he sipped. "That's probably the next fitness trend. The farmer's walk on a real farm. One pig under each arm!"

"You know," McGreevy said, sipping and eyeing Eric's arms, "there's a treadmill downstairs."

"There is?"

"Yes, by the washer and dryer." He set down his mug. "Now, it's old, this treadmill. Nothing fancy. But if it's ever storming out, or you come home late and the gym's closed..."

Intrigued, Eric closed his eyes and smiled; the coffee had cooled to his perfect temperature. He gulped. "Thanks. Not tonight, though. I want to get outside a little."

"Suit yourself," McGreevy said, standing, pushing in his chair. "Well, have a good workout. And remember, it's just downstairs."

Eric had changed into a loose cutoff tee and tight shorts. On his walk to his gym on Ashland, no one noticed him. Passing each block, he had checked his reflection in the windows of stores and coffeehouses and slowed his stride near sidewalk cafés to attract stares. When a sudden breeze hooked open his shirt, exposing his entire chest, he didn't pull it down. But still, no one looked. At Ashland he turned right and entered the gym using an app on his phone. "Have a good workout!" chirped a fit woman behind the desk, wearing a sports bra and yoga pants.

Eric noticed the crowd was light as he easily found a treadmill overlooking the basement weight room. He picked a thin workout towel off a stack and programmed a warm-up into a treadmill and began jogging. The old industrial building, newly repurposed as a gym, was the opposite of Summerdale: it looked bigger from the outside. Cardio machines lined the windows along Ashland on the first floor where Eric warmed up. On the wide-open second floor, disused machinery and heavy chains were neutered with a coat of yellow that matched the chain gym's logo. The cut-open basement level, in full view of the floors above, was named the Pit, an attempt to co-opt Chicago's gear-cranked industrial past. The sturdiest racks awaited the sturdiest humans who did the only heavy lifting in this building now.

Eric swung his arms out and cracked his neck. As programmed, the treadmill inclined and picked up speed; longer strides stretched Eric's legs. Once in motion, he realized his arms were sore from his lift the night before. But the soreness felt good, like he had done damage, a taste of discomfort to come: growth phase achieved.

"Break down, build up, break down, build up," Eric said to himself over and over as he counted the minutes to his cooldown. By the end, he was soaked. He had pushed himself hard and sweat through his shirt. Though his heartbeat was fast and his muscles felt full, the fat roll over his stomach stayed cool to the touch. His belly's resistance to warming up and burning off angered Eric. He smacked his stomach as the treadmill slowed to a stop. Drawing out his arms into a stretch, he felt stubble on his forearms and made a mental note to shave down when he returned to Summerdale.

Off the treadmill, from the corner of his eye, he sized up others on treadmills and stationary bikes, how fast they were going, how hard they were working. None impressed him. But just downstairs, a blurry mass caught his eye. It was a heavyweight lifting heavy weight. Dumbbells the size of Eric's head flew into the air and down, up again and back down. Eric slowed, craned his neck, and located a spot in a nearby mirror where he could catch the lifter's full reflection without staring. Another rep and down, another rep and down. Eric shook out his arms and did a little jog, so no one would see him watching the seated lifter. Dumbbells down, the man stood up. He dwarfed his muscular trainer; now Eric couldn't look away.

The man was tall with muscles both round and cut. Veins caught shadows from the pendant lights hanging off the first-floor railing. He wore a tight string tank and thin compression shorts that revealed the contour of his penis. The man's body was exactly as Eric had imagined his own. And the trainer guiding the big man's posing, Eric learned upon asking, was Joey.

Back home at Summerdale, after prepping meals from the food he'd bought the day before, Eric sat on his bed and stewed. He sat in his still-sweaty underwear, swinging his feet back and forth to burn off energy. He stretched back with his phone, scrolled to Megan, and sent: *Saw Joey training tonight. Make an intro again?* Then he closed his eyes and dropped his phone onto the nightstand and fell asleep.

Walking downstairs, dressed for work with his courier bag slung over his shoulder, Eric breathed in eggs and pepper. "Good morning, Mr. McGreevy!" Eric pulled his meal prep bag from his cabinet and his containers from the fridge. At the stove, McGreevy turned and smiled. "Well, good morning, Eric! How did you sleep?"

Eric paused as he closed the refrigerator door. "Actually, great. Better than in my old apartment. Bringing the rest of my sheets, but definitely dumping my old bed."

"Good. I want to be sure you're getting all the rest you need."

"What smells so good?"

"Eggs!" McGreevy said. "And coffee!"

Eric checked his phone. No text back from Megan.

"Would you like some, Eric?"

He made a face. "Smells great, but I need to get going. Thanks!"

He walked to the train with his old courier and new meal prep bag and headed to another day of goal attainment. In between calls, he listed his car for sale on Facebook and found a buyer for $3,000. It was the best offer he thought he could get, and the buyer agreed to the exchange before the end of the month. By lunch, he was ready to show off his meal prep skills to Megan.

"Why didn't you text me back last night?" Eric asked, swirling his chicken through lemon juice at the bottom of the container. "Just sold my car, by the way."

Megan stared at him, ignoring his news. "Because it didn't deserve a reply?" she answered, inflecting her answer into a question as she bit into her own plain chicken. "Because you don't need to be introduced to someone you already met?"

"I met the guy *once*, a year ago! And I don't remember him, and usually that means he doesn't remember me, either. All I need is for you to send a text and let him know I'm interested in finding out if he's taking new clients. That's all!"

She rolled her eyes. "If you saw him last night at the gym, then why didn't you talk to him?"

"He was training," Eric said, wiping his mouth and chin. "I didn't want to interrupt him. And I didn't see his card at the desk on the way out." He was on a roll and kept going. "So I had no way of contacting him, you know? I didn't want to barge into their session like, *Hey, Joey, can ya train me?*"

Unconvinced. "I know you, Eric. Someone there intimidated you."

He cut again and gulped. "Just didn't have the chance, that's all."

She cut a few more pieces of chicken and pulled out her phone from her designer purse. She tapped out a text and bounced the phone on the table. "There. Done. Now you have each other's contact info."

"Thanks."

"Next time, Eric, just talk to the guy."

"OK. Put your shirt back on. *Eric*, was it?"

"Yeah, Eric," he said, taking his shirt off a locker room bench and throwing it on. "I know my posing needs work, but..."

Joey laughed. "Posing's the least of your problems. Can't take you."

Eric rolled air into his shirt; posing had left him sweating. He sat on a bench. Joey, still shirtless from showing Eric how to correctly isolate muscle groups, sat with a smooth, veiny leg on the opposite bench.

"Why not?" Eric squeaked.

Joey pulled down his fingers one by one. "First off, you're whiny as *fuck*. Second, I'm competing in November, so my time to train others is very limited." He tilted his head back and spit in a garbage can. "And third, I'm training a newcomer for Novice in your weight class who's gonna smoke you. Trained him last night."

Eric slouched. "Well, that's direct."

"No bullshit, Eric. You're DOA." He shrugged. His shoulders bulged.

"Everyone's gonna know my client's name after November. He'll go up at Opens in March, kill it again, and we'll get him set up in L.A. with endorsements. He'll be on all the covers and websites within a year. Twelve weeks, Eric? The only way you could possibly be ready is if we spend fifteen hundred a week on gear and you get some heart. You got either?"

"Heart?" asked Eric.

"Purpose. Reason for breathing. I'm fucking looking at you right now, and I can't describe you. I'm listening to you, and I'm falling asleep. You're nothing. You have no heart and it shows."

"I want to compete because..."

Joey rolled his hand out. "Because? Because *why?*"

Eric's mouth was open but no words came.

"There ya go. Every bodybuilder can answer that question in their sleep. It's proving something, overcoming something, honoring someone. And you're just sitting there like a fat lump with this dumb look. You know what? I'm going to call you Lumpy. I'll get that going around the gym. You got something upfront for gear?"

Eric looked down. "Oh, cash? Yeah, by the end of the month. But I was kinda hoping to..."

"What, Lumpy, go natural? In twelve weeks?" Joey swung his arms back and flexed his abs. "Not even the nattys are natural. Gym's been open twelve days, and shit's run through here they don't even have a name for it yet. Guys are just fucking taking it."

"So I have no chance in November? And can you not call me Lumpy?"

He spit again. "Look, Lumpy, never say never but..." Joey stood up and studied the tightness of Eric's arms and legs. He grabbed Eric's face and stared into the whites of his eyes, felt the dividing ridge between his traps and delts. "Nope. Not seeing it. Six months might be possible if you had some heart and cash." Joey smacked Eric's chin and pulled back his neck fat. "So why now? What's so special about November? Why not train for Opens in March?"

Eric looked at Joey's ab cage, still stiff. "Age brackets are changing next year."

"And next year, you'll be in a more competitive field but placing anywhere in Novice this year gets you pre-qualified for next." He poked Eric's belly and grimaced. "If you were my client, I'd tell you to work hard now and enter Opens with the conditioning you'll need to place in the top three. It's top three or shit."

Eric frowned. "I've already told everyone I'm doing this. I'll lose entry fees..."

"When did you sign up?"

Eric thought back. "Memorial Day."

"Jesus," Joey said, rolling his eyes. "And you come looking for a trainer *now?* Look, if I was an asshole, I'd just take your money. But I only train winners because it's my reputation on stage, too. You cannot get there in twelve weeks. How do you know Megan, anyway?"

"We work together. Your wife trained her last year. She placed third."

Joey looked at his watch. "Look, Megan's bad ass, but she's gotta get her eyes checked, sending you to me looking like this."

"Well, you know women!" Eric said with a laugh, rolling his eyes.

Joey squinted. "You're a bit of an asshole. I gotta get to my next client, the one who's gonna win." Joey reached to shake but grabbed his shirt instead of Eric's hand. Walking out of the locker room shirtless, Joey called back, "Delete my number, Lumpy. Deleting yours now."

Eric sat on the bench with his eyes closed. "Fuck. You," he said loudly enough for anyone in the otherwise quiet locker room to hear. He clicked on his phone and deleted Joey.

"I don't know, Mr. McGreevy. Maybe this just isn't meant to be," said Eric, sitting down at the kitchen table with the chair reversed. He ran his index finger in the gap between the back of the chair and the table.

Turning from the stove, McGreevy threw his hands out. "I'm making plain chicken and steamed broccoli, and you're telling me this *now?* Ribeye was on sale today!"

Eric chuckled. "I don't know what I was thinking. That I could do this..." He rapped his fingers on the table. "That I could do any of this."

"I don't want to hear that kind of talk, Eric." McGreevy lifted the lid off a pan of sizzling chicken.

"I don't know what else to say. Joey doesn't think I can do it. You should've seen how he looked at me. And the guy he was training last night, who's in the weight class I'll compete in? Beast."

McGreevy walked to the table and sat. "Who's Joey?"

"This trainer at my gym. The guy I should be training with. Doubtful now."

"Doubt will get you nowhere. On stage or in life."

Eric knocked his head back and exhaled. “I know!” He sat up straight to look Mr. McGreevy in the eye. He waved his hands. “I always get myself into this. I get determined, and then someone stops me.”

“You *let* someone stop you. You’re the one you have to convince. This Joey, is he the only trainer at your gym? The *only* one who can help you?”

“No. There’s others.”

“And?”

“I know. Go talk to one of them.”

“Well? Did you?”

“No,” he said, looking at the ceiling. “I just got my stuff and left.”

“So you didn’t even stay to work out after you talked with Joey? And you didn’t seek out any other trainers while you were there?” Eric shook his head and looked at the stove. The lid atop the simmering chicken was quivering.

“You must not want this very badly, Eric.”

“I do! It’s just...you know, I get shit like this at work for not following through and then...” As he spoke, his delts poked out from his cutoff.

McGreevy returned his attention to the stove. “Stop feeling sorry for yourself.”

Eric clasped his hands and looked at them. He noticed stubble in the crease between his biceps and forearm.

“You can do this!” McGreevy pushed away and grabbed lemon juice from the refrigerator. “You can’t take no for an answer,” he said, shaking the bottle. “There’s another way. Go back to the gym right now and I'll put some of this dinner in those containers for your meals tomorrow. OK?"

Eric nodded and stood up. He flipped around the chair and pushed it in. "Thanks, Mr. McGreevy. Thanks for listening. You know what? I'm really glad I found Summerdale."

McGreevy grinned, pouring lemon juice over the chicken. "So are we."

"Back again?" asked the female desk attendant, checking a note on the monitor as Eric scanned in. "Three-a-day?"

He smiled. "Yeah, three-a-day!"

"That's dedication. Have a great workout!"

"Thanks." As he walked downstairs he held up his phone and maneuvered the Pit's neon sign for an Instagram post background. He speed-clicked and took one for Megan with his eyes closed and his tongue out. He scrolled through his pics until he found one he liked with just enough of his chest showing through his cutoff T and tapped out, *Two-a-day PART 2. Let's kill it!!* And hashtagged. And posted.

Eric kept his drawstring bag with him. He watched as each lifter took a bench at various inclines and declines. Heavy metal blared but almost everyone wore earbuds and disappeared into their own world of weights and mirrors. The only two women on the floor lifted together and ignored the random stares and aggressive smiles from men passing by. As Eric sat on a freed-up bench and stretched his arms, he noticed a lifter approaching the two. After his interest was declined, the women returned to their sets. The man walked back to his group and made a gesture indicating they weren't into men. Eric turned away and rehearsed the same gesture, new to him, and laughed at his reflection when he got it just right.

Toward the end of Eric's last set of dumbbell shrugs, his phone lit up. On the floor, he could tell it wasn't another Like for the pic he'd posted, but a text. He dropped the dumbbells and exhaled. Sweat splashed to the floor as he picked up his phone. *Hey, bud. Just saw you're training again.*

It was Mike, who had trained him on and off for years. Eric sat on the edge of a nearby bench and began rolling one of the dumbbells beneath his foot and tapped out an affirmative reply. *Yeah, for Novice in Nov. What's up with you?*

The rolling dots of a text bubble popped and dropped. *Looking for a trainer? I'm open.*

Eric noticed Joey across the floor with a client. *Yeah, I am.*

The bubble again. *Where you at now? You move or something?*

Aville.

Who hasn't moved up there?? Where u training?

New gym on Ashland.

Hardcore. I can train up there now. I pay extra but it's worth it to be there.

The clanking of a loaded-up barbell dropping into its rack distracted Eric, and he looked in a mirror. In reverse, he watched a young man dip out of a squat rack and unhook a thick weight belt. He turned and dropped the belt and rolled up his shorts, revealing thick, torn up quads. Eric stared.

A lifter passing the rack zeroed in on the dumbbell beneath Eric's shoe. “You done with that?”

Eric popped up. “Sure,” he said, rolling it away and handing the other to the lifter from the ground.

“Thanks,” said the lifter, holding them easily in each hand. “You see that guy over there squatting?”

“Yeah,” Eric said, raising his eyebrows. “What is that, 495?” he asked, totaling up the barbell. “Not bad. He gets *low*,” Eric added as a compliment of how fully he descended with the loaded barbell upon his shoulders.

The lifter smirked. “He’s ass to grass on squats. *Now*. Two months ago, that fuck couldn’t squat 135. Watched him. Couldn’t even break half.”

“He couldn’t get below parallel?” Eric said, looking/not-looking, in the mirror again.

“He couldn’t *get* parallel! Now he warms up with 225 and gets low.”

“In two months? How’d he get yoked in two months?”

The lifter nodded toward the squat rack. “Eddie.”

From behind the squat rack rounded a beast. With one hand, he tossed a forty-five pound plate onto each side of the barbell. “Get that belt back on!” he shouted, locking in the plates with thick collars. “Round five, let’s go! We’re rolling to 675. You want 705? C’mon. Let’s break seven hundred. You’ll get it tonight. Chalk up again. Let’s go!” Eddie’s T-shirt showed the logo of the gym, the same shirt that Joey wore.

The chatty lifter walked away, and Eric subtracted 705 from 135 and figured his increase in his head: *In two months?!* He gulped. He picked up his phone and scrolled back to Mike. *Hey, bud, sorry.*

Already got a trainer. Thx anyway.

Eric stayed. Long after sets of half-hearted inclines and flat bench, long after he walked around the locker room, long after he did a twenty-minute cooldown on the treadmill wearing his drawstring bag for extra weight, Eric stayed. Finally, Eddie and his client parted, and Eric darted in.

"Hey," he started as Eddie removed plates from the barbell on the squat rack.

Looking Eric up and down, he gave him a head nod. "Pull off those 45s."

Eric did as he was told. He took off the plates and reracked them on a nearby tree.

Eddie stepped away from the rack. "Now get these," he said, pointing to the side of the bar that still held plates.

Complying, Eric removed them one at a time and reracked. His heartbeat picked up. When he was finished, he went back to Eddie, who was sitting on a bench looking at his phone. He said nothing. Eric stuck out his hand to shake. "Hey, I'm Eric." Without looking up, Eddie slapped away Eric's hand and said, "Put up two plates on each side."

"Two plates? I just took off..."

Eddie looked up. "Two up. Now."

Raising an eyebrow, Eric did as he was told. Then he turned around. "OK?"

"Squat," Eddie said without looking up.

Eric loosened up his shoulders and entered the rack. He wrapped his hands around the bar and lifted it off the hooks. Now resting on his shoulders, he moved his feet into place and squatted. But he was spent from his morning workout; the depth made him cough, and he struggled to hold the bar. He couldn't get low. Standing made him dizzy. He reracked. As he turned, Eddie was still looking at his phone.

"Ten more."

"Ten *more?*" Eric yelped. He could barely finish one.

Eddie put down his phone. He looked Eric up and down. "What's your story? Why you here?"

"I want to compete in Novice in Nov..."

"Looking like this?"

Fuck, Eric thought. *I may as well go back to Joey.*

"Squat!"

So Eric turned, facing the mirror in the squat rack, and placed the bar upon his shoulders. They weren't efficient, but he cranked out ten.

"Rack!" Eddie yelled.

Eric dropped the bar into the squat rack hooks. Eddie motioned him over with an index finger. The long, veiny muscles in his hand and forearm popped and rolled. He grabbed Eric's hand and held it palm up. It tickled as Eddie rubbed his thumb across the inside of Eric's hand. "Smooth."

And then Eric looked down. *A real lifter's palms are calloused.*

"November, huh?"

"Yeah," Eric said, shaking out his legs.

"You are a fucking project. But I've done it before. What you got for me upfront?"

He took a step back. The veins in Eddie's calves threw shadows on his skin. His arms stretched out the short sleeves of his trainer shirt. His nipples showed through the thin fabric; there was no hair on him, except his eyebrows and a five o'clock shadow. The industrial lighting reflected on his shaved head.

"Meter's on, buddy? What cash you got?"

"Sorry," he said, pulling over a bench and sitting. The weight room had emptied out. "What're your rates? Do you offer a package for..."

"A package?" Eddie threw back his head and laughed. "Are you fucking kidding me, a *package?*"

Eric shrugged. "It's kinda new to me."

Eddie jogged his jaw side to side. "Lots new with you, apparently. Got pins?"

"Yeah, a full box. Maybe another fifty at my old apartment..."

"What gauges?"

Eric looked up and thought about the boxes in his closet at Summerdale. "Umm, 20 gauge 3cc, I think, and some 23 gauge 1.5-inch..."

"What've you done? What gear?"

Eric hunkered down and paused. "Umm..."

"C'mon! No lifter has to think about this shit. What stacks? Just give me the past few?"

Eric spoke low. "Test and EQ for bulking, that's been my go-to. This spring, I took Tren and Dianabol off cycle, then went on Deca with..."

Eddie twisted his face. “Amateur. Where’d you get those stacks, on the muscle sites you jack off to?”

“Umm, no…” Eric stuttered, embarrassed, sitting back. “So do you want to see me pose, or…”

Shaking his head, Eddie stood up. “Grab your little bag. Let’s go take a walk.”

They stepped outside into the cool evening air and headed toward Clark Street. The light breeze and late summer light kept people lingering in sidewalk cafés, and heads turned as Eddie passed. Conversations stopped; mouths dropped. Eddie leaned in. “You want that, don’t you, Eric?”

“Yeah,” Eric said, looking straight ahead. “I do.”

“Not just on stage, but everywhere?”

“I do.”

Eddie smirked. “You gettin’ hard thinkin’ about it?” he asked as they crossed Clark.

“A little.”

“I can get you to that stage in November. Saw you drooling over my client. Want to know how he did it?”

“Tren, Winnie, Anabol, Test?”

Eddie gave him a playful slap. “No, silly!” They began walking toward Summerdale Avenue. “So what you got for cash for me?”

Eric opened his mouth, but no words came. “I could peel off two a week, maybe two-fifty max if I…”

“Five.”

"Five *hundred* a week?" Eric shouted. "I don't have that kinda cash..."

Eddie tapped Eric's arm with his elbow. "You want to win?" He pointed up the street. "Right here."

They approached a bank on the corner—Eric's bank, with an ATM built into the wall of the Andersonville branch. The bank was dark, but the ATM glowed in the evening light. A smiley face with dollar-sign eyes bounced across the screen like a tennis ball.

"Five hundred, right now. Pull it out."

Eric stammered. "Fuck. That's..."

"You walked this far with me..."

"I didn't know you were gonna ask for that kind of cash. I don't even think I can withdraw that much."

Eddie flicked Eric's carotid artery. "But you kept walking with me. Because you want the show but none of the work."

Eric's neck prickled. He saw stars and he massaged the artery as it warmed. "That's a lot of money, Eddie."

"It's nothing. There's the difference between us. You cling to that five like you cling to your excuses. Where's that getting you, that five, all locked up? Who's that five helping right now, Eric? Anyone look at you back there? They looked at me. Not you." He leaned in closer. "Invest it. Put it to work. Pull it out."

Eric looked down. *I just wrote Mr. McGreevy a check. I don't get paid for another two weeks. I won't be paid for my car until the end of the month.*

"That five isn't earning you any interest. Get it? Not from your bank.

Not from anyone. Keep it locked up safe or grow a pair and pull it out."

At that, Eric turned. He took out his wallet and dipped in his ATM card. The smiley face dissolved, and the screen darkened. He scanned his finger and entered his PIN and withdrew the cash. He avoided looking into the blinking camera above the monitor.

Eric could feel Eddie watching his every move, and he began sweating. His heartbeat picked up as twenty after twenty dropped into the cash dispenser, like winnings from a slot machine. He grabbed the clean, cold bills and handed them to Eddie, whose hand was already out. Eddie's palm was ranged with callouses.

"OK," said Eric, turning to face him. "There it is." He gave a nervous smile, but Eddie stood in place. He stared down Eric until he spoke. "Attaboy. Be at Ashland at 4:30 tomorrow morning."

"*Four*-thirty?"

"Tomorrow morning. And you'll be back at six tomorrow night with your pins." He grabbed Eric's neck and slapped his face. "Get ready for that stage." And he walked down Clark Street. Heads turned again.

And Eric was breathless.

"Oh, my God, Eric. Seriously?"

"Yeah, isn't that hilarious? I just saw it last night."

Megan dropped her fork and reached over the table, pulling up his hand. "First of all," she said, rearranging Eric's fingers, "it's *this*..."

and moved his hand into the correct gesture. "So whoever you got that from didn't even do it right."

Eric was deflated. He looked down at the table. "I thought you'd think it was funny."

"Why would I think that was funny?" She propped her thumb and index finger beneath her chin and tilted her head. "Oh, look, little Eric learned something new at school today and wants to show it off!"

"You're always doing the..." He dropped his fork, split his fingers between his mouth, and darted out his tongue.

"Oh, my God." Megan rolled her eyes before closing them tightly. "Seriously, Eric?" she said, opening them, glaring at him. "Our coworkers are right at the next table..."

"Well, you never had a problem with it before."

Megan twisted her mouth and cut into her plain chicken. The wind tousled her hair. "So *Joey* sent me some interesting texts last night."

Pushing back, Eric's heartbeat picked up. "Like what?"

She smiled, then cut. "Like, that you're a beta."

"A *beta*?"

She smiled wider. "Yep."

Eric cut into his own chicken and bit. "Doesn't matter. Not training with him anyway." Another cut, another bite. "No way would I train with that guy."

With her arms on the table, she rested her chin upon clenched fists. "Joey's the best trainer. He doesn't bullshit. So if he told you to—"

"And see," he cut in, "that's where I doubt Joey knows shit. So because he says I'm a beta, it's true? I don't want a trainer who doesn't believe in me."

She leaned back and took another bite. "So who *is* this trainer of yours? What's his name?"

"Eddie."

"Eddie *what?*"

Eric shrugged and murmured, "Eddie Trainer."

"I don't know any top trainers in Chicago named Eddie, and I know all the top trainers. Who's on his client list? Why did he take you when Joey wouldn't?"

"Jesus, Megan, I thought you'd be happy that I found a good trainer." He took another bite. McGreevy had made the chicken and vegetables perfectly.

"I'm happy if he's the best trainer for you, Eric. But I find it very odd that a top trainer like Joey wouldn't take you, but this other guy will. Is he doing your diet, too?"

"You know, seriously? Why are you in Mommy mode with me all of a sudden?" He leaned back. "Wait, are you..." He twitched his eye. "Are you expec...."

Down went her fork and up went her hands. "No, Eric, I am not pregnant. I am not on the rag. I am not uppity. I am not anything that men say *about* a woman when they can't handle real talk *from* a woman."

Eric stood and shuttled up his containers. "Whatever." He left his chair pushed out and sped back to the office.

Megan howled, "And that's why you're a beta!"

"Fucking bitch."

The rest of the afternoon was awkward for Eric in the cubicle row. Every time Megan's chair swung back from the divider, he instinctively leaned around it—whether he had his headset on or not, it was a conditioned response to the high squeal of the wheel of her chair—but Megan hadn't looked around the divider at him. Her chair swung out because of an intense phone conversation with a customer. Or because she had to go to the restroom, to the break room, or to a meeting. Or for anything that had nothing to do with Eric.

And Eric knew her walk, a confident gait, and its lean, approaching shadow upon the gray carpet from the lights above, so every time she returned to her desk that afternoon, he overrode his instinctive head-up/hand-up/lay-up and ignored his work-wife right back.

It was difficult for cubicle-adjacent work-spouses to fight, and whispers began up and down the long row that things were not well between them: "I heard she told Eric to fuck off!" "It's about time."

And not a head-up/hand-up/lay-up from Megan as Eric left at 4:45 to run to home, change and grab pins, and get to the gym before six. He almost snuck around the opposite end of the cubicle row to leave undetected but thought walking past her without saying good-night would hurt her more. So he did. Waiting until she was off a call, he shook his meal prep bag loudly to declare he was leaving and then left without saying a word. She didn't turn.

And so at the gym, during his warm-up on the treadmill, Eric said it once again to Eddie: "Fucking bitch."

Eddie laughed. "Use your anger, brother. Let it out," he said, increasing Eric's speed from a casual jog to a run. "How're you feeling from this morning?"

"Tired."

"You don't *know* from tired. Wait 'til I cut your carbs in half."

Eric almost rolled off. "I'm barely eating any carbs now!"

"Come on. Pick it up," he said, escalating him. "Let's pick it up." Eric gripped his palms around the metal sensors in the handles and watched his heart rate soar. "Keep holding those sensors. We're getting you over 150. C'mon, work harder. You're not even at a hundred..." Again, Eddie jacked up the incline. Steadily, Eric's beats per minute increased by fives and tens. "Focus!" And finally, Eric surpassed 150 beats per minute. Gasping as Eddie lowered the incline and speed, Eric's shaky legs slowed to a level walk. He wiped his forehead with a forearm, back and forth, while hanging on the handle with his other hand. "Bring your pins?" Eddie asked, speaking low.

"Yeah. In my bag in my locker."

Eddie shook his head and headed to a flat bench, just freed up. "Good," he said, looking into Eric's eyes until Eric looked away. "Lie back. I'm going to stretch you out. You've got tension in your hamstrings."

Doing as he was told, Eric laid back on the bench and immediately drenched the hard vinyl pad. "Grab a towel next time."

"I will," Eric said as Eddie lifted and bent his right leg in slow, easy movements. Eric closed his eyes and wiped his forehead dry with his arm. The stretches felt good and relaxed him.

"Good work tonight, Eric. Now let's go get your pins."

Just behind Eddie, Eric walked into the locker room. The evening crowd, usually thick at an established gym, was absent, so they stood alone as Eric opened his locker. From the top shelf, he pulled down his drawstring bag and removed one syringe with a needle attached.

Eddie inspected. "Too small." Walking to another locker row, Eddie soon returned with needles gripped in his hand. "Use these."

Eric looked at them, shiny in their clear enclosures. The needles were thick, and the sharp ends beveled wide. "What gauge is this?!" asked Eric.

"The gauge you need." And he handed Eric two vials. "This will get you through the next week. Once a day before lifting. You always inject *before* you lift, right?"

Eric looked down. "Isn't that how everyone does it?"

"I don't give a shit how everyone does it. Everyone isn't my client. I asked you a question. You always inject *before* you lift, right?"

Eric cleared his throat. "Yes. Always before I lift."

"Good."

Eric carefully dropped the gear in his bag. "So, what *is* it?"

Eddie smirked. "It's once a day, 3 cc before you lift. This will get you through the next week." He curled his massive arm and popped himself lightly on the forehead. "Oh, one more thing!" Eddie said, looking back at Eric from the locker room door. "First inject is tonight. All of the vial marked START. Every drop. Right in your scrote. See ya at 4:30..."

Eric latched his legs together. Eddie laughed as he walked out. "My balls?" he said aloud, squishing up his face. "Wait! Eddie, are you serious?"

Walking to the sinks and pulling away long sheets of paper towels, Eric cradled the glass vials within his bag. Outside on the weight floor, Eddie was nowhere to be found. Upstairs, he stopped at the front desk. “Hey, hi! Is Eddie still here?”

A muscled young man in a string tank looked up from his cellphone. “I don’t know who Eddie is.” He returned to texting.

“Eddie!” Eric scolded, looking at the photos of trainers directly above them. “Eddie, you know, my trainer...” He stopped talking, as he found no picture of Eddie. “I’m just trying to find his pic. I’m new here.”

“Everyone’s new here, dude. Don’t know him, OK? So why don’t you go and have a good one.” And he hopped up on a stool, dropped his flip-flops to the floor, and sunk his eyes into his phone.

Eric walked home to Summerdale slowly, dreading every passing block. *My scrotum?* As he opened the front door, the historical plaque caught his eye again. “That date is just not possible!”

He locked the front door behind him and ran upstairs from the kitchen and dropped his bag on his bed. He pulled the curtains closed and took off his shirt. In the bathroom, he started hot water and washed his hands and dried them on a dingy white towel hanging from the shower door handle. “Christ,” he said softly, bouncing his pecs in the vanity mirror. In his bedroom, he took off his shoes and socks and dropped his underwear and shorts to the floor. His phone vibrated; it was Eddie with his next few workouts. He checked that his cellphone alarm was set for four a.m. and took out the START vial and a syringe from his bag.

In the bathroom, he turned on the hot water again. He opened the vanity and pulled out cotton balls and rubbing alcohol. And he laughed out loud; he was about to inject something—he had no idea what—into his scrotum. *Maybe Eddie was fucking with me. I should text him. But I don't want him to snap at me again. Can't be that bad. Just the first time, he said, right?* Stalling, Eric washed his hands again and opened the sealed syringe.

He closed one hand around the glass vial, shaking it gently to warm the oil. The word START, written in marker, smudged his fingers blue. He soaked two cotton balls with rubbing alcohol and cleaned the vial's soft rubber top, then wiped his scrotum. He plunged the draw needle into the vial and sucked all the oil into the syringe. He pulled out and untwisted the draw needle, throwing it into the sink, then screwed on the long, thick inject needle, eyeing every inch. "Fuck!"

Feeling around his scrotum, he rolled away the veins floating between his testicles. He began sweating; his heartbeat picked up. *Am I really doing this?*

Raising the syringe to eye level, he pushed the plunger to expel trapped air. A few drops of oil leaked out, and he shook them off in the sink. Drawing the sharp point to his scrotum, he stopped just shy of puncturing himself. "Fuck. Seriously, Eddie?" he said again as sweat rolled down his forehead. "OK, OK," and he took a breath and injected. Once pricked, his scrotum took the needle easily, and he secured the syringe between his fingers and pushed the plunger with his thumb. Oil streamed into his scrotum, awash inside loose, baggy skin.

"Owwww..." he said softly. Every so often, he looked down at the syringe and how much oil was left. Finally, the plunger reached the stopper, and he pulled out. Blood dribbled onto the floor, and he pressed fresh cotton balls on the puncture. The warm buzz in his scrotum ranged through his stomach, his chest, his legs, his arms, and finally, around his neck. He turned off the light in the bathroom, then his bedroom, and lay on his bed. As Eric stretched out, the oil tingled every bend and crease and fold of his body. He became drowsy. And then, as if a switch were pulled, his skin chilled. He felt refreshed, awake, alive. He sat up and shook sweat from his hair. Walking into the bathroom, Eric turned on the light and caught his reflection in the glass shower door. His body, in the reflection, was thickly muscled. He opened the shower door and activated the RainArray.

As the nozzles pulsed steaming water throughout the glass enclosure, Eric flexed and tugged at his penis. On a table in his room, his phone beeped. It was Eddie: *Keep yr hands off yr dick!!*

Eric was awakened by the alarm on his phone. As he howled a yawn, he felt his scrotum: no tenderness.

He turned on lights and walked to his mini-fridge, which was stocked with protein shakes, and downed one. In the blur of early morning, he reached a hand out to the wall and stretched his shoulder, leaning forward and back. It was only that morning that he realized his mini-fridge always had protein shakes in it, and always his favorite brand and flavor. And he smiled, stretching out the other shoulder. *That's how it should be.*

Looking around his room, he admired its order and masculinity: deep colors, dark wood, clean lines. Everything in its place and everything as it should be. *I should be catered to, just like the big boys. This feels right.*

He threw on compression underwear, mesh shorts, a dark green cutoff T, white, webbed socks marked L and R, and laced up his shoes. He took off after checking that his drawstring bag held wraps and straps. He scrolled back to Eddie's text and looked through a workout focused on his shoulders/delts. The dark morning air was cool, and the neighborhood quiet as he crossed Clark Street. Bright lights, no people. Chairs inside the sidewalk cafés were cabled and locked; a cyclist in reflective pants raced toward the lakefront. Eric reveled in the quiet, and as he passed beneath the street lights, he watched his shadow enlarge and thought, *When I'm bigger, I'll take pics walking to the gym, right under this light. Empty street. Just me. Just like an ad. But I'll hold my weight belt so that's in the shadow, too.* He immediately thought of texting Megan his idea, but stopped. *I was a dick. I need to apologize to her.*

Turning on Ashland, he opened the gym door and heard clanking from the weight room below. “Morning,” he said, holding out his cellphone for a scan.

“Have a good workout!” said a fit young woman sitting behind the desk. As he grabbed a workout towel, he glanced above the desk; Eddie's photo was there.

He walked downstairs and found Eddie, set up with heavy dumbbells around a flat bench. And then he stopped on the last stair and closed his eyes. *I didn't inject. Fuck.*

“Hey, Eric,” Eddie said, clapping his hands. “Let's warm you up. Got a 5:30 right after you, so let's...what's wrong?”

“I, umm...” Eric started, clenching his teeth, eyes still closed.

“You forgot your gear.”

“Yeah, I did do it last night, exactly like you said to, and...”

“C'mon,” Eddie said, giving a head nod toward the locker room. “Do this quick. Leave your towel on the bench. Got your pins in your bag?”

“No. I don't,” Eric said, opening his eyes and following.

Eddie walked quickly to his locker; the veins in his quads and hamstrings showed through his white compression shorts. The thick muscles in his ass separated lengthwise as he tried and failed to open his combination. Both lats spilled out the back of his racer-back tank top. Eric tried not to stare.

A quick look, a quick grab, a quick slam. "C'mon," Eddie said, walking through the empty locker room. "Gonna make this quick and painful."

Into the handicap stall they went. Eddie motioned for Eric to turn around as he closed and locked the door.

"Pull your shorts down."

And Eric did.

"OK, on *three*. One, two..." But on two, Eddie jammed the needle into Eric's right glute. He shuddered and threw his palms onto the cold wall tiles for support. The needle kept going in and in and in. When the base of the needle finally stopped, Eric felt oil leak down his hamstring; the trail tickled, but he dared not turn.

Time passed slowly until Eddie reached for toilet paper, rolling away so much that his hand look mummified. He pulled out and dropped the syringe to the floor. With his covered hand, he pressed against Eric's ass, and then thumbed it away for Eric to take. "Stay in here and keep that on for a minute," Eddie said, closing the stall door as he began washing up at a row of nearby sinks. Pulling up his shorts, Eric reached down for the syringe and tucked the point into the bloody toilet paper. He walked out of the stall and buried the syringe down a half-filled garbage can.

Eddie noticed and yelled, "Don't *ever* stick your hand in a garbage can here! Not everyone has manners like you." He gave Eric a quick smile and headed out. "C'mon. Let's get this shit started." As Eric washed and dried his hands, he felt the oil crawl through and tingle every inch of every limb. This was unlike any steroid he had ever injected. He walked out of the locker room and faced an array of dumbbells up to 105 pounds. When the tingling burned off, he picked up the weights Eddie rolled toward him and attacked his first set.

"Morning, Mr. McGreevy!" said Eric, returning from his workout, dropping his drawstring bag on a chair at the kitchen table. He opened his cabinet and pulled down a large tub of post-workout branched chain amino acids.

Standing by the coffeemaker, Mr. McGreevy turned and smiled. "Morning, Eric! You're up early."

Eric fussed through the cabinets, opening and closing them. "I keep forgetting where you keep the glasses..."

"Here, right by the sink," Mr. McGreevy said, nodding just over his left shoulder. The coffeemaker began spitting and steaming through the filter; the carafe was almost full.

Eric grabbed a glass and scooped in green powder from his tub. He reached by McGreevy and filled the glass halfway and swirled.

"Only halfway?" McGreevy asked, pulling away the carafe and looking for mugs.

"Yeah," said Eric, taking his first swig, wincing. "Not something you want to prolong." He sat at the table and set down the glass and stretched out his arms. "Man, that last set was killer! Total growth phase."

McGreevy sat at the table opposite Eric and set down his black mug. *Palmaris Longus* was inscribed in gold cursive.

"How's your new trainer?" McGreevy asked, sipping. "Coffee?"

"No, thanks, Mr. McGreevy," said Eric, sipping his drink. "There's caffeine in this. I'm good 'til I get to work." And another sip.

"So, how's Eddie?"

"He's great. I mean, he's tough as shit. He's *huge*."

"Well, I see a difference already..." he said, eying Eric.

"Really?" Eric asked, popping both shoulders. "I was hoping it wasn't just me." He stopped himself. "Umm, how did you know my trainer's name?"

McGreevy shrugged and sipped. "Well, you told me."

"I did?"

"Of course. How else would I have known?"

"I guess I did." He laughed and sipped again. "This whole week's a blur. Oh! I sold my car, so I'll make a few runs down to my apartment for more stuff this weekend."

"That's great, Eric! And whatever Eddie has you doing, it's working."

Eric swirled and sipped. "Thanks. It's a hardcore gym. Real industrial vibe."

McGreevy sipped and leaned back. "That building used to be industrial. All those old buildings over on Ashland and Ravenswood, too. That whole area was warehousing and light manufacturing. Right next to the Chicago & North Western line. All gone, or condos now."

"There's so much about this area I want to know. Especially this house."

"You'll have plenty of time to explore this house, Eric," McGreevy said, standing with his mug. “Well, I have a full morning to get started. You have a great day!”

“Thanks. You, too!” He turned as McGreevy walked out of the kitchen and then went upstairs to shower and shave down.

On the Red Line, Eric thought about how he’d approach Megan. He knew that he needed to make the first move. But how to be sincere when he was always so sarcastic? *Just make it on her terms, on her time, not mine. If she’s on the phone, I don’t interrupt. If she can’t make lunch today, I’ll offer to meet her after work tonight or over lunch tomorrow. This apology isn’t about me; it’s about her.* And as the train rambled on through darkness toward the Loop, he felt relieved. Even after a sleeping man in a nearby seat woke up and snarled at him.

When Eric walked down the cubicle row to his desk, he noticed Megan was already on a call. She swung up her headset mic as he dropped his meal prep bag onto his chair and held the cubicle divider. His heartbeat soared. “Hey, Megan,” he said softly, smiling.

She turned slightly. “I’m on calls.” She scrolled through her Contacts window and dialed.

“OK,” Eric said, shrugging. “Lunch today?”

Her call connected. “Good morning, this is Megan returning a call from Don about the install. Yes, I’ll hold. Thank you.” She faced Eric, expressionless. “I’m on calls all morning, but let’s talk at lunch. And you better make this worth my time.”

He tapped the cubicle wall twice. “Will be.”

A few hours later, she tapped his side of the cubicle wall. "Let's go."

"OK!" he said, bounding up and taking off his headset. They walked quietly to the break room refrigerator and took out their meal prep containers, his slightly bigger than hers, and utensils and napkins and bottled water. Out the window, he glanced at the city skyline and clouds rolling in over Lake Michigan. "Rain's coming," he thought of saying, but held it. *First words to her gotta be apologetic, not trivial.* The elevator to the lobby was quiet. On the ride down, he thought of complimenting her flowery bolero sweater but thought better of it. They found their regular café table overlooking the river. Eric grabbed a chair and sat, holding his breath repeatedly to steady his heartbeat. After she sat, he spoke.

"I'm really sorry, Megan. I was a complete dick. I regret what I said, and I totally disrespected you and everything you've done for me. I'm sorry."

She opened her container and began cutting into her chicken. Eric opened his container and followed. She rolled back her shoulders, and the loose ends of her bolero waved in the breeze. She looked him in the eye. "Thank you. I accept your apology. But if you *ever* talk to me like that again, we are done. Understand?"

"I do." Eric smiled and stared at his food.

"I know you, Eric. You are beautiful and true and vulnerable, and I can talk to you about anything. Do you know how few people in the world I feel that way about?"

Eric teared up. He shook his head. "No."

"Of course, you don't. And until just now, you probably didn't care that you were one of them. So it's going to take some time to get back there. OK?"

He smiled and held up his hand for a lay-up.

She lowered her eyes and focused on her next cut of chicken. "Too soon."

"All right-y then." He chuckled as he cut his.

"Your meal does look amazing..."

Eric was about to admit that Mr. McGreevy had made it but held back. "Thanks. You know things are falling into place. I've had killer workouts this week."

"Looks like it." Megan took a bite and moved her chair away from the sun.

"Yeah. I shoulder-pressed 105 for reps."

"For *reps?*" she asked, widening her eyes.

"Yeah, just burned out on them."

"You do look bigger, and you're losing your belly."

Eric smiled. "See, I told you Eddie was a good trainer!" And he stabbed a piece of chicken and swung it through the air like an airplane. "Gettin' swole!" He took a bite.

"I love that you're so dedicated." She swirled her sweet potatoes. "I asked Joey about Eddie."

Eric closed his eyes for a moment and dropped his fork. "And?"

"I don't like him." She reached out her hand as he jutted back in his chair. "Eric? Hear me out. You owe me that."

Eric nodded and pulled back to the table. As he clasped his hands, he noticed new veins over his wrists. He unbuttoned both cuffs and rolled up his sleeves, revealing long, spongy veins, like buoys roped together.

"Eric? Listen to me. Joey and Eddie were trainers at the same gym two years ago. Would you stop looking at your arms for just a minute?"

He darted his head up. "All right."

"Look, I didn't tell Joey that you're training with Eddie. I just said I was curious because I'd heard some things about him at my gym in Oak Park. He said the last two guys Eddie trained won their weight classes."

Eric leaned back and folded his arms. "OK then! See? My guy trains winners."

She smirked. "So what are you taking?"

Eric cut and chewed. "Nothing."

"Eric? This is *me* you're talking to." Megan rolled out her hand. "Your arms get bigger and your belly gets smaller in a few workouts? What are you on?"

He swallowed and shrugged. "Nothing."

"Nothing. Really?"

"Yeah, really" he said, shrugging, stabbing his sweet potatoes. "Just hard work."

"You know, you can be a real sumbitch..."

"Oooh, *real* talk!"

She smacked his arm. "Eric, listen! He takes guys too far, too fast. One of the guys he trained wound up in the hospital. Ask Eddie what happened to Kyle after he won Novice two years ago."

"Well, he *won.*" Eric fluffed up his sweet potatoes and scooped them into his mouth. "That's all that matters. So Joey doesn't like Eddie. He's probably jealous." He swallowed hard. "They're trainers. They're constantly poaching each other's clients. So what about the second guy? What happened to him?"

Megan pursed her lips and closed her eyes. "He moved to L.A. and got immersed in the gym scene. He got a sponsorship and a magazine feature, and Joey's lost touch with him."

"So other than the guy that wound up in the hospital, this doesn't sound bad, Megan. I mean, I bet I could dig up dirt on Joey, too, right?" He dragged the last of the chicken through the sweet potatoes and chewed. "Delicious!"

"I just don't like the guy, Eric. And I'm worried about you training with him."

He swallowed and smiled. "Megan, thank you. But I know what I'm doing."

She stuck up her palm for a lay-up. "I sure hope you do."

He smirked and smacked.

Friday morning, Eric awoke seconds before his 4:00 AM alarm sounded. He frowned as he turned off his phone. *Fuck. You. Alarm.*

He rolled over and felt stubble across his arms and legs again. *Why is my hair growing so fast now?* But as he flattened out his pillow, he felt an engorged delt, bigger than the day before. And on the lightest touch upon his shoulder, a new vein mounded up. He flipped around and set his feet on the floor and yawned, shaking out his arms.

In the bathroom, he turned on the light and looked at his reflection in the vanity mirror. *Yes*, he told himself, his shoulders were bigger. And there, as if a twisting blue line had been drawn on with a colored pencil, another vein popped through his other shoulder; it wasn't as prominent, but it was there with new separations between cords of muscle.

"Cutoff Ts every damn day," he said to himself as he stood at the toilet and peed. He touched each shoulder with the opposite hand, feeling the gap between muscle cords. And then he thought, *Cutoff Ts every damn day. That's a good hashtag.* He flushed and washed his hands and took a shirtless selfie in the mirror and settled on *#cutoffT #ripped #killinit #livinit #ILNovice #bodybuildingislife.* Posted.

He brushed his teeth and cupped his hands and drank. Then he took a deep breath and reached into the vanity cabinet for his vial.

It was almost empty.

"Huh?" Eric said aloud, holding it up to the light for a closer look. "How can this be almost empty? It's supposed to last a week." The vial wasn't cracked or leaking; no oil had settled out upon the cabinet shelf. *Where did my gear go?*

Aware of the passing time, he did a quick inject, put on compression underwear, a pair of mesh shorts, socks, and shoes. Grabbing a yellow cutoff T-shirt from a drawer, he ran out the front door with his drawstring bag and headed toward Ashland shirtless.

Another punishing workout with Eddie, and it was only on the walk back at a quarter to six that Eric realized he wasn't sore. While he expected less soreness as an advantage from any gear he injected, he had never worked out so hard and felt no soreness afterward. And he felt pumped up for the entire day. Even the door of Summerdale House, a heavy masterpiece of carved mahogany and leaded glass, now felt light in his hand.

Eric walked into the kitchen and dropped his bag on the table. He found his BCAAs and leveled off a scoop in a glass from the drying rack. He ran the sink faucet to chill the water, then slowed the flow and dipped the glass beneath. The white granules foamed up from the cold. He swirled the half-full glass and began drinking.

"Well, good morning, Eric!" said Mr. McGreevy, walking in from the backyard. "Back from the gym already?"

"Just now!"

He noticed the sour look on Eric's face. "Those BACs of yours still tasting no better?"

"BCAAs. Yeah, bleech!" He sipped again.

"Hold your breath while you down anything distasteful. Dulls your tastebuds."

"Really?"

McGreevy smiled. He wore a long-sleeve plaid shirt and a leather tool belt. "Trust me," he said, spinning an awl.

So Eric tried it. "You know, that does help."

"See?" said McGreevy, walking to the fridge and hooking the awl into a hanging loop on his belt. He pulled out a small bottle of orange juice. "Well, I'll get back out there soon and water before the ban starts at six."

"I know, it's been so dry. I thought it was going to rain yesterday." Eric rinsed out his glass in the sink and sat down at the table. "And thank you for making my lunches yesterday. They're perfect!"

McGreevy patted him on the shoulder. "There's another set in there for you today."

Eric grinned and stood and threw on his drawstring bag. *Wash the glass. He makes my meals, the least I can do is clean up after myself.* As McGreevy walked down the hall, Eric walked to the sink and blasted hot water. "Oh, wait, Mr. McGreevy?" Eric called after him. "Do you have plastic bags anywhere? Little ones, the kind that zip at the top?"

"In the drawer!" McGreevy answered from the stairs.

Eric swirled out the remaining granules from his glass and soaped up a sponge. "Which drawer?" Eric asked, washing and rinsing the glass and setting it upside down in the dish rack. He dried his hands on his mesh shorts and opened the fridge and found plastic containers, each with measured servings of chicken, sweet potatoes, green beans, and brown rice.

As he closed the refrigerator, a small plastic bag swept by his shoe, followed by a second, and then a third. He turned and noticed a narrow drawer fully open. Eric took the bags off the floor and picked up three more from underneath the table. Inside the drawer were dozens upon dozens of small plastic bags, each with a sliding closure. Eric had never seen bags so perfectly sized for vials. "Thanks, Mr. McGreevy!" he called through the hallway as he grabbed a handful and ran up the kitchen stairs to get ready for work.

That evening, Eric walked in the gym a few minutes before his session time and started on a treadmill. All day, he had wondered how to ask Eddie about his gear evaporating. Soon enough, Eddie walked up, but Eric had his eye on a young man down in the Pit who was reracking a barbell with five 45-pound plates on each side.

"Man, shorties have it *so* easy," Eric grunted with an upturned lip.

"What did he just squat down there, 495?"

Eddie glanced into the Pit. "Yeah, looks like it. He'll get over six before he's done tonight. C'mon, focus on your workout, not his."

"But I am right, Eddie. I mean, he's five-foot-nothing. Short limbs and a low center of gravity. You can't tell me he has to work as hard as a guy who's 6'4..."

"You're not 6'4, Eric." Eddie smacked his arm. "C'mon, focus. Going into a run," he said, upping the speed and incline. "And don't think you're slacking over weekends. I'll send you your diet for the next week. Follow it. Make your two-a-days tomorrow and Sunday, and no alcohol. Plenty of sleep. Got it?"

"Got it." Eric pulled in his lips and grimaced. "You know, whatever I'm taking, I haven't been sore yet."

"Good," said Eddie, ramping up the speed again. "Now let's get that heart rate up. How's your diet going? You look like you're cutting weight."

"There's someone at my new place who likes to cook. It's super clean, almost exactly the meals you've sent me. Kinda freaky how close it is, actually."

"Diet's everything. Abs are built in the kitchen."

"You know, I wanted to ask you..."

Once Eric was in a steady jog, Eddie upped the speed again. "You know how I know you got more in you? You talk, talk, talk. When you're focused, you shut the fuck up."

Eric kept his eyes on his pace and said not another word until Eddie turned down the machine for his cooldown. He stepped off and wiped his forehead. "So, Eddie. I gotta ask. What *am* I taking?"

Eddie smirked. "Test and EQ."

"OK. I've done that. I get a little bloaty but..."

"Oh, no, no, no. Sorry, that's not right. It's Tren and Winnie."

"Tren and Winnie?"

"Oh, wait, sorry!" He put his thumb and forefinger to his chin and twisted his neck to the ceiling. "Hmm..."

"C'mon, this stuff isn't cheap, and it's almost gone. I need to get you another five, and I'm almost broke 'til payday. I can't sell my car until the end of the month."

Eddie gave Eric a look of mock pity. "Maybe you should move into your car."

Eric did a double-take. *I was just talking about that with Mr. McGreevy.*

"Let me ask you something," Eddie said, tapping Eric's shoulder. "You think *anyone* knows what they're taking? How much bad gear have you taken over the years?"

He nodded. "Yeah, a few sources were bad."

"And when you bought it, what did they tell you it was?"

"Test and EQ. Got bad Deca once."

"And those kiddie cocktails you buy for after your workout? You really think those labels tell you the truth? From an industry that regulates itself?"

Eric thought of the granular separation that remained in each glass of his BCAAs. *Is it sawdust? Crushed rice? Why doesn't it blend?* "Maybe not."

"Maybe not is right. And do you think all the bodybuilders holding up those tubs of bullshit in the magazines and on Instagram are actually taking those supps to get big? Honestly, Eric?"

He wiped his forehead. "No."

"No. So it's a little fucking insulting that you *know* you're living in a world of bullshit and you hand over good money for bullshit, but you're complaining to me about something that's finally giving you results."

Eric looked down and gulped. "So no post-cycle therapy, then?"

Eddie shook his head. "Now I'm sick of *your* bullshit. Let's go downstairs."

But before he led the way, Eric, feeling emboldened, pushed a bit more. "Tell me about Kyle."

"Who?" Eddie furrowed his brows.

"Kyle, who you trained two years ago?"

He cocked his head to the side. "My client that won his weight class at Novice? *That* Kyle?"

Eric nodded. "Yeah. What happened to him *after* he won?"

"Get back on the treadmill."

"But we just finished..."

"NOW, Lumpy!"

Eric stepped back on, and Eddie jumped the speed to maximum. "Let's work your legs some more, so you stop working your mouth."

Eddie pushed Eric to his limit. When the treadmill finally slowed, Eric raced around the floor to slow down his speeding heart.

Afterward, they ran through a few sets of weights, grunting only necessary words to one another for the rest of their session. Eric darted into the locker room as soon as they finished. He took a bench and began scrolling through his phone for Instagram likes but found a text from a local contact he named Car Buyer: *Sorry, man, found a car today with a better price. Thx.*

Eric held his temples with both hands. "Fuck," he said to himself. "I'll relist it tonight and find another buyer. But I need money fast." He took a few deep breaths and dropped his phone into his drawstring bag. On his way to the urinals, he took off his shirt. Others in the locker room noticed, and a few stopped their conversations as Eric passed. He lowered his shorts and jangled the flush to start his stream.

The row was empty, but someone took the next urinal. "Hey," said the man.

Eric said nothing back.

"So you've really packed on muscle," the man said as he began peeing.

Eric rolled his eyes but kept them forward. "Thanks."

"Welcome." The man leaned back a little. "You do private posing?"

Eric's stream stopped. He wanted to tell the guy to fuck off. Instead, he closed his eyes and whispered, "Yeah. Three hundred."

"So, Eric, how was your first week at Summerdale House?" asked Mr. McGreevy, sitting at the kitchen table with a newspaper in hand.

"I can't believe it's been a week already. I just feel so focused. Ready for anything. This place is amazing. Workouts are tough. My trainer's tougher. But I feel like I can do anything here. Like all my dreams will finally come true."

"And then some."

Eric nodded. "You know, I never appreciated how a home can affect you positively. My car buyer fell through, but I'm OK. Eddie and I had a fight at the gym, but I'm OK. This house just resets my mind and makes me feel good about myself."

Just then, Eric thought to ask about the date on the plaque. "Oh! Mr. McGreevy? Speaking of Summerdale, the date of the house, on that historical marker outside?"

"Yes?" He was engrossed in an article and didn't look up.

"It's wrong. Foursquares didn't exist until the 1890s. That plaque says 1837."

McGreevy looked at his mug, which showed a faded pot of gold. "No, it doesn't. This house was built in 1893."

"Mr. McGreevy." Eric chuckled. "I've seen that plaque every time I've walked in this house. I just keep forgetting to ask you about it. It says 1837, and that's not possible. It's like some marker saying the Sears Tower was built in 1950. It couldn't have happened."

McGreevy turned down his lip and shrugged. "I don't know what to tell you, Eric. It says 1893. Go have a look."

As Eric bounded away, McGreevy called after him. "Wait, Eric! I'll make you a bet. If you're so sure that plaque says 1837, I'll give you a month's rent free. But if it says 1893, you owe me an extra month on the thirty-first."

"Oh, come on!" Eric said, returning to the kitchen, mouth agape. "Is that even legal?"

McGreevy smirked. “Would you ask if it was legal if you were so sure about the date? I’m the one who’s going to lose, right?”

“OK!” Eric said, tossing his hands up. “What the hell? Deal!”

Dropping his newspaper, McGreevy stood. “Let’s shake on it. C’mere.”

Eric took a few steps forward, and suddenly his heart began beating faster. “All right,” he said, extending his hand. McGreevy glared at him as they shook.

And then, Eric bounded outside. “One free month’s rent coming up!” *Now the car won’t matter,* Eric thought as he opened the door and looked at the plaque.

It read 1893.

“No? Wait. This isn’t right!” Eric shouted, touching the raised gold lettering and black relief. He closed the door and sat at the kitchen table. “Circa 1837, that’s what it said every time I’ve seen it! Even this morning, when I walked back from the gym,” he said, returning to the kitchen table where McGreevy had returned to his chair and newspaper.

Dipping a corner of the Arts section, McGreevy exhaled loudly. “I really don’t know what to tell you except that double rent will be due at the end of the month.”

Eric took a seat and cleared his throat. His heart raced. “Can we? I mean, *could* we, Mr. McGreevy, maybe...”

McGreevy stretched his mouth to the side. “Could we *what*, Eric? A deal’s a deal and your word’s your word. You shook.”

“But, Mr. McGreevy! I can’t...”

"You *can,*" he demanded, folding up the section, "You have time." As he stood with the paper in one hand, he dug into Eric's shoulder with the other. "And I'm just certain you'll figure out a way to get it."

"And now the last thing I want to say, because we have so much good news to share, is to call out someone whose numbers have shot through the roof in the last few weeks!" said Britt, looking around the long aisle of employees with their chairs turned toward the cubicle aisle. "Eric Saunders? Come up here, Eric! Come on!"

"Holy shit!" Eric mouthed, standing up as the entire cubicle row, all fifty coworkers, clapped.

"C'mere, big man!" Britt shouted, waving him into the center. Eric held his hands to his face, smiling, and waddled to Britt. They shook. "One-hundred twenty percent increase in outgoing calls in the past two weeks. Thirty percent increase in incoming orders!"

The applause was half-hearted, even from Megan, but it was applause nonetheless.

"Hey, let's get some enthusiasm here?" Britt scolded his team. "'Cause all of you looking at your phones at the end of the row, down there...right now, down there? I see y'all! I don't think you heard me. By increasing outgoing call volume, Eric increased incoming sales. Get that? Let me say that again for you kindergartners still not making the connection. More calls *out* equals more sales *in*. Has anyone else noticed that Eric is now in the top three associates every fucking day?"

Grumbles. Everywhere.

"Eric, can you share with the team what's brought this on? Because when I got here a month ago, God damn, big man, you were on the edge of being walked out of here."

After clearing his throat, Eric looked down. "Well, Britt," he started, looking over his chubby supervisor. The short sleeves of Eric's thin work polo rolled up his biceps as he spoke. His nipples and top two abs showed. "It comes down to this. I think it's about being fully invested in our team and, more important, being fully invested in our customers. Knowing what they need before they even know they need it. When our new product was launched in Miami last week, I got on the phone with my Top Fifty and let them know about it. Not an email, a phone call. Like, 'Hey, guys, here's something really special that's coming, and I want you to get in on our low pre-release pricing before your competitors pile on...'"

"Out! Fucking! Standing!" Britt shouted, hands clapping overhead. Others in the crowd followed, and as soon as their tepid response died down, Eric held up an index finger. He was about to make his self-loathing coworkers furious and his self-loving supervisor positively high. "One more thing, Britt. No coincidence. Hundred-percent here. My numbers went up *after* you transferred here from Atlanta and started leading this team."

Britt threw back his balding head and blasted a laugh. "Out! Fucking! Standing!" he snorted and put an arm around Eric's shoulder. "Damn, big man! I can barely get my arm around you! Would you look at this beast?" As Britt playfully poked Eric's arm, he noticed that Britt was getting hard. Suddenly, Britt began clapping low to hide it. "So here's the word, everyone. Here's the word. Listen up because this is the *Atlanta* way for all of you here in the Chicago branch just dialin' it in every day. You can choose to complain that Big Bad Britt took away your free bagels and donuts..." He crouched down and rubbed his eyes. *"Oh-boo-hoo! Boo-fucking-hoo!* and get back at me by doing the bare-ass minimum on your daily call outputs, or..." He pressed on both knees to stand and held the silence. "...Or you'll be replaced. It's that simple. Now get back on the phones and let's fucking KILL it like Eric!" Britt clapped his hands overhead, ending the pep rally. But before parting ways, Britt pressed his fingers hard into Eric's shoulder. "Well done, big man. Well done!" As Britt walked away, Elliott came out of nowhere. "Nicely done, Eric. I knew you could do it all along!"

As Eric shook Elliott's outstretched hand, he wanted to spit in his face. Instead, Eric simply muttered, "Thank you."

Half-hearted applause fizzled away as chairs, and backs, were turned as Eric jogged to his desk. Those who faced Eric glared at him. *Fuck you all*, he thought with each cocky step. *Every one of you, fat, lazy fucking losers, go fuck yourselves.*

As he pulled out his chair, he glanced at the seat to make sure no one had left a tampon or stale yogurt upon it, as he would have done just weeks ago to any coworker with a nose as deeply brown as his.

After seeing, and feeling, nothing on the chair pad, Eric sat. As he woke up his monitors, he began thinking of how to use Britt's newfound interest to his advantage. Just then, Megan rounded the cubicle with her hand up for a high-five. "Congratulations, work-husband," she said as Eric met his hand to hers. She scrunched her nose. "Now go fuck yourself."

He laughed and put on his headset. And Megan said just loud enough for their end of the cubicles to overhear, "Well, I guess I need to go attack my Top Fifty customers now!"

Coworkers rolled into the aisle and cheered her.

As their applause died down, Eric blurted out, just as loud, "Wouldn't hurt."

That night, after an evening workout and picking up groceries, Eric came home to an empty house and prepped meals of chicken and vegetables. After eating some of what he'd cooked and washing the dishes, he went upstairs to his room, closed the curtains, and took his clothes off. In the bathroom, he looked at his body in the mirror and posed front, left side, right side, and then threw a double-biceps and turned. As he flexed, he thought of wearing another fitted polo shirt and doing a few hundred push-ups in the supplies closet before popping into Britt's office just to say hi.

The bathroom light was nearly perfect, so Eric worked in shadows just right, closed his eyes, and stuck out his tongue. Opening his eyes, he threw back his shoulders. He could see veins across his upper chest. His waist was lean; his quads thick. And all so suddenly.

But in the glass shower door, he was bigger still. Attracted to his reflection, he pressed his palm to the glass, looking back and forth between fantasy and reality.

At the sink, looking at his reflection in the vanity mirror, he was less impressed. *Still*, he thought to himself, *no acne, no rashes, no bloating, no itching, no volcanic pin marks, no cough, no gyno*. It worked better and faster than any gear he had ever used.

He stepped into the shower and activated the RainArray and lathered up and shaved down. Out of the shower, Eric felt relaxed. He dried his hair, which he double-checked wasn't falling out, and threw the towel across the room onto the bed.

But the towel didn't land on the bed; it hovered over the bed and shook, bunched up. Eric's heart skipped a beat, thinking himself fooled by his eyes, for the two hollow rounds beneath the hovering towel suggested legs. Legs that were moving, one left, and then one right.

Slowly Eric stepped toward the bed and jumped away when the towel dropped from the air to the floor. Eric rubbed his eyes. With a shaking hand, he leaned down and pulled the towel off the floor and threw it over the bathroom door.

Keeping his eyes on his bed, he opened his dresser and put on mesh shorts and a tank top. He rubbed his eyes again. *I'm seeing things. I'm just working out too hard. Too little sleep. Too much worry about money*. Then he felt his biceps, lobbing an index finger around new, bulbous veins that had surfaced, and smiled. *Who cares what I'm injecting? It's working*. As he walked into the bathroom, Eric heard a man's voice behind him.

"Eric?"

Eric heard a gunshot in his bedroom and turned quickly. A man sitting on his bed fell backward, bleeding through his eyes. He reached out his hands and shouted Eric's name again.

Eric ran into the hallway, ears ringing. He shook his head and covered his eyes. A shiver ran down Eric's spine. His heart raced; he began sweating. *It wasn't real! That wasn't real. There's no one in my room!* Minutes passed and he slowly peeked around the door and looked into his bedroom. It was empty.

Stunned, Eric returned to the hallway and stood still until the evening light faded and his bedroom was dark. The only light around him was the low-flickering hallway lamps. He pulled his bedroom door closed and jogged to the kitchen.

Downstairs, all the lights were on, but Mr. McGreevy didn't answer Eric's calls. He sat at the table, facing the rear stairs, in McGreevy's usual chair. Sitting motionless, Eric could think of nothing but the man's shot-off face. *Maybe I'll sleep down here tonight, on the couch in the parlor. That wasn't real. I'm just seeing things.* He took a few deep breaths and stood, pushing in the chair before leaving the kitchen.

As Eric walked out, he bumped into Mr. McGreevy and screamed.

"Eric!" McGreevy said, surprised, setting down a grocery bag and reaching for his shoulder. "Eric, are you all right?"

"Sorry, Mr. McGreevy! Upstairs, in my room, there's a..."

"There's a...*what?*"

But Eric was speechless.

"Here, sit down," McGreevy said, leading him to his regular chair. He returned to the hallway and picked up his bag. "Let's see here," he said, hoisting it onto the counter and feeling around. "I just bought some tea that might help you..." He pulled out a small tin and faced the label to Eric. "'*Chill the Fuck Out.*'"

He laughed. "There's a tea called *Chill the Fuck Out?*"

McGreevy squinted at the label. "It's from Wolfe's."

"Wolfe's Tea Exchange, in the Loop?"

"That place is a goldmine. They're in all the stores now, and they're opening a wine bar over on Clark & Farragut, did you see that?" But Eric closed his eyes and pressed his palms onto the table and breathed slowly. McGreevy mumbled, "I'd better get this tea started," and quietly filled a kettle and set it on the stove over a high flame. He pulled out his chair and sat. "What happened upstairs?"

Opening his eyes, Eric stared at the kettle, beyond McGreevy. "I don't know. It was a split-second. I saw someone. I know no one is really up there. But can I ask you, Mr. McGreevy? Has anyone here ever…" And he stopped.

"Has anyone here ever…*what?*" he asked, reassuring Eric with a smile.

Eric held the next words for a long moment. "Shot himself. Has anyone ever killed himself at Summerdale? In my room?"

McGreevy widened his eyes. "Oh, Eric! Is that what you saw?"

Eric watched the flames reach up like dozens of fingers beneath the kettle. "Yeah. I mean, no! I'm just really tired, and I know I'm imagining things. But it was so clear; it was so real. I heard the gunshot. My ears were ringing. He was looking at me and calling my name. This guy, he knew I was there. He knew my name." Eric shivered and rubbed his biceps to warm himself up. He rocked gently. "How would he know my name?"

The kettle spit a whistle. But McGreevy stayed at the table, watching Eric slowly fall apart. He began sniffling.

Soon the kettle wailed. "Let me go get that," McGreevy said, turning off the stove.

For himself, McGreevy filled a mug that read *PRINCIPIUM* with hot water and squeezed in a cut lemon from the refrigerator. The teabag spun and dipped as he poured hot water in another. He carried both mugs to the table, and Eric put his hands around his, *ET FINIS*.

"This man you saw, Eric. Tell me if he looked familiar to you."

"I couldn't tell. He didn't have a face anymore." Eric tested the water by sipping slowly. The tea bag attached itself to his lip, which brought a passing smile. "His face was bloody, but his eyes were wide open. He was looking right at me."

They sat at the table, without saying anything, each one sipping his mug until each one was empty. As soon as Eric looked drowsy, McGreevy put both mugs in the sink. "How about you go back upstairs now?"

Eric closed his eyes and exhaled. "You know, Mr. McGreevy? Could I just sleep down here tonight, maybe on that couch in the parlor? Just for one night?"

McGreevy frowned. "Eric, you have a perfectly good bedroom upstairs. You just paid for it twice. I knew you'd find a way to make the money. And you didn't even have to sell your car."

Eric opened his eyes and inhaled. "Would you mind..." he started, looking to the kitchen stairs.

"Of course, Eric, I'll go up with you. I'm curious myself who it was." McGreevy walked up first, followed by the heavy, slow steps of Eric just behind him. Grabbing the knob, McGreevy slowly opened the door. Suddenly Eric stood upright, as if preparing for an attack. "That's the idea, Eric! Walk back in with your head up and shoulders back." But what occurred to Eric as he opened his door was if any vials and needles were out, or if any were lying in the wastebaskets. He dimmed the lights.

As McGreevy walked toward his bed, he turned, "I'd want the lights on full blast if I'd just had a scare like yours..."

Eric scanned the bathroom for anything that reflected light: glass or metal. Finding none, he walked to the bed and pointed. "Here. He was right here," he said, drawing a circle with his index finger where the man had reached for his hand.

"I don't see anything, Eric. Doesn't look like anything's disturbed." He chuckled. "You keep a very neat room, I'll say that." As he walked to the door, Eric sat on the bed, steadied himself, and smoothed out the bedspread into wide swirls. Every few seconds, he looked over his shoulder to the wall. *Is he behind me? Is he still on this bed?*

"Can I ask you something, Eric? This training you're doing. It's very intense, isn't it?"

"Very."

McGreevy leaned against the fireplace mantel. "And you're keeping up a full schedule at work. I see you leaving early and not coming home until dinnertime or later, then working out again."

He nodded. "Yes."

"Are you getting enough rest?"

"Probably not. But there's no other way. I can't back out of this. I've told everyone, and I want to win too badly."

McGreevy smiled kindly. "You're on your way. Well, it looks like everything is in good order here. Good night, Eric..."

As McGreevy reached to close the door, Eric called out for him.

"Yes?" he answered, turning around. Eric looked behind himself again. "Could you just...I mean, would you stay in here with me? Just until I fall asleep?" And then he shook his head. "I feel really silly asking you."

McGreevy dimmed the light. "There's no need to feel silly, Eric," he said, pulling out the chair from the desk. "I'll be waiting right here until you fall."

Eric swung his thick legs inside the covers, peeled off his sweaty shirt, and dropped it on the floor. The dry sheets made his damp skin tingle. "Thanks, Mr. McGreevy. I bet you've never done this for another tenant."

"You'd be surprised what I've done for my tenants, Eric. For every one of my boys, including you. Now close your eyes and imagine yourself in November, bigger and stronger than everyone else on that stage. Everyone is looking at you. Flexing. *Winning*."

"Thanks, Mr. McGreevy. Good night."

As Eric closed his eyes, he noticed McGreevy licking his lips. Softly, he said, "Good night. Sleep tight...Lumpy."

CHAPTER TWO

"You're going the wrong way!"

"No, *I'm* not!" Aaron yelled back, waving a middle finger.

"Aaron! Aaaaaaarrrrronnnnnn!"

"Go home!" Aaron tripped on an upended sidewalk square and fell. His friends, walking the other way, didn't look back when he called their names, so Aaron rested atop the slab. The gravelly cold felt good against his sweaty forehead. He closed in his limbs and began the acrobatics of standing while drunk. On his way up, he felt his mouth for blood. Finding none, he smiled, but noticed a few drops from his arm on his shoe. "Fuck! These are new!"

As he wiped dry his bleeding arm, he looked up at a large house. Aaron had never noticed the intersection of Summerdale & Wayne before, but this house had a FOR RENT sign in the window. He walked up the stairs to a wide porch and looked closer at the sign, finding a lucrative, handwritten detail: PRIVATE FULL-FLOOR SUITE AVAILABLE IMMEDIATELY. *That would be perfect,* Aaron thought. *Red Line right there. Clark Street right here. I'll outbid anyone. I can afford it. That suite will be mine.*

"I've always liked the names around Milwaukee. Everything sounds so idyllic," said Mr. McGreevy at the kitchen table. "More coffee, Aaron?"

"Thanks!" McGreevy poured and Aaron dropped in milk from a creamer in the shape of a cow. "I guess. I've never really thought about it."

"Like Greendale or..." McGreevy looked up. "Bay View! Every name up there sounds like a depot on a model train headed straight for *Leave It to Beaver*."

Aaron laughed out loud. "I guess they do!"

"Where are you from?"

He laughed again. "Elm Grove. Oh, my God, you're right! Milwaukee does sound like a model train. Like, what am I thinking of? That one Christmas movie? Where they all take the train to Vermont..."

"White Christmas?"

"Yes! And they all get off the train at this really quaint little station. We have one in Elm Grove." He looked out the window. "I love Christmas. It's my favorite time of year. We always put up a big, real tree, and our whole family goes to church on..."

McGreevy cringed. "Well now, that's enough about *that* holiday!" He smacked the table. "So, Aaron, the suite that I showed you upstairs. You seemed to love it. Tell me a little more about what you do for work."

"Of course!" He sipped, and then again. "You must get a ton of people wanting to live here."

McGreevy widened his eyes. "A *ton*."

"I'm looking for a place to settle down, and I love Andersonville, and I think I'd be a really good and responsible roommate or *housemate*. It's going to be announced this week that I got a sweet promotion, so I can afford to rent that whole floor myself. I don't have my car anymore, and the train is just a few blocks away, so that's convenient, too."

McGreevy looked impressed. "All right-y then. Aaron, I think you'd be a great addition to Summerdale."

Aaron stood. "Really? That whole suite, the one you just showed me, with the pine floorboards and concrete tub and all the mid-century furniture?" He made victory fists and threw them into the air, shortening his sleeves.

"Whoa, Aaron?" McGreevy asked, standing with him. "What happened to your arm?"

"Oh, right," he said, tucking in to hide the scrapes. "I fell down some stairs at my building. I'm so clumsy sometimes."

McGreevy pulled Aaron's arm and peered in. "Well, that looks infected. Have you put anything on it?"

Grabbing his mug, Aaron sat and pulled down his sleeve, stretching the hem at the wrist. "No, I'll be fine." He hugged himself. "Not the first time I've fallen down."

"I don't know, Aaron. I'd hate for that to turn into something..."

Aaron sipped. "That's really sweet, Mr. McGreevy, but I'm sure it's fine."

Bonking his head gently with a palm, McGreevy jogged to a cabinet. "I just remembered, Aaron. I've got just the thing. Come over here by the sink." And he pulled down and uncapped a clear bottle.

"Sure," Aaron said, half-emptying his mug. "Your coffee is so good. I'm not much of a coffee drinker, but that may change here!"

"It will. C'mon, let's see that arm. Right over the sink."

Aaron raised up his sleeve, and McGreevy poured clear liquid onto his swollen scabs. After a wince, Aaron massaged it in. His body immediately tingled. He closed his eyes. "Oh, wow. What is this?"

When Aaron opened his eyes, McGreevy poured on a little more. "Just a little *something*. It's right here, Aaron," he said, putting the bottle back on its shelf. "In case you need it again..."

Mesmerized, Aaron watched the liquid funnel and drain into his scabs. But once dry, his arm felt numb. His smile, and buzz, faded. "Can I have a little more, Mr. McGreevy?"

"Of course, you can, Aaron!" he said, pulling down the bottle again. He opened the cap and held it beneath Aaron's nose. "Isn't that pleasant?"

"It sure is!" he chirped, eager to please.

McGreevy drizzled the liquid lightly over Aaron's scabs as if he were dressing an heirloom salad. Aaron nodded his thanks and returned to the table. As he sat, he sipped the rest of his coffee and enjoyed the buzz.

McGreevy also sat and took a long swig from his mug. "But still. Tell me you'll stop at Walgreens on your way out?"

"I will," he said, looking into his empty mug. As he rested his arms, he brushed his scabs against the scrolled edge of the table. He ducked his arm beneath to check if the wound had reopened. It hadn't, but the accidental brush recharged his buzz. Aaron smiled at McGreevy, who was droning on about his rose garden, and kept his arms low in his lap. Every few moments, he pressed into his scabs. A fresh hit was at the ready, at a touch.

"Well, you certainly look very content, Aaron!" McGreevy said with a chuckle.

"You know, it's just nice to have someone worry about me and my scabs."

"Not enough worrying at home?" McGreevy glanced at the coffeemaker.

Aaron looked down. "Not much...anymore. They just don't get me." He pressed his lips and stared out the window over the sink.

"More coffee?"

"Well..." He pushed his mug forward. "Maybe a *little* more?"

"I was just thinking of putting on another pot," McGreevy said, walking to the coffeemaker.

"You know, Mr. McGreevy, I think this will be good for me, this house. New start on things. There's more bars up here now, but it's not like Boystown or River North. Just seems quieter up here."

"And you live in Logan Square, you said? That's some distance from here."

"It is," he said. "That's part of the reason I wanted to move. When I had my car, I could get everywhere, so I wasn't so isolated, but all my friends live along the lake, up here, or farther north. Just easier, especially with all the summer festivals and Hollywood Beach."

The coffeemaker perked up.

McGreevy sat down.

Aaron's mug was full.

"What the..." he yelled, bolting up.

"What's wrong, Aaron?" asked McGreevy calmly.

He looked at his mug, then at McGreevy, then at the coffeemaker on the counter, which now had a full pot and was turned off, and back at his mug, and to McGreevy's mug, also suddenly full.

Grabbing the back of the chair, Aaron tried to control his breathing. "Didn't you just..."

"Didn't I just *what?*" McGreevy asked with a laugh. "Aaron, are you all right? Maybe I should switch you over to decaf?"

Glancing around the sunny kitchen, Aaron rubbed his arms and shook his head and sat. "I'm sorry, my mind must have wandered."

"You relax and enjoy your coffee! I have just a few house rules, before I show you the full lease."

Aaron nodded his head. "Sure. Rules." He sipped cautiously.

"There are to be no guests."

Aaron nodded. "Fine."

"Even *overnight* guests."

"Great," he said, looking at his mug and the coffeemaker, then the coffeemaker and his mug. "No overnight guests. Got it."

"You can use the barbecue pit out back as long as no one else in the house is using it. A rooming house runs a little different than an apartment building." He swung out his hands, but Aaron wasn't paying attention. "You're welcome to take a cabinet for your groceries and things. You're welcome to use my plates and glasses. Aaron?"

Spooked, Aaron continued to stare at his mug. He pressed his scabs. "Sorry. Ready to sign! I love the room you showed me."

"Cheers!" McGreevy smirked and raised his mug.

Just as Aaron raised his mug, McGreevy lowered his. "I think we can do better than this." He walked to the refrigerator and pulled out two oversize beer cans.

"Oh! Wow," Aaron said, taking a can as McGreevy sat. "Thanks!"

"Look at this!" said McGreevy, turning the can. "It's a small-batch Hefeweizen from Milwaukee!"

Aaron giggled as he popped the tab. "That is quite a coincidence."

McGreevy popped his tab. "You have to drink the whole can, Aaron! Alcohol is never wasted at Summerdale House."

"Cheers, Mr. McGreevy!" They clinked and Aaron sipped. And again.

"Welcome to Summerdale, Aaron. I'm so glad you found us."

Upstairs in his new bedroom the following Sunday morning, Aaron began unpacking. He looked the bedroom over, admiring the neutral pine floors and warm teak, mid-century furniture—a low, wide dresser with swiveled legs and a beveled mirror. A narrow highboy with tapered legs for his socks and underwear and T-shirts and shorts. Mirrored closet doors with rounded, padded cedar hangers dangling upon a thick rod. Richly grained bedside tables with shelves and shallow drawers in matching walnut: perfect, he thought, for his books, his gunmetal gray cylindrical sleep monitor, his reproduction mid-century lamps, and his cockring, dildos, and lube.

Upon the bed, which had a solid frame and crisscrossed dark and light ellipses inlaid in the headboard, Aaron bounced playfully. The mattress was high; the pillows were down. *Mr. McGreevy has astonishingly good taste for an old man,* Aaron thought, scouring his bedroom for a design flaw. He found not one.

Dark blue walls contrasted with eggshell baseboards and trim. *Picture railing!* he thought. *I've always wanted picture railing. So many art festivals coming up. I want to buy some really good, undiscovered artwork, and I'll post pics in this perfect room and help them get discovered. Art is such a good investment. This room should be in a glossy. Hell, I should be in a glossy.* He fell back and swiveled his arms joyfully, as if making snow angels, until a sleeve hem curled over his forearm and ripped off a scab. He sat up and pulled up his sleeve. He was bleeding.

Fuck. He darted into the bathroom and opened the vanity. Empty. He glanced back to an unopened box in his room marked *Bthroom SHIT* and remembered that he had packed only the essentials: razor, deodorant, shampoo, soap, washcloths, half-empty toilet bowl cleaner, and shower spray, and had thrown out the rest. *Now that was smart,* he thought, chiding himself at packing everything except the one thing he suddenly needed. *Why is that, when you move, you suddenly need the one damn thing you can't find?* He unrolled toilet paper, on a tall brass stand—not cupped into the wall—and dabbed it onto his arm. He rolled and tightened his loose sleeve until it held the toilet paper and ripped open the *Bthroom SHIT* box and found lemon verbena soap. At the sink, he stretched back the sleeve and lathered and let the red toilet paper disintegrate down the drain. Finally, the bleeding stopped.

He thought to run downstairs for the salve that Mr. McGreevy had used. *No, I just got here! He'll worry. That'll be the moment he walks into the kitchen. He'll pry: 'What's wrong, Aaron? What happened? Are you OK?' The last thing I need is more of that.* So he rolled off more toilet paper, dabbed it on, and raised his arm. In the mirror, he looked over his face, his stubble, his green eyes, his thick brows, his thicket of sandy, shiny blond hair. *Damn, the light in here is really good,* he thought, glancing at the skylight. *Why is everything here so perfect?*

As he lowered his arm, he noticed a bottle on the sink—a premium, small-batch vodka—in wavy, artisanal glass with a red bow on its neck. *How did I not notice this before?* On the retro gift tag was a handwritten note: *Welcome to Summerdale, Aaron!* Touched by his landlord's gesture, Aaron unzipped the foil and pulled off the cork and took a swig. And another. He closed his eyes and felt the burn mellow into a buzz and drank again. *Damn, that's good. I should pick some up.* He recorked the bottle and examined the label, embossed and hand-numbered. Above the hot water faucet was an empty, shallow, rectangular impression for a bar of soap. But to the right, above the cold, was a jagged, round hollow that met each contour of the bottle's uneven base. With a quick turn, Aaron locked the bottle back in place. And then, smiling, he removed it for another shot. And another. And yet another, until the bottle was half empty and Aaron had passed out.

The light of the moon crossed Aaron's face, and he awoke to a vibrating hiss. The high strain came from the foot of his bed. *Fucking radiator*, he thought and threw a pillow across the room. *But it's summer. And I don't think there are any radiators in here.*

Yet the sound came in waves flowing in and out by his ear, and then high and low by his legs. But in the light of the moon, Aaron saw nothing. And just as suddenly, the sound was gone, and he curled his pillow around his ears and fell back asleep.

"Cut it off! C'mon, cut it off!" Aaron shouted as a pair of scissors approached and snipped off his clown tie, wide, red, and polka-dotted, and a small crowd of people cheered. Aaron held up the cut, frayed end and took a selfie, showing as much of his glass-enclosed corner office as he could fit in. "This is amazing!" he said over the hollers of those gathered and posted the five-second video that looped back and cheered him on endlessly.

"Congratulations, Aaron! Our new boss!" said a young man. "Things are finally going to change around here!"

Cheering again, and a tray of shots went around. Aaron grabbed one and wiped away tears. "This is so amazing. Thank you for having confidence in me. Seriously, everyone, thank you. I worked really hard to get here, and I will lead this team to even greater heights this year. I'm so honored. You guys have no idea!" He clinked shot glasses with the others, and he threw his back, setting it down on his glass desk. Others followed, which set off another round of toasting clinks.

"Aww," said a young woman who bounced to his side and tapped his shoulder as Aaron wiped away another tear. "We love you, Aaron! We're so proud of you! We were all in the same onboarding group three years ago!"

They clapped for him again. Aaron fussed around his desk drawers, opening and closing each in order, top to bottom, over and over. "I don't even have anything in my desk yet! Anyone have a thumbtack?"

Someone darted out and returned with a red thumbtack. Aaron examined it. "Red? Red on red, that's so matchy-matchy!" he said, tacking up the end of his tie on the wall. "I love it. Keeping it there always, to remind me of this moment with all of you!" And he finished with a laugh. "OK, get back to work. I'm your fucking boss now!"

"It was amazing, Mr. McGreevy! I mean, I knew this was coming, but wow!" Sitting in a chair at the kitchen table, Aaron beamed. "Sorry, I'm still kinda drunk right now. We all went out and celebrated..."

McGreevy sat back and sipped from his mug that read *A Pot of Ale & Safety*. "Really, Aaron? I couldn't tell. Would you like a first drink at home today?"

He rolled his index finger over the scrolled tree rings in the wooden table. "I'd love a *first* drink at home. You know what I just realized? This table. It was alive at one time. But now it's not alive."

As McGreevy walked to the refrigerator, he turned. "You might be surprised, Aaron."

"Oh! And that vodka bottle that you left for me upstairs? That was so sweet. Thank you."

McGreevy pulled a bottle from the freezer and uncorked it. Into a rocks glass, he cracked ice from a small bucket. The vodka misted as it coated the cubes. "Here we go," said McGreevy as he set the glass into Aaron's waiting hand and sat. He raised his mug. "Cheers, Aaron. Congratulations. You're on your way!"

"Thanks so much, Mr. McGreevy." They clinked and drank.

"Why don't you tell me all about this new position? How long have you been at your agency?"

He nodded and held the sweaty rocks glass between his fingers, drinking every few words. "So many people I onboarded with said that I'd never make it to team leader."

"And look at you now."

"Look at me now." He smiled and sipped again. "I have a team of eight. But I usually say it's twenty. Mostly marketing and public relations like me. I have this really big meeting tomorrow with my new bosses and I'm ready. Now I'll report directly to the bigwigs on the forty-fourth floor about our creative accounts and new business. And they'll review my proposal for the city's summer clean-up campaign. It's such a great agency. I'm really good friends with my boss, Dahlia. Well, she *used* to be my boss. Can I have another, please?"

"Of course, Aaron!" he said, taking the glass with him to the freezer. He looked back at Aaron as he dropped in fresh cubes.

"You know what, Mr. McGreevy? I feel like I can tell you absolutely anything."

"You can."

Aaron snuggled back in the chair and grinned. "I love Summerdale already."

"Aaron, congratulations on your promotion to team leader. Well done! For those up here on 44 who don't know him, Aaron has been with us for only three years, and in just the last sixteen months, he's brought in $2.1 million in new business. Did everyone know that? He's a networker like no other and exactly what we need in his area downstairs." The white-haired, well-dressed gentleman stopped talking to allow a hearty round of applause. Aaron half-arose from his boardroom chair and beamed. "Two-point-one million *and* Aaron is about to be featured in Chicago's annual Top Forty Under Forty List. We expect big things from you in the next year, and we're very excited to see the final edit of your thirty-second spot for the City of Chicago. Dahlia's told us all about your concept."

All eyes were on Aaron. He stood and tugged at the collar of his crisp white shirt. "Thank you, Mr. Godfrey. Thank you so much! I'm excited to show this final cut to you this morning."

Everyone around the long conference table smiled. As Aaron sat, Dahlia, at his side, tapped his arm. "You made all the changes I sent you last week, didn't you?"

Aaron looked down. "No. It's fine the way it is. This is my job now."

Dahlia gritted her teeth and rolled back.

The room darkened, and a large white screen came alive with the colors of the Chicago flag waving in the wind, against the glittering morning sun upon the Chicago River. One man's voice, then another's, in quick succession with images of many people: "It's summer in Chicago, when our city comes alive. And in our very windy city, the garbage flies. And that gives the wrong impression. To our visitors. To our residents. So if every Chicagoan picked up just one piece of garbage every day, there wouldn't be any left. That bag in front of your apartment? No, you didn't leave it there. But someone else did, and now it's our problem. So pick it up. Pick it up! Chicago is one of the cleanest big cities in America. But this summer, we can all do better. You will. *I will.* Pick it up! Pick it up and throw it out. Garbage. It's no longer beneath us." The last shot was of the Chicago flag waving behind the summer clean-up logo. And the video ended.

"Thank you so much, everyone!" As the lights returned, Aaron stood and held out his hands for praise that didn't come. He looked around the boardroom table. Silence. So he sat.

Godfrey spoke first. "Aaron, I'll start with the only two positives I saw. The theme music is strong, and I like the beauty shots of downtown and the river. You worked the city's campaign logo into the visuals and the city's motto *I Will* into the copy. So good work there. Now, onto the problems..."

A woman raised her hand, and Godfrey called on her. "It's a bunch of white guys on the North Side! Where's the West Side? Where's the South Side? Where's the diversity in the voices narrating?"

Another man: "Aaron, the point of this campaign is to represent all of Chicago, not just downtown and the North Side. The commissioners were very clear with us."

Aaron nodded. "I understand that and I actually did include a few women picking up garbage at the end..."

"A *few*!" said another woman at the table. "In a city that's over half female, we get a few women. Picking up garbage. At the end!" A round of chuckles.

"I only counted two," said the first woman, who added, "so we get two women, both white and the only ones in the entire spot picking up garbage. Because for some reason, it's beneath white men to pick up garbage, even though that's your campaign message. Any women of color, Aaron? Or *people* of color, anywhere? Did that occur to you?"

Another at the table waved his hand. "Dahlia, this'll be torn apart if we present it like this. Can we postpone a day or two, so Aaron can make this right? This can't be what we submit to the city."

Dahlia cleared her throat and tapped Aaron's shoulder. "As you know, I'm no longer Aaron's supervisor. But we'll continue working together to ensure we include the goals that were laid out by the commissioners. We were chosen because our commitment to diversity aligns with the city's, and we will deliver an outstanding campaign for them."

"Running for alderman, Dahlia?" asked one.

The table burst into laughter until Godfrey spoke again. "Aaron, this needs to look like Chicago and it doesn't. Why would you call us in to see something this unfinished? The city is expecting this tomorrow! Dahlia, you supervised this..."

She straightened her collar. "We will absolutely be ready, Mr. Godfrey. What's important this morning is to get everyone's feedback before the deadline."

"I'm surprised by this, to tell you the truth," said Godfrey, glaring at Aaron. "You've done some great work for us in the past, but not today. Fix it."

"It will be," said Aaron, forcing a smile.

"It *better* be." Godfrey stood, and everyone followed his lead. "New cut tomorrow morning, eight a.m."

"Tomorrow morning?" Aaron gasped.

The group was silent. Godfrey leaned on the waxed table. "Aaron, your promotion was based on the two previous wins you delivered for us and a glowing recommendation from Dahlia. Fix this or you'll find yourself unpromoted."

The others followed Godfrey out. Only Dahlia stayed.

"Aaron..."

Walking from her, he pressed a button on a wall console and raised the blinds. The window, chilled from the icy blue sky above, let in little of the sunlight warming the buildings and people below. Looking down, Aaron spied an elevated train bounding a curve as another slid along in the other direction. He smiled, as if he were watching a model train set.

"Aaron?"

He turned. Leaning against a sill, he threw out his hands. "I think that was really unfair. All of it."

"Welcome to 44, Aaron. I'm not presenting your rough drafts for you anymore. And I brought up every objection they voiced a *week* ago. A week ago! What were you doing all that time? Once you knew this promotion was a done deal, you should have been finishing up all your old projects."

As Aaron looked down and clasped his hands, Dahlia massaged her forehead. She stepped closer, until he looked her in the eye. "Aaron? It's not the message, it's the actors. And I need to tell you something. You need a home run tomorrow. Godfrey wasn't kidding. Use your new team. Bring in Sofia and Tommy. They've done amazing work for municipal clients before. They won two Indies for their Wheaton project last year. Did you know that?"

He nodded. "I did," he said, pursing his lips. "Yeah, I did."

"So why didn't you bring them in? I'll put Theo and Graham on this. *Everyone* wants them for their video projects. They're a genius team. They'll fix your shots and pacing. Did you know that *they're* nominated for two Indies this year?"

Aaron frowned and looked out the window again. "*I* should be the one fixing my cross-shots and pacing. It's what I went to school for."

"Hey?" She tucked a finger beneath his chin. "I want to see you succeed." She took back her hand and smiled. "You earned this, Aaron. But this isn't about you anymore. You're leading a team. You win; they win. You lose; they lose."

"I'm the only one who lost here," he said, his eyes fixed out the window. His mouth was dry.

"Aaron," she started, leaning into his view out the window. "C'mon, look at me. I need to ask you something, something real tough that's been on my mind."

He shrugged. "Sure."

She paused. "Are you drinking again?"

And he looked away. "No."

"No?"

"No *more* than I can handle."

"So that's yes." She cocked her head. The incoming sunlight just reached her dark brown eyes. "And *there's* your problem."

Aaron walked to the conference room table and bounced a swivel chair between his hands. He scowled.

Dahlia followed, but he wouldn't face her. "*This*, Aaron. This is exactly where we've been before, you and I. I speak some truth, and you run."

"I'm right here!" He stretched out his arms on the back of the chair. "I'm just realizing that this job's a lot of pressure."

"It is," she said, stepping even closer. "I've been there. And now, I have even more pressure on me. But you know what? I welcome it. Because that's how I prove myself." She rolled out the chair next to his and leaned her elbows on it. "Proving that I earned my seat at this table." She stood up and swung her arm. "And I have to earn it every day that I'm in here. And you know what, Aaron? You earned it, too. You've been sober and focused, and you've brought in more new business than anyone else in the past sixteen months. So they rewarded you for that. But do not think for one second that you can start coasting. Now, you get to work even harder."

He turned. "I can handle the drinking, Dahlia. I've worked hard for over a year, and now I deserve to enjoy myself. I can loosen up if I want to from time to time."

"There is no *from time to time* with you, Aaron! There's no halfway with you. You are either sober and focused, or you're a fucking mess. When did this start?"

He returned to the window, folded his arms, and stared outside.

"And now you walk away again. Do you see your pattern? But here's the thing, Aaron. I vouched for you. I was a part of your promotion because I saw how dedicated you are to the agency. When you're *sober.*"

"I do not have a drinking problem anymore!" he snapped. "OK? That's over. So would you please stop saying..."

"Do I need to call Andy?" She walked to the windowsill and folded her arms, mimicking Aaron's pout. "Do I need to call him again? I've still got his number from last time." She took a breath and held it. After a moment, she said, "Let me put this as clear as I can. If you fuck this up, it affects my reputation on 44. It was the strength of my recommendation that got you promoted. When you're sober, you're brilliant. *That's* the Aaron I want to show up and sit at this table. Not the Aaron that showed up today." As she leaned against the sill, sunlight glazed through her hair and illuminated every kink and curl. "Are you still writing?"

He shook his head no.

"Aaron, that book is your dream! It's good. I'm still waiting for the second half! What's stopping you?"

He began tearing up. He thought of distracting her by complimenting her turquoise blouse and hoop earrings but didn't.

Throwaways like that won't work anymore, he thought. "I just can't find the time right now. But I'll finish it. I'll get to it soon, and then I'll add all the feedback you gave me last year." Forcing a smile for her, he wiped his eyes. "Look, I just moved to a new place. I have a lot going on. But I *am* the same Aaron that earned this promotion."

Forcing a smile for him, she pushed off from the sill. "Prove it. Do whatever it takes, Aaron, but fix this before tomorrow." Walking out, she paused at the door and turned. "Now dry your eyes and get to work."

"Hello, Aaron! How was your big day today?"

Slumping in a kitchen chair opposite McGreevy, Aaron dropped his messenger bag to the floor. With both elbows on the table, he rested his frown upon his fists. "I don't even want to talk about how terrible today was," he mumbled.

McGreevy dropped his paper. "I'm sorry to hear that! What happened?" He folded it in neat quarters and set it on an empty chair.

He sat up. "You know what, Mr. McGreevy? I just want to go to bed. I mean, I spent the whole day making changes and doing everything they told me to do, and I brought in all these new actors, and they were really difficult to work with and wouldn't do anything I told them to do, and by the end, I totally lost my patience. This one girl, oh, my God. She was driving me crazy. Total diva and I just gave it right back. So everything's going to be fine now, but no, today did *not* go well. Not at all."

"I'm sorry, Aaron. You were so excited about everything this morning."

"I was," he said, running his hands through his hair, then massaging the dark circles beneath his eyes. “I really was. I look horrible, and I had to do a media interview. And I haven’t even eaten anything.”

McGreevy stood and pushed in the chair. “Well, why don’t you let me put something together? It won’t take but a minute. I was just starting to think about a late-night dinner myself,” he said, opening the refrigerator. He began shuffling through the crisper.

“I don’t want to put you to any trouble.” He pulled out his phone. “It’s late. I’ll just get something off one of the apps and have it delivered.”

McGreevy walked back and put his hand over Aaron’s, stopping him from unlocking his phone. “It’s just the oddest thing,” McGreevy said, pressing down hard. “Delivery drivers have such a hard time finding this house...”

Once Aaron left his phone facedown on the table, McGreevy returned to the stove. He looked perplexed. “I know, Aaron, it makes no sense to me either. So let me put something together for you. I know just what you need.”

“Well,” Aaron said, leaning forward as his stomach grumbled, “after a day like I had, I guess a home-cooked meal would be nice. Can I help with anything?”

“No, no, no!” he said from the sink as he began rinsing chicken breasts. “You just keep telling me about your day. I’m so curious why it didn’t go well.”

“I mean, if it wouldn’t be too much trouble to listen to all my problems?”

Facing the stove, he dropped the breasts into a skillet. “It’s never too much trouble to listen to all your problems.”

Aaron peeked at his phone and returned it facedown.

"You're not ordering now, are you?" McGreevy asked, back still turned.

"No. Just looking at my likes. I put up a post earlier, lots of inside jokes about that diva bitch. I love your stove, by the way. It's not original, is it?"

McGreevy washed his hands and grabbed a butcher's knife, then cut up vegetables and dropped them into a large pot. He settled a high flame beneath it, and the chicken, in the skillet, began crackling. "You have such an eye for detail, Aaron. It's not original to the house, but that kitchen table is. How about a drink now?"

"Yes! Anything with vodka."

Nodding, McGreevy grabbed a rocks glass and picked ice cubes from the bucket in the freezer. A bottle of vodka, identical to Aaron's upstairs, lay astride a wire rack. The cubes steamed and popped as McGreevy poured chilled vodka over them. As he set down the rocks glass, which had frosted over, Aaron peered in and turned it by its rim gently, quizzically. Back at the stove, McGreevy fussed with dinner.

"Huh! This is really odd, Mr. McGreevy," Aaron said, glass in hand. He sipped, looked over the frosted glass again, and set it back down. "You don't leave any fingerprints."

McGreevy turned. He glared at the glass, and it split in half.

"Oh, my God!" Aaron said, jumping back, felling the chair. Aaron reached for paper towels on the counter and rolled a handful around the spill. Ice cubes spun and sailed to the floor. "That glass must have been really hot before you put the ice in it." Aaron said, sopping up the vodka cascading into his messenger.

"*Must* have been." McGreevy smirked as he tore off the last of the paper towels and took over. "Now, now, Aaron, I don't want you cutting yourself. Here, let me get that and I'll make you another drink..." McGreevy pulled a garbage can from beneath the sink and slid broken glass into it. He kneeled for the wayward ice cubes and wiped the floor dry. "There," he said, dropping the can by the sink and wringing out a sponge. "Let me wipe down that table." He passed the sponge carefully over the wet, wooden tabletop. "I sure hope that alcohol didn't strip the stain," he said. He squeezed out the sponge over the sink and ran hot water over his hands. He turned as he dried them with a plush hand towel.

Aaron fanned the table with his arms. As it dried, Aaron gave a thumbs-up. "Table looks OK."

"Good. So tell me about the rest of your day. What else happened?" McGreevy tossed the hand towel aside. He remade Aaron's drink, placing it before him; this time the glass was chilled but not frosted.

He drank. And again. "Thanks." Aaron closed his eyes for a moment. "I was so excited. I really was, when I left the house this morning. And then they ruined it for me." And he drank again.

At the stove, McGreevy turned the flames down. "How's that?"

Aaron sipped. "They said it wasn't good enough, the way I envisioned this spot. They said I have to bring in more *diversity*," he said, adding air quotes before sipping again. "The message was fine, they said, just not the people delivering it. But it was perfect, Mr. McGreevy, it really was. I think I'm not ever going to be understood in my lifetime." He drank.

McGreevy turned. "You've said 'they' a few times, Aaron. Who is *they*?"

"My new bosses. The quote-unquote *bigwigs* on the forty-fourth floor. The meeting was up in their conference room. Oh, my God, it was so ostentatious and dated. Lots of eighties gold fleck and onyx inlay, like, from *Dynasty*. Not my aesthetic at all. Or *anyone's*, if they have any taste." He rolled his neck and sat up straight, then sipped. "You know what, Mr. McGreevy? I think they're jealous. Because I'm so much younger and I have all this talent. Whatever. I did what they wanted." He swirled the ice and drank the last. "Can I have another? You know I feel bad drinking all your vodka and eating all your food."

McGreevy lifted the lid from the pot, inhaled, and reset it. "Another ten minutes and this will be perfect. Aaron, I need to be honest with you. May I?"

Aaron noticed McGreevy was looking at him by the reflection in the greenhouse window. He gulped and made eye contact between the basil. "Sure."

"You made a big mistake today. You really did. By giving in." McGreevy stayed turned.

"I did?"

McGreevy held Aaron's anxiety tightly. From the window, McGreevy watched Aaron's every tic and twitch.

"I did?" Aaron asked again, his voice a little higher, as if McGreevy hadn't heard him, and his knee started bobbing up and down. Only after Aaron looked into his empty glass did McGreevy turn. "You compromised. You compromised your vision. Never, ever do that again. And for what? To pacify some old suits who want their agency to look relevant, by *using* you? By satisfying some quota they don't even believe in? Ridiculous."

"You know, that's exactly what I thought. But it was my first meeting with everyone on forty-four, and I didn't want to be *that* guy."

"Let's have another drink."

"Mr. McGreevy! It's like you always want a drink in my hand or something."

He gave Aaron a little shrug and collected his glass. "Well, you want my advice, don't you?"

Aaron sat up like an eager puppy. "Of course!"

McGreevy shook his head as he returned to the freezer. "Be *that* guy. They got you to compromise today. See how that worked, Aaron? It was a test. They knew it was your first time in the tank, and now they think they can push you around."

Seconds later, Aaron had his next drink.

After some talk about his rose garden that Aaron ignored, McGreevy took the chicken off the burner and the lid off the pot. A deep, spicy steam rolled through the kitchen.

"That smells so good!" Aaron said as he breathed into the now-empty glass, melting and shifting the cubes. He drank, then returned to McGreevy's advice. "You know what? You're right, what you said earlier. I compromised."

"You're the boss now, and you'll know better next time. And there *will* be a next time. There always is with people like that."

Aaron pounded the table. "Yes! There's this new account I've had my eye on, and now that I have a big title behind my name, I'm going to send them a proposal."

"Really? Tell me about it."

"Actually, it's right here in Andersonville. Well, they're in the Loop, but they're opening in Andersonville. And I've got the perfect pitch to take their retail global."

McGreevy grinned. "Attaboy." McGreevy took plates out of a

cupboard and set them on the table with silverware and napkins.

Aaron marveled at the picture-perfect scene before him. He wondered, only for a moment, if it were all staged. "A home-cooked meal in this amazing kitchen? I should post this on the 'gram. That really was faster than delivery."

A moment later, Aaron's plate was full, and he had a fresh drink. McGreevy pulled a Hefeweizen from the fridge and pulled the tab. "Cheers, Aaron."

They clinked and drank.

"Cheers, Mr. McGreevy. And cheers to my new start at Summerdale!"

That night, just past 2:00 a.m., Aaron woke to a hissing sound. He rolled out of bed for the bathroom. He swatted the wall to find the lightswitch, stood at the toilet, and peed. He tilted his head side to side and massaged his warm temples with one hand while he guided his penis with the other. *I drank too much. And I need to be up in a few hours. Fuck.* As he tapped his penis, the hissing sound behind him returned, only louder.

Startled, he raised his shorts quickly and caught his hand in the waistband. "Dammit!" he shouted, while looking down at his knuckles, where glass shards wedged out of creases between each finger. Bleary-eyed, with his other hand, he pulled at the shards, but his fingers were too large to remove them. *Do I have tweezers? I wonder if Mr. McGreevy does. No, I can't wake him up. Where the hell did this glass come from? I wasn't cut at the table.*

As Aaron fussed, the shards sailed like paper cuts into shallow nerves and poked deeper, dripping blood onto Aaron's shorts. He rolled toilet paper around his hand and walked downstairs. *Gotta be a junk drawer in the kitchen. Everyone has a junk drawer. Even Mr.*

McGreevy must have a junk drawer.

In the kitchen, Aaron turned on the pendant lights and opened and closed drawers high and low, finding nothing. He looked under the sink, seeing only cleansers and the garbage can. And then he looked up, at a high cabinet from which McGreevy had pulled down the bottle that soothed his scabs. *Which shelf was it?*

Aaron wasn't tall enough to see all the way back, so he grabbed a chair, turned the lights brighter, and set the chair by the fridge. Quietly, he searched around many bottles and found the one he thought was the right one and stepped down. He uncapped it, looked at the label, faded and warped, and hoped.

Holding his breath, he unrolled the reddened toilet paper and poured the bottle over the back of his hand, letting the runoff drain into the sink. It worked. Instantly, he felt a light buzz. He set the bottle at the edge of the sink and held the counter as a rush—the same rush as before—chilled his body. Tingling pulses closed in on his heart, and he needed both hands to keep standing. His scrotum toughened; his penis stuck out of the slit in his shorts. Turning, he lowered himself to the floor and leaned back against the cabinets. He pressed his palms to the tiles for support. And he passed out.

"Aaron!" McGreevy yelled, snapping his fingers. "Aaron?"

Aaron came to. He shook his head and looked up. "Oh, my God!" he shouted, standing quickly. He threw a hand onto the sink for support. Deep breaths, in through his nose, out through his mouth, in through his nose, out through his mouth, and he rounded his palms on his cheeks to wake up. "What happened?"

"I was about to ask you the same thing," McGreevy said, moving the chair back to the table. He turned on the faucet. "Here. Let me get a...

here it is!" He reached to a nearby drawer for a tea towel and ran it under cold water.

Then Aaron realized that he had on only a pair of shorts. And his penis was sticking out. He passed a hand by the slit and covered himself. He stumbled away from the sink. "I'm so sorry, Mr. McGreevy, I..."

"Here," said McGreevy as he wrung out the towel. "Put this on your forehead."

Nodding, Aaron took it. "Thank you. I'm so sorry! I just woke up last night and felt all this glass stuck in my hand..." He held out his hand as he spoke. "This won't happen again." He rolled the towel over his forehead. The cold, coarse dampness refreshed him.

"No need to explain, Aaron. Here, take this up with you, so it's always close by," said McGreevy, handing Aaron the bottle.

Aaron darted his eyes toward the rear stairs. "Thank you. I should get ready for work. And this really won't happen again."

As he turned for the stairs, McGreevy called his name. "There's more. There's another bottle right here in this cabinet." He pointed, smiling kindly at his tenant. "There's always more."

"So where are you now, Aaron? Kel said he heard you left Logan. I can't remember the last time we all got together for a drink. Was it last summer? Or Kel's Christmas party two years ago?"

"It's been forever. I'm up here now, in Andersonville." Aaron finished his drink and looked through the open bar windows to Clark Street. "I really like it here. My place is just a few blocks away. It's this really nice old house, and I have the entire third floor for my bedroom and office. The whole floor is mine!" He pointed toward Summerdale Avenue and then got the bartender's attention. "Best tequila. Two shots."

"Sure thing, Aaron," the bartender replied.

"You just moved up here, and the bartender already knows your name?"

"I tip well." He smiled and sipped.

"Such a sweet neighborhood, Aaron. How'd you get out of your old lease so fast?"

"I was month-to-month. And I did that whole 'living with less' thing last year, so I had almost nothing to move. And my room was furnished. It's a big bedroom with all this amazing mid-century furniture, a private bathroom, and this kind-of-nook area where I'm doing all of my writing. I'm just writing nonstop right now. So I'll save up while living here and buy a place closer to where you are."

"I love the Gold Coast. I have a view of Barney's from the rooftop pool, and I can see the lake from my bedroom. I walk to work every day, and I can get to my boat so easy..."

"Yes! Your boat," said Aaron, beaming. "Let me know the next time you go out! I haven't been in the Playpen in forever. Is that the last time we were all together? You know, what happened to Billy after Kel broke up with him?"

"Total mess, Aaron. He moved back to Florida and disappeared. You know Billy stole thousands from Kel. Right out of his bank account. It was so *bad*."

Aaron rolled his eyes. "Poor Kel. He was really in love with Billy. I should text him, I guess. But he's fallen out of touch with me."

"You two used to be so close. You know that Billy was jealous of you. He always thought you and Kel were..."

Aaron's mouth dropped, so he filled it with the last of his drink. "Me? And Kel? We were best friends since high school!"

"He talks about you a lot. And you're meeting us out Friday night, aren't you?"

"What's going on Friday night?" Aaron asked as the bartender dropped both shots and filled their water glasses from a bottle. "Thanks," Aaron said, pressing together his thumb and index finger and scribbling in the air. "On mine. My tab."

"Wow, thanks, Aaron! But if we're celebrating something for you, then I should get these."

"Too late," Aaron said, winking at the bartender.

"So what are we toasting?"

Both shot glasses went up. "My promotion at work! I'm going to lead a team of *twenty!*"

"Aaron! Congratulations!"

They drank. "Damn," Aaron said, setting down his shot glass. "That was really too good to do as a shot."

"Yeah, no lime and salt needed here. You're at the same agency, right?"

Aaron nodded. "Three years to the day after transferring down from the Milwaukee office. Been on this awesome team from the start. And now I'm their boss."

"Wait—was it you or Kel that grew up in Whitefish Bay?"

Aaron nodded his head. "That's random. That was Kel. They moved to Elm Grove right before our freshman year. We already lived there. But I knew Kel because our families have houses on Lake Geneva. Our dads are partners in the same law firm. Why?"

"Kel was talking about you the other day. You know, can I be real honest here, Aaron? He's worried about you. And so am I..."

"Why? Hey, sorry?" Aaron turned and raised his index finger. "Can we get two more? Yeah, same shots. My tab. Thanks."

"Ummm. *Yeah.*"

Aaron shrugged. "What?"

"This is your third drink and your second shot. And we got here half an hour ago..."

He grimaced. "I had a day and a half at work today, and I thought we were having a good time catching up."

"Aaron! I'm sorry. We're all just worried about you. You've pulled away from everyone. Since last year, we don't hear from you anymore. You got a sweet promotion, and I'm so happy for you. But people are talking. Scott and those guys said you got so drunk last weekend, and that you that fell on the sidewalk. Then someone else said you broke your arm."

He waved both arms like a dummy. "As you can see, they're perfectly fine." He pushed back. "You know what? I fucking hate the cliques in Chicago. It's *so* high school with guys here. Scott and his whole group are so small-town. No one seems to mind me drinking when I'm the one buying." Aaron looked at the full sidewalk café outside; everyone had a drink at their table. "You know, why don't you go lecture them? I don't drink any more than anyone else here does. I grew up in Wisconsin. I grew up around it. I don't have a problem. The only judgment I ever get is from people who are from here."

"Kel's from Wisconsin, too, Aaron. You both call it a *bubbler*. Look, we all used to be close. For whatever reason, you're not in touch with any of us anymore." He reached out his hand for Aaron's. "We're just worried because we know where you've been. Andy is..."

Aaron stuck up an index finger. "I do *not* want to talk about Andy, OK? He's a liar. He's made up so much bullshit about me, and he's so holier than thou! He thinks he's better than EVERYONE!"

"Shhh...Aaron, come on. Come on?"

"He's not going to be out with us on Friday, is he?"

"We're going to a *bar*, Aaron. No, Andy won't be there."

He nodded and sipped his water glass. "Good. Which one are we going to, anyway?"

"Helen of Troy."

The bartender dropped the shots. "Thanks." Aaron made a face. "In Boystown?"

"No, Helen of Troy up here. But it's the same shitty dive. It's on Ashland & Summerdale."

"Oh, no way, I live on Summerdale now! OK, I'll be there. So let's toast...let's toast to *you* this time."

Shot glasses were raised high. "Awww, Aaron! Thank you. We really do care about you."

"Seriously. I'm so glad you texted me. Here we go—to our friendship. And to your boat."

"How about just to *our* friendship?"

And at that, they clinked.

"Hi, Mr. McGreevy!"

"Well, hello, Aaron! How was your day today?" Seated at the kitchen table, he glanced up from his paper.

"So much better. Seriously. Each day's better than the last. I go in every morning thinking I'm the boss, acting like the boss, being the boss, and you know what?"

McGreevy chuckled as he removed his glasses and folded his paper. "What's that, Aaron?"

"I *am* the boss!"

"Attaboy, Aaron." He stood up and walked to the sink, leaving his paper on an open chair and glasses on the table.

"Hey, Mr. McGreevy, can I get a drink? I just got dinner and caught up with a friend over on Clark Street, and I only had one drink." He set his messenger bag on the floor and sat. He gently pawed McGreevy's glasses.

"Now, now, Aaron..." McGreevy started as he reached in the cabinet for a rocks glass. "Don't undercount for me."

"Undercount *what?*"

He turned. "There's no shame at Summerdale." He opened the freezer and dropped a handful of ice cubes into a glass. Then poured vodka over. He closed the freezer door with his elbow and set down the glass before Aaron. "Now, I have to go get some things taken care of. So *you* have a good evening!" He grabbed his paper and glasses, and Aaron's eyes followed. "Those frames are so on-trend."

"I try to keep up."

"Thanks, Mr. McGreevy. You have a good night, too," Aaron said, sitting at the table as he sipped. "Damn, that's good vodka," he said to himself. "Hey, Mr. McGreevy?" he called. "There's some weird hissing sounds in my room. I don't know where it's..."

But there was no reply. Aaron took another drink and thrust upward to pull the bar receipt from his pocket. He looked at the total he had just spent. "Two-hundred forty-two dollars and eighty-three cents. God, those shots were thirty each. And it's not even the weekend yet." He swung his messenger over his shoulder and took his glass upstairs.

In his room, he looked for a place to set his drink. There were no coasters, and too much beautifully stained wood for a sweaty glass, so he turned on the bathroom light, placed the drink on the sink, and flipped up the toilet lid to pee.

And he then noticed his vodka bottle. Full.

After flushing and washing his hands, he swirled the glass and drank the last. There was enough ice for another, so he opened the bottle and poured it in. The melting cubes spun with glee as Aaron poured vodka on them. He recorked the bottle and clicked it back into the sink.

At his desk with his drink, he pulled out a chair and sat with the glass on his knee. He leaned back, staring at the bottle on the vanity, partially emptied, and made a mental note of its volume: *Almost down to the top of the logo.*

He looked at his laptop, which had remained closed since moving in. He ran a hand through his messenger bag and pulled out his phone. On the home screen, he found several Instagram updates and mentions of his agency on Twitter. Smiling, he unlocked his phone and read through each. "What the fuck!" he shouted.

There was a new voicemail from Dahlia: "Aaron, look at your Twitter. Let's meet in my office on forty-four and get ahead of this. I want an update first thing." He turned off his phone and shook his head. "I don't answer to you anymore..." He took another sip and looked at the bottle on the sink. No change.

Sleepy from dinner, he finished his drink and set the empty glass on the floor. Aaron took off his shirt and unbuckled his belt, walking out of his pants. Off came his socks and T-shirt and underwear. He dove into the light cotton covers and kicked his legs around. And as he began tugging at his penis, he fell asleep.

"Aaron?" hissed a low voice, slipping by his pillow and teasing his neck with a tongue.

Tickled, Aaron smiled in his sleep and gently pet the coil sliding along his body. Now beneath his bedsheets, the voice repeated, "Aaron?"

He turned on his back and buried his head between both pillows, exposing his throat. "Drink..." it said, licking open Aaron's lips. "Drink from me."

A fang secreted into Aaron's mouth. "Drink from me," it hissed once again.

As Aaron swallowed the sweet, cool drip, both fangs swung high into the air and gashed down on his neck.

Aaron sprang awake, eyes wide. He screamed, but he had no voice; his throat was coated and silenced. The coil wrapped around his legs and arms, pulling him deep into the mattress. Cold, sweet fluid rose up over his naked body. "Drink from me," it said again, turning Aaron's mouth into the swirling pool above him. As he lapped down fluid, he gulped air and coughed up. Slowly, the pool receded. Aaron's stomach was full. And he passed out.

"Aaron, I want you to know that I'm already in contact with the model. And now I want *your* side of this story."

"It's ridiculous."

"Is it?" asked Dahlia, cocking her head to the side. "Because it doesn't sound ridiculous to me." She swiveled her chair gently side to side. "Did you reach out and pull down this model's hair?"

Aaron rolled his eyes. "Only to get it all in the frame."

"Her *hair?*"

"Yes. She had..." He pulled a bottled water from a nearby cooler, uncapped it, and drank. "We were outside, and it was so windy and..."

Dahlia held up a palm to Aaron. "Here's what the model tweeted: *Humiliated to be told that my hair, in its natural Black beauty, wasn't the right look for this agency. Director pulled down all my hair and said, 'NOW you look right.'* Should I go on, Aaron?"

"I was under a deadline! Her hair was beautiful, but it wasn't in the shot. I had a tight shot and..."

"I am not understanding you. You told a black woman that her hair looked good *after* you pulled it down? And then you told her, which is her next tweet, *Now I can feel you in this shot?*"

"That's not how I meant it!" Aaron stood up and walked to the window. "Yes, it was entirely the wrong choice of words, but if I wasn't under this *insane* deadline you all put on me..."

"Whoa there, Aaron. This *insane* deadline was because you didn't listen to what I told you almost two weeks ago." Dahlia shook her head and scrolled her phone. "And here's a retweet to *Now I can feel you in this shot* from someone with 200,000 followers: *You know white people can't feel unless they touch.* That's a hashtag now, Aaron. And it's trending on the back of our agency."

He sat and sipped. "I'm sorry. It was wrong to..."

Her eyes were wide, and her hands were gripping her chair. "You know what, Aaron? Maybe you're not ready for this job."

He stood. "What!"

"Sit down! Rolf and the social media team have this contained. I'm meeting the model and her agent this morning to apologize in person." She leaned forward and massaged her forehead.

"Maybe I could join you, if..." he started, sitting.

"Oh, no! No, Aaron!" She threw out her hands and clasped them behind her head. "You have done *quite* enough already. Now I have to take time away from my projects and my new team to clean up your mess. Just like the old days, isn't it?"

"I'm sorry, Dahlia." He wedged the bottle cap in the soft gulley between his thumb and index finger. He began flicking it every few seconds as he slouched.

"I'm sorry, too, and would you stop fidgeting? I may not be your boss anymore, but I am on the executive committee, and I've recommended to Rolf that we put you on a warning."

"For *this?*" The cap dropped to the floor as he stood up.

"Yes, Aaron, for *this*. For damaging our agency's brand and goodwill. That is not something we look for in a leader. And now you need to think about how you're going to explain this to your team because

EVERYBODY knows about it."

He walked to the door and took a swig. He glanced at the cap on the floor and left it. "Anything else?"

"There is," she started, locking her eyes into his. "I'm not the first one to notice this, Aaron, but recently I smell alcohol on your breath. Including right now. Were you drinking this morning before work?"

He clasped the doorknob with his free hand. "No, I wasn't. Anything else?"

"Were you drinking on the shoot, when that model was present?"

Aaron looked down. He paused and chose the lesser trap. "No, I wasn't."

"I see. Noted, Aaron," she said, combing her fingers through her hair. "Noted."

"Can I go now?" His voice shook as he opened the door. "Is there anything else?"

"Yes," she said, pointing. "You can pick up that fucking bottle cap off my floor."

"Oh, my God, I need another drink!"

The bartender nodded at Aaron and delivered. Someone behind him tapped his arm. "Kel's here."

"OK," Aaron said, sipping. He made a motion to the bartender to tally his bill. Once dropped, Aaron looked it over and pulled out his credit card. He turned. "Is that everyone?" he asked, looking over the seven others behind him, talking around highboys with several empty glasses on each. They nodded their thanks, and Aaron clicked the pen. He roughed out 20 percent of the total and wrote an overly large $202.00 on the line and signed his name with a smiley face. He closed the check presenter and slid it over the metal rail on the bartender's side of the relationship: Poured. Paid.

"Okrrrr..." Aaron said, sliding off the torn bar stool. "Hey, guys, I'm going to go chat with Kel, but I'll be back."

"Thanks, Aaron!" said one. A few others smiled passingly, passively, and went back to their conversations. Two didn't look at Aaron at all. Almost out of earshot, Aaron heard them say, "He's such a fucking mess." "I know. He really had it together for a while."

Down the long, dark bar, Aaron passed wooden crates, unopened boxes of rail liquor stacked high, a large garbage can on wheels, half-full of empty cans, and a dimly lit EXIT sign above a black, dented wooden door with a diamond cut-out window, the only light in the back bar.

Outside on the patio, Aaron squinted in the evening light. It was warm, and the breeze scrubbed away the smell of bleach and stale beer from the back hallway. Wooden picnic tables, each with loose, rusted bolts and curled up planks, sat here and there on weed-lined concrete among whiskey half-barrels with their metal rings down at their base. Each warped barrel was held together by the precast dirt of cigarette butts, plastic wrappers, and seasons of disposed well drinks. Aaron found an open seat on a wobbly bench. "Hey, Kel."

"Hey, Aaron."

The two others at Kel's table smiled and quickly left the patio. For a moment, both he and Kel were silent. Aaron put down his drink and went first. "So how are you?"

"Good. You?"

"Good."

"That's good."

Kel drank. Aaron drank. Silence.

The door opened and then closed. Aaron and Kel were the only ones on the patio, enclosed by a high wooden fence and exit gate. The breeze picked up.

"Warm out."

Kel nodded. "Very."

Aaron drank. "So what's going on?"

He reached for Aaron's free hand. "You're in trouble, Aaron. You really are," Kel said, looking away. In the evening light, Aaron noticed fresh wrinkles around his blue eyes, but Kel's hair was as blond and wavy as when they met as children. "There's no easy way to say this." He took a deep breath. His voice was shaky. "But I love you, Aaron, so I'm going to say it anyway."

"Why am I in *trouble?*"

"Because I used to be your best friend. And you were mine. As long as I can remember it's been Kel-and-Aaron, Aaron-and-Kel. And I've been there for you so many times, and this time, this last time, you were doing so well. You really were! But I can't..." He started tearing up. He let go of Aaron's hand. "I can't do it anymore. You're not giving me any hope."

Aaron sipped. "I'm not giving *you* any hope? About what?"

"That you're ever going to stop. That rehab, even if you go back, is finally going to work. That you can admit to anyone, including yourself, that you didn't give up your car, that it was taken from you by a judge. And it's sitting, right now, on Circle Drive between our parents' houses." He rubbed his eyes. "I went up to see them a few weeks ago. I texted you that. You *knew* that. And I asked if you wanted to go with me to see your mom and dad, and you just...you couldn't even reply. And when I got there, I just sat in my car, and I stared at yours and I cried. You know what, Aaron? We taught each other sign language at two in the morning in our bedroom windows. I came out to you first, sophomore year, and then you came out to me, right after. Remember? And we both cried for what seemed like forever because we were both so scared and we felt so alone, but at least, we were scared *together*." He dropped his face into his hands. He wiped his eyes with his palms and smiled. "You're my best friend, Aaron! There's no one like you in my life. But I can't...I can't help you anymore. I can't apologize for you anymore."

Aaron hunched down. And said nothing.

"Your mom keeps asking mine how you are because you never call them back. You never text them..."

"Kel. I'm OK. I just got a big promotion. I can handle..."

"No!" he said, standing. "You can't, Aaron! That's the thing. You *can't*. I know you better than anyone, and you can't!" He wiped his eyes and sat. Kel reached out for Aaron's hands, but Aaron drew them in. "You're not even listening to me. Or Andy."

"Don't bring up Andy. *Andy* is the reason I don't have a car anymore."

"*YOU* are the reason you don't have a car anymore." Kel stood up again. "You know, lately, you just disappear. No one hears from you. No one can find you. Scott and those guys told me you moved from Logan Square. So that's something *else* you couldn't bother to tell me." He wiped his eyes. "I love you. But I can't do this anymore." Kel rounded the bench and huddled over Aaron, dropping his arms into a long hug. He kissed him on the forehead and walked back into the bar.

And Aaron was alone.

He sat hunched over the table for a long time, as people came and went, drank down and emptied their plastic cups, and went back inside for more. Aaron sat as the evening light drained into darkness, and finally, he stood up and went back inside. He hadn't touched his drink. He left it as others standing nearby took the table.

"Hey, Aaron," said someone from earlier, when it was still light out. "A few guys are still here. Hey, everyone, Aaron's back!"

"Hey. Is Kel still here?" Aaron asked, as a few went up to the bar to order a new round.

"No, he left a while ago. Didn't say anything, just bolted. Looked like he was crying or something. C'mon, you look like you need a drink."

Aaron lit up. "I do. I *really* do."

"Aaron! Hey! Aaron!"

"Fuck you!" he yelled back at the group of four trailing behind him.

"Where are we going?"

"Fucking Aaron. He wants to show us where he lives now."

"C'mon! One more block. Where are we, Balmoral?"

"Yeah," answered one, trudging along.

"So where do you live, Aaron?"

"I'm on Summerdale, Scott."

"We're on the wrong block. That's another one down!"

"OK, turn right on Wayne, and we'll be there. Hey, stop being an asshole," Aaron yelled back.

The four behind Aaron followed and then stopped, mid-block. "There! That's where I live now."

"Which one?" asked a friend in the group.

"That big house. On the corner."

"What corner?" asked another.

"Oh, my God! Right there!" Aaron said, pointing at Summerdale House.

"Yeah, but which house?"

Aaron ran up the stairs, kicking past the ivy. "Here!" he shouted as loud as he could, "Right here!"

"Aaron! Shh...that's someone's front lawn..." said one.

He walked onto the porch and waved. "Isn't this old house so beautiful?"

Across the street, a porch light turned on. A front door opened.

"Shit," said one in the group.

"Do you know what time it is?" an elderly man yelled, pointing. "Whoever's out there?"

"Aaron!" said one, teeth clenched.

"Keep it down!" scolded another.

"Aaron?" the man yelled out from the porch. "Aaron? Is that your name, wherever you are?"

"Come on, Aaron. Stop playing!" they yelled.

"Oh, fuck off!" Aaron yelled from the dark.

"Young man, go home or I'm calling the police." He threw up his hands. Two more porch lights went on across the street, and another door opened. A man wearing a coat over his pajamas stepped outside and greeted his neighbor. "You see this, Bill? Look at this! More problems..."

"Let's just go." "Aaron is so drunk..." the group said as they walked away. "Fuck him," another said as they turned the corner.

But one in the group stayed back.

"Assholes," Aaron said, fumbling for his key at the kitchen door. He replayed the dialogue out loud: "Which house is it, Aaron? *This one, the one I'm fucking pointing at.* We can't see it. What corner? *If I can see it, why the fuck can't you?"*

"Hey," said a voice behind Aaron.

Aaron turned, surprised. "Hey!"

"I'm Lucas. I was with Scott and everyone. Not sure if you remembered me or not."

"Ummm, sure..." Aaron said, looking him up and down. "I bought you a few shots. But I didn't think you were interested in me..."

"I'm just shy. And I'm really drunk and horned up."

Aaron reached for his hand. "Good enough for me. And you're kinda my type. So, wait. You can see the house, too?"

“Yeah, but I have no idea where we are. Those guys must be more drunk than we are.”

“Must be. What was your name again?”

He laughed. “Lucas!”

Aaron’s eyes hadn’t adjusted to the dark; no porch light had come on. But there was a slice of moonlight upon the door, so Aaron toggled Lucas into it. He touched the contours of Lucas’s face, freshly shaved and boyish, and in turn, Lucas gently bit Aaron’s finger as it crossed his lips. Aaron passed his other hand over Lucas’s crotch. “Nice. Come in, Lucas.” As Aaron opened the door, he shushed his guest. “But be super quiet inside. I don’t want to wake anyone up.”

Quietly, Aaron closed and locked the kitchen door. They tiptoed up the back stairs. On the first landing, Aaron bucked his hand up and down, enforcing silence. In the moonlight, Lucas gave a thumbs-up.

Once they were in his bedroom, Aaron closed the door slowly and locked it softly. After double-checking that it was locked, he found Lucas already on his bed. Aaron went to him and kissed his neck, running his hand through his thick, dark hair. Lucas turned, reaching back to meet Aaron’s mouth. Their tongues played at the tips, until Lucas pressed into Aaron and began unbuttoning his shirt. Aaron did the same and felt Lucas’s soft shoulders and arms. Aaron pulled down Lucas’s pants and underwear and opened his mouth. Lucas exhaled loudly and pushed his hardening penis into Aaron’s throat.

Aaron pulled away and threw off the last of his clothes. “I’m really drunk,” Lucas said as Aaron began undressing him.

“So am I!”

Lucas felt Aaron’s lithe body and playfully reached for his asshole. Aaron smiled and whispered, “Fuck me. I want you to fuck me,” and opened his bedside table. Inside, Lucas found lube and toys. "Kinky!" he said, excitedly, turning Aaron onto his stomach.

But atop Aaron, Lucas's arms sank into the mattress. Around his hands, fluid pooled up. "What the..." As Lucas sat up on his knees and flicked his arms dry, long red marks appeared on a forearm.

Aaron, drunk, didn't notice. He laughed and poked Lucas. "You're really handsome." He turned for a kiss.

"Why does..." Lucas started, as he pulled away from Aaron.

"What's wrong?" Aaron asked, turning, sitting up.

Lucas shot out of bed and plunged his forearm into the moonlight. He looked at the ceiling, the floor, the window, and then peered into Aaron's bathroom. He walked to the bedroom door and turned on the lights. "Why does my arm have scabs on it again? Where are we?"

"My apartment!" Aaron squinted and put his hands over his eyes. "God, that's so bright!"

"Look at my arm!" Lucas said, returning to the bed and jutting his wet forearm in Aaron's face. "Look! These weren't there when we came in."

Aaron touched his arm and peered in. "I don't see anything, Lucas."

And then, with a loud click, the lights turned off. Aaron peered into the dark as Lucas whispered, *"No, no, no, no, no, NO!"*

As his eyes adjusted, Aaron found Lucas fumbling at the bedroom door. The knob slipped from the grip of his wet hands, spinning over and over.

"This isn't happening! I can't be back here!" He swatted at the lightswitch, turning it on and off and on and off, but no light came.

Aaron tiptoed over to him and whispered, "Shh...Lucas..I'm really not supposed to have visitors over!"

But Lucas wasn't listening. Frantically, he spun the doorknob and began pulling at the heavy wooden frame.

"What's wrong? Did you used to live here?" Aaron asked, tugging at Lucas's arm. "Come on. Let's go back to bed," he said with another tug. "We don't have to fuck around, let's just chill and cuddle. OK?"

Lucas pushed him away. "But the kitchen, the back stairs! It's not the same. It doesn't look the same. Where are we again? What street are we on?" Lucas passed Aaron and reached down for his clothes. He began dressing. "Aaron! Where are we?"

"My apartment!"

"Where?"

"On Summerdale."

"On Summerdale?"

"Yeah. Summerdale & Wayne."

Lucas shrieked, "Is there a landlord here?"

"Mr. McGreevy."

Lucas fell to the floor.

"Shh...Lucas! I'm so serious. I can't have guests over. It's a rule here."

And then, from the hallway, knocking at Aaron's door.

"I...I'm sorry," Aaron said, softly, putting on his pants. "I'll keep the TV down..."

Aaron helped Lucas up. They looked at each other in silence as the knocking stopped. And then, a soft voice from the hallway: "Lucas?" The doorknob was being turned from the outside. "Is that you, Lucas?"

Aaron's mouth dropped. How would anyone know his guest's name?

And the door opened. "Come out here, Lucas," said the voice again from the dark hallway.

Lucas hid behind Aaron and began crying. "Why did you bring me back here?"

Aaron saw no one at the door, but Lucas tightened his grip as if someone were approaching. He dropped to the floor and began spitting up. Aaron knelt down and hovered. "What's wrong, Lucas? Should I call an ambul..."

An arm reached around Aaron's neck and pulled him onto the bed. When the arm let go, he watched Lucas stand up and stare into the moonlight, as if in a trance.

He backed up to the wall. And Lucas ran out the window.

"Lucas!" Aaron shouted.

Glass shattered and Aaron covered his eyes. A breeze whipped through the room, and a fanlike carpet of glass shards swirled into the dark corners of Aaron's bedroom. He shook his head and wiped his face with the bedsheet. His heart raced.

Aaron's door slammed shut.

After minutes frozen in place, Aaron pulled off the bedsheet and threw it on the floor. One foot, then another, and he walked carefully toward the open, empty dormer. The entire window was broken out and hanging off the gutter.

Carefully, Aaron leaned on the broken sill and looked into the front yard. Lucas's body was caught in a tree upside-down, lifeless. His arms had dropped outward, and he was bleeding out both eyes onto the lawn.

Backing away from the window, Aaron noticed insects flying in and out of his room. One settled on his arm. It was a wasp. He flicked it away as hundreds settled like a cloak upon Lucas and drank up the trail from his eyes. The swarm lifted Lucas's arms, untangled him, and set him on the lawn face-up. The dark swarm separated into two figures, and both stood. One became Lucas. The other, Mr. McGreevy.

Awakened, Lucas ran, but McGreevy flew inside him and pulled him back. They struggled. Once Lucas gave up, they separated and their bodies reformed. And they both walked through the front wall into Summerdale House.

Aaron fell to his knees and threw up. He crawled back into bed and passed out.

The morning sun awakened Aaron. He rolled onto his side and lifted himself up. The night before came back to him in bursts.

Jolted by the memory, he shot up and looked out the window—unbroken—and surveyed the front yard of Summerdale from the gutter to the sidewalk, to the old tree, to the houses along Wayne Avenue. Nothing out of place. And no sign of Lucas.

Curious, Aaron unlocked and opened his dormer window. It ran smoothly on its track and relocked with precision. There was no glass on the floor, and the sheet he had spread down was back on the bed, tucked in.

He walked into the bathroom and started the shower. Over and over, he cupped his hands beneath the faucet and drew warm water into his mouth. He turned, looking at his unmade bed. Lucas wasn't there.

After a long shower, Aaron dried off and sat on his bed naked. His mind raced. He couldn't talk to Mr. McGreevy about Lucas, nor could he text his friends—what would he say? Aaron wondered aloud if he could slyly ask anyone Lucas's whereabouts without inciting panic. Aaron didn't even know his last name.

Just then, he noticed what would calm him down—the bottle on the vanity sink. He put on shorts, uncorked the bottle, and held the neck to his mouth. The bottle was full.

It was a dream. The whole thing, just a vivid dream. There was no Lucas. I don't know anyone named Lucas. Someone slipped a drug into my drink, and I hallucinated the whole thing. It didn't happen. He smiled at himself in the mirror and took a swig. Then another.

Aaron smelled bacon from downstairs, and he was suddenly hungry. He recorked the bottle and set it back in place, throwing on a college T-shirt and flip-flops before darting downstairs. *It was all just a bad dream!*

He expected another tenant or two at the table, but found none. "Morning, Mr. McGreevy!" He pointed to a placemat, utensils, and a mug of steaming coffee. "Is this mine?"

"Well, good morning, Aaron!" McGreevy turned, spatula in hand. "Of course, it is! How was your night? You look a little pale."

Aaron sat. "I'm fine. Just fine."

"You want eggs and bacon, I assume?"

"Sure." On the counter by the sink, Aaron noticed an empty hurricane glass and leafy celery stalks.

With tongs and a spoon, McGreevy filled up Aaron's plate first, then his own. McGreevy set both at the table and then returned with more coffee for himself and sat. "Go ahead, Aaron. Don't let it get cold."

Aaron put the cloth napkin in his lap. With each quick bite, color returned to his face.

"So, Aaron! What's on your agenda for this beautiful Saturday? Looks like sunshine all weekend, from what I read in the *Trib*."

"Not really sure what I'm doing yet," Aaron fumbled. He glanced at the hurricane glass.

"Oh, my goodness," said McGreevy. "I forgot your Bloody Mary!" He opened the refrigerator and pulled out a bottle of premade mix.

"Actually," called Aaron, holding a hand out. "I'm OK without it. Really, I don't need one."

"Now, now, Aaron. If you had a bad night last night, this is just what you need to get back on track. A little hair of the dog that..."

"I'm really OK. This coffee is great! And this is just like brunch on Clark Street!" he said, holding up his fork as a toast. "Really delicious."

McGreevy poured vodka to the top of the glass. The celery swirled. "I know you want it, Aaron." And he set it down.

"Thanks," he said.

"You wouldn't want to hurt my feelings, now would you?" McGreevy asked, frowning as he sat.

Aaron shrugged. "Of course not."

McGreevy snapped his napkin and put it on his lap. He gave Aaron a confident look. "Drink."

And Aaron raised the glass. It was the saltiest, sweetest, strongest Bloody he had ever had. And once it was gone, he felt better: more aware, more awake, more alive.

"There now," said McGreevy, chewing bacon. "Isn't that better?"

Aaron wanted to say no, but he couldn't. It would be rude. "Can I have another?"

McGreevy wiped his mouth on his napkin and dropped it on his chair. "Of course, Aaron. You never have to hesitate to ask for seconds."

By his third Bloody Mary, Aaron wasn't buzzed but focused. McGreevy had talked about feeding his roses for the entire meal and excused himself when he checked the time. "I'll need to get out there and water the yard now. My boys are thirsty..."

"Thanks, Mr. McGreevy, for breakfast and everything."

"Of course, Aaron!" But he stopped before walking out the kitchen door. "Actually, I wanted to ask you about something. Did you call up to me the other morning after I went upstairs? Something about some hissing noises in your bedroom?"

Aaron rolled in his lips, then smacked them out. "Nope!"

"Something about a..."

"All good, Mr. McGreevy! Must have dreamt it."

McGreevy opened the door and chuckled. "Well, you be sure to let me know if those hissing noises come back..."

After his landlord left, Aaron gathered the empty plates and began washing them in the sink. There was no leftover food, so he soaked and washed the large pots and wiped out the cast-iron skillet with paper towel, washing only the heat-scarred bottom and handle. And he went upstairs, locked his bedroom door, and passed out.

It was evening when Aaron awoke. He stretched his arms and legs and watched a shadow from the setting sun soak and flatten the detailed inlay of his dresser. It looked like a magazine layout, his bedroom in the light of evening, and he thought of taking pictures to post on Instagram. *My phone can't capture this. It's too perfect. Everything here is too perfect. It doesn't feel real. But it is.*

He lingered in bed, in his thoughts, then got up and peed. As he washed his hands, he looked at the vodka bottle, full again, but he didn't drink. At his desk, he opened his laptop, which released dust into the air. But he didn't enter his password. Instead he recharged his phone and caught up with texts and Instagram posts, and though he searched, he found no new messages from Kel.

I'll start writing again tomorrow, he told himself, closing the clamshell. *Maybe I'll show something to Dahlia again; she gave me some really good feedback last time.*

But then, one Instagram post caught his eye, from his favorite bar a block off Sheridan. "What the?" he said aloud, scrolling down the post and skimming comment after comment. The post had thousands of likes. "Tomorrow night? Fucking shit!"

"There you are!" said McGreevy, turning from the oven. He grabbed mitts. "I was about to call up and ask if you wanted to join me for a

Sunday pizza dinn..."

"Hey." Aaron yanked out a chair and sat.

"Anything wrong?"

"No!" He rapped on the table.

McGreevy pulled the pizza from the oven, on a rectangular stone. "Don't dent my table there..."

"Sorry. That smells really good."

He set the stone atop the stove and inhaled. "Mmm! Nothing like fresh basil and tomatoes from your own little garden. Picked this morning!" He rummaged through a drawer and pulled out a cutting wheel. "I might even have a beer with you tonight."

Aaron twisted his mouth and looked at his clasped hands.

"Aaron, what's wrong? Your eyes are *extra* green."

"It's bullshit. I'm sorry, I shouldn't swear at the table. But it is. It's bullshit!"

McGreevy began slicing. "I'm listening..."

"It's just unfair. This bartender. A fucking *bartender!*"

"Did he water down your drinks or something?"

"No! He just...this is *so* unfair."

McGreevy looked at Aaron and rubbed his temples. "Words, Aaron. Let's use a few more..."

"It's this bartender!"

"Yes, we've established that." He pulled cheese off the wheel and ate it. "It's some *fucking* bartender..."

Aaron pounded the table. "He got a book deal! This *nobody* bartender got a book deal!"

McGreevy looked impressed. He reached up for plates.

"I found out yesterday. It's been killing me all weekend. It's all anyone is talking about. And now that he has a book deal, you *know* a movie deal is next."

McGreevy set plates on the table, then opened the freezer. "Let me fix you a drink. Can I ask why this is getting to you? Is he a friend of yours?"

"No!" Aaron looked up and smiled. "I mean yes, Michael is an acquaintance. We're not friends on Facebook or Instagram or anything. I just know him through the bar. This guy isn't a writer. He's just a bartender!"

"Just a bartender, Aaron? A little snobby, don't you think?" McGreevy asked as he broke up an ice tray and knocked a few cubes into a rocks glass. "It sounds like his hard work has paid off." He smirked as he poured in vodka and watched Aaron in the reflection of the greenhouse window. "I'd think you'd be happy for Michael. Tell me why you're not..."

"Because he's not a writer! He works at a bar. And he's in one of these fucking cliques that posts all their brunches and vacations together. He's *nothing*."

The cubes swirled as McGreevy set down the glass. "Now that sounded *very* snobby, Aaron..."

"You're right. I'm sorry. Just let me drink this, so I can think coherently..." He threw back the drink and caught a drip with his thumb, drawing it back into his mouth. In a few sips, Aaron exhaled and relaxed his shoulders. "Thank you. That's better. You're skipping the tonic lately, I notice."

Pulling in his chair, McGreevy clasped his hands on the table and smiled. "Another minute and that pizza will be perfect. So tell me about this bartender. Why is this getting to you?"

"Because this deal just falls into his lap, and did you know that *I'm* a writer?"

McGreevy turned down his lip. "I certainly didn't! Tell me about it. Is it a novel you're writing?" He returned to the stove, cut apart large squares, and set a few onto each plate. From the fridge, he grabbed a bottle of beer and set everything down on the table.

"It's just a first draft. I mean, it's pretty much ready to send out as a proposal." Aaron pulled a plate onto his placemat and put the napkin in his lap.

"What's it about? I'm a voracious reader, you know," he said, popping the cap of his bottle and taking a swig.

"Oh, I know! I looked through your books in the parlor. Like, Chaucer and Dante and Shakespeare."

He smirked. "I see a little of myself in them all. Hey!" he said, prompting Aaron to look up. "Maybe *I* could read your draft and give you some feedback."

"Really?"

"Of course, Aaron!" McGreevy said, pulling cheese and dropping it in his mouth. "There's nothing I enjoy more than developing the talents of my tenants."

"Well, basically, it's about this group of gay friends who meet at this one bar when they're just out of college in their twenties, and *then* the bar gets demolished."

McGreevy looked startled. "While they're inside?"

"No!" Aaron laughed and took another slice. "I mean, it's twenty years later, and then the bar gets demolished." He bit and chewed. "Oh, wow. This is amazing. Totally worth the evening carbs."

Silence but for chewing.

"This is like a gourmet pizza. You know what, Mr. McGreevy?" Aaron started, looking around the kitchen, and finishing off a crisp square. "Everything here is perfect. And I feel like I can tell you anything. You're great with all your advice."

McGreevy bit. "Well, that's why I'm here, Aaron. Tell me more."

"So, like, the characters have all gone their separate ways, and then twenty years go by, and then they all come back and reminisce *before* the bar gets demolished."

"I'm not following."

"Like, it was on the news, the demolition of this iconic bar, and then they come back, but none of them knows that the other is coming back, and they meet for one last drink."

"So it sounds like the reunion is an opportunity for these friends who've lost touch to compare and contrast how their lives may have been better had they stayed close, or if they would have drifted apart regardless, as their differing values and politics are revealed over dinner that same night."

Aaron pursed his lips. "Exactly!"

"And with the finality of a demolition as a symbol of the end of their shared experience in youth, you're also symbolizing that as something in their memory ends, new memories will begin for others."

Swirling his ice, Aaron nodded. "That's perfect." He drank.

"And you'll *have* to have some reference that all four of them…it is four, isn't it, Aaron?"

"Yes. Four." He bit into his next square.

"Four friends, and one rediscovers a lost love within the group, and they all re-ink their faded Pride tattoos to commit to their renewed friendships."

"That's really good!" Aaron said, darting his finger into the air. "Because friendships, like tattoos, will fade. But friendships can be renewed."

"Profound, Aaron." He swung his head beneath dripping cheese and bit. "I can tell you've put a lot of thought into this story."

"Well, my draft is *nearly* done." He swirled his glass again. "It just needs another few rounds of edits. I think I need another drink before I go back upstairs."

"More pizza?" McGreevy asked, half-standing.

"No, just the drink. But seriously, this pizza is so good!" he said, curling over the hanging cheese and biting.

"Is it a party later? At someone's house?"

"No, it's at his bar off Sheridan. This is his last night before he moves to L.A. and focuses on this full-time. I mean, if he's moving to L.A., you know a movie is coming. He got a huge signing bonus. His book agent will be there, too…"

McGreevy perked up. "His agent? I think it's a great idea that you go. You need to find out who his agent is and tell him about *your* novel."

"Really, Mr. McGreevy? Isn't that a little shady?"

"Absolutely not. Here, let me get you that drink. And you go upstairs and dust off that laptop and get to writing!"

"Take some chances and meet that agent? Is that what you mean?"

A moment later, McGreevy handed Aaron his drink. "Absolutely. And there's no time like the present."

"So congrats again, Michael. I'm *so* happy for you. Really, I am."

"Thanks, Aaron!" Michael said, leaning over the bar for a kiss. "*So* appreciate it. I just can't believe all this is happening, you know? I'm fucking moving to L.A.!"

"You'll fit right in."

"Hope so," he said, looking over a line of new people walking in. "Wow, look at all the people here! So, just the one drink?'

"Yeah, can you open a tab for me?" he asked, reaching for his wallet.

Michael smiled. "I'm sure gonna miss your bar tabs, Aaron!" He swung around and swiped his card, then handed it back.

"Well, we'll certainly miss you around here. Hey, you know what? I heard your agent will be here. Is that true?"

"For sure. He's doing some press for me in Fulton Market. I guess there's a big LitCon there this weekend. But he'll swing by with someone who's going be on the book cover. The model's actually from here, so he was excited to sign on. He's got a huge Instagram following."

"Nice." Aaron sucked down his drink. "And what's his name?"

"The model? It's, umm..."

"No, your *agent.*"

"My agent? Why do you want to know my agent's name?"

But Aaron had no answer. Which was his answer. Michael raised his eyebrows and noticed a new chit in the printer. "See ya, Aaron." He shook his head and walked away.

"Asshole," said Aaron under his breath. He took a stool at the far end of the bar and began texting friends. He glanced through the crowd but saw no one worth losing his bar stool for. A few texted back that they'd be at the bar soon.

And then he scrolled back in time to Kel and read through years of messages that ended with one, unanswered by Aaron weeks ago: *All right. Gonna stop texting u. Just please call ur mom and dad. They love u and so do I… ALWAYS xxoo*

Aaron tapped EDIT CONTACTS, highlighted Kel's name, and deleted him. He jangled his half-empty glass to catch the eye of a different bartender. "Another? My tab. I'm Aaron. Thanks."

By his third drink, Aaron was surrounded by three friends. One of them brought up Lucas, and Aaron's ears perked up.

"It's so odd," said one. "He's not texting me back, and he's not picking up. Hope he's OK. Didn't he stay back with you Friday night, Aaron?"

"Oooh-oooh-woo!" said another. "You and *Lucas?* But he's so innocent!"

"He's not that innocent," said the second friend. "He went through rehab a year ago."

"Alcohol?" asked Aaron.

"Heroin," said the third friend. "His track marks just started fading."

"Jesus!" said Aaron. "I had no idea."

"Honestly," said the second, reaching into the drinks he ordered on Aaron's tab. "I was surprised to see him out drinking with us. I mean, aren't you supposed to be *totally* sober, like no drugs at all?" he asked, sipping.

"Alcohol isn't heroin," said Aaron.

The first friend darted his eyes discreetly at Aaron. "Alcohol's a drug. Obviously."

But it didn't get past Aaron. "What's that supposed to mean?"

The second and third friends grabbed their drinks and slinked away.

"Nothing. I just..."

"You just *what?*" Aaron asked, finishing his drink.

"Hey!" Aaron shouted. "Michael! You still work here, right? Even though you got a FUCKING book deal?" He pounded the bar.

"Aaron, why have you turned into such an asshole?" asked the first friend.

"I'm not. I want to find his agent. Is his agent here?"

"His *agent?* Are you kidding me? For what, that novel you've talked about for years that no one's ever seen?"

"Yeah. I have a story here that he needs to know about. One a lot better than Michael could write." Aaron pounded the bar again. "Hey! Can I get my drink already?"

"Jesus, Aaron," he said, turning away. "You are a fucking mess."

More people piled in from outside, crowding Aaron to the edge of the bar.

"I don't know why everyone is against me all of a sudden," Aaron said, throwing a hand in the air. "We used to be really tight. Now we're nothing. *You're* nothing. All of you are just nameless, faceless nobodies. We have nothing in common anymore."

And his last friend closed in. "It's not that we don't have anything in common anymore, Aaron. It's that we don't have *alcohol* in common anymore. So when you finally hit rock bottom, and you will, don't come crying to us. Because no one deserves it more than you." He walked to a nearby circle of friends, and Aaron overheard their first words: "Aaron is such a fucking mess. I'm over him." The others replied, "I don't want to be around him anymore." "Trust me, nobody does."

"Assholes," said Aaron as he turned away and faced the door. Behind him, a thud.

"Your drink, Aaron. And your check." As Michael walked away, Aaron found a dollar bill from his wallet and threw it on the bar, then spilled his drink over it and ran.

"Fuck them," he muttered, throwing open the door. He pulled out his phone. "It's all gonna come out."

"Pretty angry there, Aaron. C'mon, let's get outta here."

Aaron took a step back. "Do I know you? Are you friends with Michael and those guys? Or with Scott? I can't remember."

"Yeah, we met Friday night. You were really drunk. Come on. Let's get out of here. There's a new bar just up the street."

"Thank fucking God. ASSHOLES!" he screamed at the door and stuck up his middle finger.

"Post that!"

Aaron's eyes lit up. "Really? I totally should. You know, you're really good looking. Are you sure we met Friday night?"

"Here," he said, taking Aaron's phone. He maneuvered Aaron's hand. "I'll take it for you. Move your middle finger over a little...there! Perfect. You got the bar sign and your middle finger just right." He snapped.

Aaron grabbed his phone and looked at the pic. "Oh, my God. That's fucking beautiful composition with the neon. Are you a photographer?"

He chuckled. "No, but thanks."

"No, really! I work for an agency. This is ethereal, or something. We should hire you."

"Post it," the man commanded. "And tag the bar so it shows up in their feed."

"Yeah?"

"No time like the present. Here, I'll do it," he said, taking back Aaron's phone and tapping away. "There. Done. Let's go."

"Hey, wait! What did you post? Was it something bad?"

He smirked, and Aaron poked playfully into his lightweight jacket. And again. "Wow. You have really big arms."

"Come on. Let's go to that bar up the street."

"Hey, wait. Wait! Before we go. Remind me your name. What's your name?"

He kissed Aaron's neck. "Does it matter?"

In his bed, Aaron awoke, drunk, and remembered nothing of how he got there. "Oh, my God," he whispered through his dry mouth. As he felt around the mattress, a hand reached back for his. Their fingers intertwined gently. With his other hand, Aaron felt a solid forearm and massive bicep. "God, you're so muscular..." he said, coughing up. An arm wrapped over his chest and massaged his sternum. His coughing stopped. "Thanks. You're sweet. I'm gonna be so hungover tomorrow," he slurred, "but you feel so good. It'll totally be worth it." Aaron giggled, still drunk.

The arm around Aaron's chest dissolved, and beneath his legs, Aaron felt two limbs kicking softly back and forth. Aaron snuggled down until the limbs melded into one. "God, your legs!"

A nuzzle rose up from the mattress and cradled Aaron's neck. He closed his eyes, feeling safe in the embrace.

Hissing began, softly at first. Soon, over and over, it whispered, "Drink from me," and secreted into his mouth. Aaron suckled and drank it down. Metal springs popped and fabric tore as a warm, striated limb from inside the mattress massaged Aaron's neck. He nuzzled into the nook. "Drink from me," it said again, as Aaron felt coiling around one leg, and then the other. The hissing grew louder as the soft limb scoped up his thigh and circled his penis.

He giggled as the limb edged playfully against his balls—exactly how Aaron liked to be warmed up for sex. As the limb pressed through Aaron's pubic hair, it let off a lubricant. Immediately Aaron began thrusting against the wet limb, speeding his hips until the limb broke open a warm hole.

"Oh, fuck," Aaron whispered, entering with a deep thrust. "Oh, fuck!" he said over and over until the suction around his penis coaxed his release. Aaron grunted and shook as the soft opening absorbed every drop. The thick limb around his neck receded and returned his head to the flat mattress. The back of his neck was sweaty, and Aaron drew up his hand to wipe away the residue. "Hey?" he called. "Hold me again. Just a little more?"

A forked tongue gently darted around his chin. His penis softened and dribbled onto his leg. Aaron giggled as the tongue, as rough as sandpaper, zigzagged over his throat. From the corner of his eye, Aaron spied two shiny fangs. Frightened, he flipped onto his back. "Drink from me, Aaron..." it said again.

And bit.

Aaron's eyes popped open, and he screamed, but no words came. Above him, he saw two red eyes staring down as the fangs sliced into his neck. Aaron grabbed at the punctures, but oily residue slicked over both hands.

Within seconds, Aaron was high.

And now he wanted more. He pressed the fangs into his neck and jostled them, tearing the cuts deeper into his flesh. With his other hand, he felt the contour of dripping nostrils and cold, bulging eyes. As the fangs dislodged from his skin, he coaxed both leaking tips across his mouth.

He turned and thrust the fangs into the other side of his neck. His eyes rolled back; he swiveled his legs across the mattress, feeling higher than before. Once spent, the fangs pulled out slowly. Aaron swiveled his limbs back and forth across the mattress.

Freed, Aaron skimmed his chest, his stomach, his legs, and licked his hands dry. Pressing his mouth into the wet mattress, he slurped down the sweet fluid that pooled up. Hundreds of fingertips rose and retreated beneath him—a calming surf that lapped the lanky bank of his body. One by one, the fingers hardened into a cradle, and Aaron passed out in its warming kiln.

"Good morning, Aaron," said Mr. McGreevy from the stove. "Well, you look happy!"

"Morning, Mr. McGreevy! I just had the most amazing *fu*..." He giggled and stopped himself. "Dream! I had the most amazing *dream* last night."

"Really?" McGreevy asked, flipping bacon in a frying pan. "Tell me about it..."

Aaron found a placemat, juice glass, coffee, napkin, and silverware, opposite Mr. McGreevy's place setting, at the kitchen table. "Now it's going to feel like Sunday again. This is for me, right? This side of the table?" he asked.

McGreevy turned. "Of course, it is, Aaron."

"Thanks!" He sat and put the bright yellow napkin in his lap. "You're so nice, always making me breakfast."

"I like to keep my boys well fed," he said, turning, taking the skillet off the flame.

He sipped his coffee. "But I'm the only one ever down here!"

"So," McGreevy started, draining off bacon fat into a jar, "tell me about this dream you had. I'm intrigued."

Aaron frowned. "I'm not bruised or anything, am I? On my neck?" he asked, pushing on both sides of his throat. "I mean, I must have slept wrong. I didn't see anything in the mirror upstairs, but could you look? Would you mind?" He lowered the collar of his plaid button-down shirt.

McGreevy peered in as he set a full plate before Aaron. "No, not that I can see. So come on," he prompted with an upturned voice. "Let me live vicariously through you. What was this dream?"

"Well, I *dreamed* that I picked up a hot guy outside the bar, and I'm not normally into super-muscular guys, but we had sex, and then we cuddled the whole night. And it was really sweet. Oh, my God, his arms. And his legs!" Aaron held his hands far apart. "His quads were just *unnfff!* Like, his body was insane." He picked up his fork and dug in.

McGreevy sat down and blew on a forkful of steaming scrambled eggs. "Well, it sounds like a great dream, Aaron."

Another stab at the bacon and he closed his eyes as he chewed. "Oh, my God," he mumbled. "Is this *maple* bacon?"

"With my homemade cinnamon-maple-honey glaze."

"I am *never* leaving Summerdale! I've never seen anyone else here, but does anyone leave?"

"Some try," McGreevy said, biting the bacon. "But one way or another, they always find their way back. So, anything else about this dream? Did he have a name?" he asked, looking away.

Aaron gulped and smiled sweetly. "You know, now that I think about it, there was a point where I got really scared, and then I wasn't. But I don't remember why." He grinned. "I know I need to leave for work soon, but could I get a Bloody Mary? Just a little one? I'll brush my teeth again before I head out."

McGreevy stood up and walked to the refrigerator. "I can put something together."

"Thanks!"

Just then Aaron's phone buzzed. He scooped eggs onto his fork and pulled his phone from his pocket. As he scrolled with one hand, he downed the eggs with the other. "Shit!" he said, and mouthed *fuck* over and over.

McGreevy returned to the table with a Bloody. He sat and sipped his coffee. "Anything wrong, Aaron?"

Aaron drank. "Fuck! Oh, sorry. I'm at the table. It's just..." He put his phone down and forked up the last of his bacon and scrambled eggs. And drank again.

"There's more of everything, Aaron, if you'd like some?"

"No. I really need to get to work now." He leaned his cheeks into his palms and muttered, "Fuuuuuuuuck!" as his phone vibrated again and again.

McGreevy guffawed. "It's not even 7:30! Whatever's going on, it can't be that bad."

"It is, on the other side of the world." He exhaled and reset his phone upside-down. "I posted something I really shouldn't have. But I don't remember posting it."

"What was it?"

"It's not the post. It's the comments. I'm just going to delete it. I need to delete that post. Right now. But I should probably read the comments my friends are leaving first."

"I suppose that's best," McGreevy said, shrugging.

Aaron scrolled and read: *Got a screenshot you POS, so even if you delete this, I never will. Fuck U ASSHOLE AARON.*

He scrolled to the top, activated the Actions arrow, and hit Delete. He ran upstairs and brushed his teeth, grabbed his messenger bag, and took off.

"No, this layout is getting better, but it isn't quite right yet," Aaron said, taking a breath, looking out the window. "Let's have another look today after..." His desk phone rang. It was Dahlia. Aaron looked at the few seated across from him and stuck up an index finger. He put the call on speaker. "Hey, Dahlia, I'm actually meeting with my team about the..."

"Aaron, take this call off speaker *right now.*"

He did. The others began talking among themselves.

"OK. I'm here."

"Aaron, I am making this call as a courtesy. Rolf and Mr. Godfrey are in my office. Come up to the conference room on forty-four immediately. Bring your security ID, wallet, keys, *everything.* Come directly up, or we will send security down. Do you understand?"

He gulped. "I'll be right up."

"OK," Aaron said, ending the call and standing, "So, I need to go meet with Dahlia about something, but let's meet again after lunch?"

Those seated arose, nodded, and left. He gathered the items Dahlia requested and glanced at his cut red tie, still tacked up behind his desk. Aaron closed his glass door and pressed his palm to it. *'Come up to the conference room on forty-four immediately,'* he repeated to himself in Dahlia's rushed, low voice. He took a few deep breaths to calm his heartbeat. He put everything into his bag, and as he walked to the elevator, he pressed his palms on his pants to dry them.

"So long, Aaron!" someone yelled as he pressed the elevator button. Soon, one arrived and swept him upstairs. When the doors opened on the executive floor, Dahlia was waiting.

"This way," she said, tapping Aaron's shoulder. They walked into the conference room where Godfrey and two other executives were already seated.

"Aaron," Rolf said, coldly, closing the door.

He motioned for Aaron to sit, and Dahlia chose the chair beside him.

Rolf sat and spoke first. "Aaron, answer yes or no. Did you post this on your personal social media account last night?" With his cellphone, Rolf showed him the photo of the bar's neon sign with Aaron's middle finger in front of it.

Aaron said nothing, so Rolf read the post: "Fuck you, backstabbing self-hating homos, and fuck this bar..."

Godfrey held out his hands. "All right, Rolf, all right. We get it. We've *all* seen it."

Rolf put his phone on the conference room table facedown. "Shared 915 times so far overnight, and on an early share, someone posted that you work for us with a link to your team leader bio. Now, we're being flooded with messages saying that we hate the LGBTQ community and asking how can we employ someone who posts things like this."

Silence, until Godfrey ended it. "It doesn't help, Aaron, that the owner of that bar is the sister of the alderman who sat on the summer clean-up committee. Had a *lovely* chat with both of them at seven a.m."

Dahlia turned to Aaron. "The city has pulled our campaign. So tell us, Aaron. Why did you post that?"

He looked at the floor. "I don't know. I don't remem..."

Dahlia turned and threw down her arms. "You don't *remember?* And why is that?"

Aaron wiped his forehead. He looked up. "Yes. I posted it, but I don't remember doing it."

Rolf stood. "This is the second disaster you've caused us, just since being promoted."

Dahlia tapped Aaron's chair. "Based on what the model told me when I met with her and her agent last week, she called your behavior misogynistic and racist. And I'd have to agree."

Rolf sat and clasped his hands on the table. "We have every right to fire you."

Aaron began tearing up. He opened his mouth, but no words came.

"You need help," Rolf continued. "Given your past success, Mr. Godfrey has agreed to offer you an arrangement."

Aaron looked down and wiped his eyes. Dahlia shook her head and looked at the ceiling. The two seated executives simply took notes.

"Aaron, look at me," Rolf said sternly. "Look at me. Here's what we are offering. If you agree to enter a ninety-day rehab program immediately and commit to your full recovery, Mr. Godfrey will continue your employment upon your return."

Godfrey leaned back in his executive chair and held out his hands. "We don't throw people away here." The executives nodded along. Dahlia gave them both a look.

Turning, wiping his face, Aaron nodded. "Thank you."

Rolf spoke next. "Is this agreeable to you? It is binding and it is immediate."

"Yes, it is. Thank you."

"Good," said Rolf. "Dahlia arranged for your sponsor Andy to be here. He's in the next room. We've shared with him only what is legally necessary and he's offered to..."

Aaron stood. "I know what this is. I know what's coming next."

Dahlia stood as well. "Aaron, I hope that you use this time to reflect on the harm you've done to a lot of people, including me. Will you?"

"Yes. But can I go home first and..."

Rolf rushed up from his chair, as if blocking that possibility. "No. You leave now with Andy and check in. The facility is downstate, and it will have everything you need. We were able to confirm your arrangements just before Dahlia called you up. Are you on any medications?"

Aaron laughed and wiped his face. "Just alcohol."

Dahlia frowned. "Aaron, if you don't go with Andy directly to the facility and complete the program, you are fired. Do you understand?"

He nodded yes. One of the executives passed Aaron a clipboard and pen, and he began reading and signing forms.

"Good," said Dahlia as she crossed her arms. She backed away from them all. "Now there's one more thing I need to say, and I'm gonna signal this out to everyone in this room." She snapped her fingers at the seated executives. "And you better make sure *this* makes it into the minutes of this little HR meeting. You can call what you're doing for Aaron forgiveness or redemption or second chances or, in Aaron's case, *third* chances, or you can join me in calling this what it really is. White. Fucking. Privilege."

Rolf looked shocked. “That’s not fair, Dahlia.”

“It *isn’t* fair, Rolf! It. So. Is. Not. Fair! Because I’ve sat in this same room and watched my brown-skinned colleagues being exited for a helluva lot less and with zero offers of redemption. *ZERO!*”

Aaron signed the last form and put down the clipboard. He folded his arms and started crying. “I’m sorry, Dahlia. Everyone, I’m so sorry!”

Dahlia laughed. “Save your tears, Aaron.” She opened the door and turned. “Good luck. The hard work will start when you get back. I’ll make sure of that.”

Rolf followed her out. Moments later, Andy walked in.

Aaron hugged him. “I’m so sorry, Andy.”

“It’s OK. Come on, let’s go. Do you have your wallet and cellphone and everything?”

Aaron opened his bag. “Yes. Everything.”

“Your ID?” Rolf asked, hand out.

Aaron scooped it out of the bag and handed it over.

“Thank you, Aaron. Your email and net ID have been revoked. You’ll get everything back upon your successful completion of the program in ninety days.”

Andy rubbed Aaron’s arm. “You can call your primary doctor on the way and let him know where you’re going. Are you taking any meds, anything that needs to be refilled?”

“No.”

“C’mon, Aaron. Time to go.” Andy put an arm around Aaron’s

shoulder, and smiled at the group. “Thank you, everyone. Rolf, I’ll send over his intake papers to you as confirmation of his check-in. And you have my contact information. We’ll stay in touch.”

“Good luck, Aaron,” said Mr. Godfrey, tapping his shoulder.

Aaron nodded his thanks to everyone as Andy led him from the conference room. An elevator opened, and they were gone.

“Hey, Andy? It’s Aaron. Hey, I’m sorry I’ve been out of touch for a few days, but I really need help right now. I’m at our old place on Roscoe. I’m outside, and...” The phone rang back.

“Aaron! Did you just call me? Where have you been? Where are you?”

Aaron fell to the sidewalk and began crying. He ran his free hand over the coarse, cold concrete. “I’m sorry! I’ve...”

“Aaron, stop saying you’re sorry. You’ve been doing so well since you came back. You called me. You did the right thing. You called me, so forget everything else. OK? So you’re on Roscoe? At our old apartment?”

“Yes,” he said, wiping his eyes.

“I shouldn’t be here, Andy! I shouldn’t be here!”

“Aaron, are you alone?”

“Yes, I’m alone.”

“Remember what we talked about, Aaron? Months ago when I took you to the facility? On your first day, when I was still with you, what did they tell you to do when you want a drink?"

Aaron nodded. "To call you. To call my sponsor." He wiped his face again. "The call means that *I'm* in control."

"Exactly, Aaron! *You* are in control. Right now. Not the craving. Not the alcohol. Not whatever triggered this. Not our old apartment and everyone who abused alcohol and drugs there. You took control and called me."

And then Aaron shouted, "I don't want to be back here!" He held the wrought-iron fence and pulled himself up. "It looks exactly the same. The mailbox lid is still broken. Andy, it looks exactly like when we lived here..."

"Are you dressed warm right now?"

He nodded. "Yes."

"Good. I'm leaving work. I'm leaving work right now. I'm twenty minutes away. Can you meet me at the diner on the corner? Aaron, can you do that for me? Just go inside and warm up, and I will meet you. Order some food. I'll pay for it if you don't have any money on you."

He nodded again.

"Aaron, will you be there?"

"Yes. I'll be there."

"Great, Aaron!" There was rustling through the phone—the sound of quickly gathering things and taking off. "Aaron, stay with me. Now let's do this again, remember? You did this so well last time, and I know you can do it again. Look away from the house..."

He gulped. "Why am I here, Andy? Why did I come back here?"

"Aaron, listen to me. Just take one step backward and look away from the house. Do it, Aaron."

"OK," he said, shaking, tearing up again, and taking one step back. "I did it."

"That's great, Aaron. Now, take one *more* step back and make it a big step. A big step away."

Aaron did. "OK."

"Take another step. You're doing great, Aaron! Can you take one more step away?"

"Yes," he said, smiling as he wiped his cheek dry. "I just took another. And I'm going to take another step."

"That's great, Aaron. Are you still looking away from the house?"

"I just need one drink, Andy, and I'll be fine. I just need *one...*"

"Aaron! Take another step back. You're the one in control. Right now, Aaron—you are the one in control!" and under his breath, he said, "Come on, come on!" And then, the soft bell of an elevator. "Aaron, take another step. I may lose you for a minute but stay with me, OK? I'll be there at the diner in..."

Andy's call dropped.

Aaron could still see the house on Roscoe. He took a step back, and another.

And then Aaron stopped. He began crying again. *Just one. That's all I need.* He wiped his face and took one step forward. And another step forward, and then another. He looked down at the sidewalk, stepping forward again. And once more, turning a walk into a jog. And from a jog into a run. He ran as fast as he could, as far as he could, until he ran up the stairs of the porch and knocked on the door.

And the door opened. “Aaron?”

“Hi,” Aaron said, dipping his head low. “Can I come back?”

“You’ve been gone a while...”

“I know. Things just didn’t work out like I thought they would,” Aaron said, smiling sweetly, rolling his shoulders.

“Never will, Aaron. Come in.”

Aaron exhaled, bringing his hands up to his wet eyes. “Thanks, Mr. McGreevy.”

“You must be freezing! It’s been snowing all day.”

“It has been. Wow, it’s so warm in here. I’d forgotten...”

“You’re always welcome here, Aaron. You’ll always have your room at Summerdale, just like every other tenant who finds his way back. My boys all come home, one way or another. Go have a seat in the parlor. I just put on a fire. Warm yourself up,” he said, taking Aaron’s jacket and hat, both with the logos of upmarket brands. “My, these look expensive. Are they new? You must still be doing well for yourself.”

“They’re new. And, I am. Same job. Same agency.”

“No gloves?” he asked, closing the door.

“I must have lost them on the run up here.”

McGreevy rolled his head back. “You *ran* here? From where?”

Aaron pressed his lips together, as if holding a secret. “Doesn’t matter.” He took off his shoes and left them on a mat by the door.

McGreevy grinned as he hooked Aaron's jacket and hat on the hall tree. "Now, now, Aaron. Don't be coy with me. You have to tell me about these past months. I'm curious who you've been spending all your time with. I have to tell you, I was a little hurt when you left..."

"I was just with friends. They're not really friends, though," Aaron said, sitting on the edge of the couch. A tall Christmas tree covered with ornaments and white lights stood by the fireplace, which had a fresh bough upon its mantel and holiday cards strung across the mirror. An angel with wide wings capped the tree, and stared down at Aaron. He smiled at the cheery scene before him, and thought of childhood Christmases in Elm Grove, and began crying.

McGreevy put his arm over Aaron's shoulder as he wiped his face. "Aaron! What have these friends done to you? You're in a shambles!"

He shook his head and looked down, bringing his cold hands to the fire. "It's nothing. They..."

"It doesn't look like *nothing*. And they certainly don't sound like friends to me. No one who treats you this way is a friend, Aaron. You need to get those people out of your life."

"I want to."

"You need to," McGreevy said, sitting on a plush leather chair with a red throw on its arm. "I just feel so bad that you felt you had to leave." He stared at the tassels on the throw and wound them between his fingers.

Aaron nodded. The warmth of the fire lit up his face. "It was a mistake. I'm sorry. Your pine tree is so beautiful. We had an angel just like that one, growing up." He kept his hands at the fire.

"There's no need to apologize, Aaron. You're home now. But I am curious. You must tell me these friends' names and how you all know each other." He returned to his tassels and winding, unwinding, winding, unwinding.

Aaron smiled. "Of course!"

"Wonderful. Let me go make you a drink. The usual or something festive to celebrate this *blessed* season?"

"Yes!" he said, taking back his hands and clapping. He looked up at the angel looking down at him. "Something festive!"

"Craft cocktails are *all* the rage now," McGreevy said, smoothing down the throw and walking into the kitchen. "I try to keep up with what you young people want!"

Just then, Aaron's phone vibrated. It was a text from Andy: *Where RU? Yr supposed to be at the diner. And were bth suppsd 2B at a mtg now.* Then his phone rang, and he declined the call.

McGreevy soon returned with two frothy drinks. "Here you go, Aaron!"

He put his phone facedown on the couch and took a glass. "Thanks."

Another text made his phone vibrate. And then another.

"Someone really wants to get ahold of you," McGreevy said, sitting in his chair.

Aaron rolled his eyes. "Andy."

"A friend of yours?" he asked, rolling the tassels between his fingers.

"Used to be. Not really." As Aaron raised his glass, his phone vibrated again. "Stop it!" he shouted, smacking his phone with his free hand.

"Now, now," Mr. McGreevy cooed softly with an outstretched hand, "you let me take care of this." He stood and reached for Aaron's phone and dropped it into his pocket. "I should meet Andy sometime." He curled his fingers around the glass as he sat.

"Oh, totally. But he can't see me drinking."

"Mmmm, I wouldn't be so sure about that, Aaron." About to raise his glass to toast, McGreevy lowered it quickly. "I have an idea! Why don't you invite Andy over? Perhaps I've met him before..."

Aaron pursed his lips. "I thought we couldn't have guests over? That's a rule, right?"

McGreevy looked down and tapped around the hardwood with his wingtips. "Well, Aaron, this wouldn't be the *first* guest you've had over, now would it?"

Then Aaron looked down. "No. It wouldn't."

"It would *not*. But that's OK," McGreevy said, winding up the tassels. "That's OK, Aaron. You broke a rule, but I'm not upset. Because..." He paused, unwinding one tassel and winding up another. "Lucas lives here now."

Aaron took his eyes off the fire. "He does? Is he here now?"

"I saw him yesterday. We were just talking at the kitchen table. He asked about you, how you're doing, things like that."

"I had the craziest dream about Lucas, the last time I saw him. That something bad had..."

"Aaron, you stop that!" McGreevy scrunched up his nose. "These friends of yours have gotten you *paranoid*. Come on. Let Andy know where you are right now. Text him back. Let's see if Andy can find Summerdale House."

"Yeah?"

McGreevy scrunched up his nose. "Yeah. I'm sure once Andy's here, he'll feel just like he's been here before."

"OK!" Aaron put his drink on the floor as McGreevy handed him his phone. A text sent; a vibe back. And another. Aaron smiled. "He's on his way!"

McGreevy lifted his glass. "Well done, Aaron. And now that you've come home, you'll have to get back in my good graces. Just like Lucas is doing."

Aaron shrugged. "How so?"

"Well, Aaron, people like to be around you. Or they will again soon. So your task is to start bringing more friends to me."

"I'd love to bring more friends here!"

"Wonderful, Aaron. So what shall we toast to, you and I?"

"To Christmas!" he said, looking at the twinkling lights on the tree. But then he listened closely to the soothing crackle of the fire. In the corner of the parlor, a new album dropped on the Victrola and played a familiar carol. Aaron closed his eyes for a moment and mouthed its solemn first line. When he opened his eyes, he exhaled. "No, Mr. McGreevy. Let's make a toast to your house."

McGreevy stuck up an index finger. "*Our* house."

Up went both glasses and Aaron raised his voice: "To Summerdale!"

McGreevy clinked. "To Summerdale! And to new tenants in the new year..."

CHAPTER THREE

STEVE

"If you're honestly concerned about cellphone tracking and facial recognition software as the biggest threats to your privacy, you are hopelessly behind. That technology is Victorian compared to where surveillance is and where it's going."

"Can you shed some light, professor?"

"Of course. So that clip you just played, where the police chief in that rural district interrupted the brain waves of the protestor. It's referred to as a scrambler. That's not the trade name, but that's what the police call it. It's a nonfatal, targeted wave that enters a subject's brain through the optic nerve. And because they're waves, they bend, they flow. You can suspend the wave midair and hover it over a suspect. Once it reads your brain waves, it scrambles them, and it induces a seizure."

"So that was a seizure? Is that what we heard in that clip you just played? An induced seizure? Because there's been widespread disagreement about what happened there."

"Yes, without going into very technical medical terms, it was a seizure. And it remembers you."

"Remembers you? How?"

"So the gun sends a signal out to the subject, but it also sends information back. Once a suspect has been seized, the brain wave is then recorded by the gun and uploaded into central processing. It's not a criminal record per se, but it's a record that, at this time, on this day, in this place, the police, as an authorized agent of the state, administered a corrective weapon."

"And then what?"

"Well, first I need to say, this collection is free of name, address, physical description, or any other traditional identification. No fingerprints, no social security numbers, no notes, no cards, no judges. Those things are not needed anymore. Your identity is stored as a biomarker and it's permanent."

"And what's the point of that?"

"They ban you by encoding Wi-Fi signals, which are everywhere, private and public. We're bombarded with Wi-Fi signals all the time. And the signal can be encoded to block to your particular brain wave. Just like our DNA and corneas and fingerprints, our brain waves are unique. So if you're suspected of committing a crime..."

"The police can administer a seizure? Through Wi-Fi?"

"That's exactly right."

"Now, let's say, professor, you're fine in one jurisdiction, but if you cross the line into another, you'll start experiencing a seizure?"

"If you've been seized in that jurisdiction, yes."

"And then, if I'm following you correctly, the only way to stop the seizure is to physically leave that area, like that rural area where the young man was seized."

"That's exactly how it works."

"OK, I'm getting a cue from my producer. We have only a few more minutes with you, but the other thing that shocked me in your report was weaponized insects. Can you explain?"

"It's not a coincidence that a wasp attack followed the unrest in Union Park last spring. Remember that?"

"I remember. We covered it."

"By weaponizing an insect like a wasp, you can program a target using GPS such as Union Park or the Red Line subway. Suddenly, there's thousands of wasps attacking people. Wasps are soft-bodied, and they can find the tiniest opening through a window or an exhaust fan. Any way to get inside a home, even inside a moving train. Think about this. No arrests. No trials. No records. Just a 'freak of nature' like what happened on the Red Line last year, which has also never been explained..."

"The Cannibal Train?"

"Yes. And the running theory, which is so ridiculous, is that it was caused by a homeless man having a psychotic episode when that train stalled in the subway between Grand and Clark & Division. But not one of those passengers that died on that train had a human bite. They were attacked, but not by a human. So this turned into some story about a homeless man living in the Red Line tunnels who broke into a stopped train and started eating people?"

"It was absolutely bizarre."

"And the suspect *has* to be a homeless person because they're not vilified enough, right? It shut down the city, this thing. Six people dead inside a Red Line train and no suspect. But people just accept that it was a homeless person. What went unreported, even now, was that twelve dead wasps were found inside that train car. And remember, this happened right after New Year's."

"That wasn't in the official report."

"Of course not. How do you explain that there are wasps in Chicago in January, let alone inside a train car, in the subway, with six dead people inside? And I need to add, the wasps were only in that car."

"I'll have to look back at my notes on that file. That story stays with me."

"Can you imagine it? You hear people screaming in the next train car. What do you do? Open that door between the cars and try to help? Or gather everyone up to hold that door shut and hope to God that whatever's in the next car doesn't get into yours? There's nowhere to escape. And they'd shut off the power in the tunnel, so there was no Wi-Fi. So here are two completely different events with the same outcome. The only connection is the wasps. The Union Park case is starting to move through the courts. But the train? Complete silence."

"I wish we had more time with you today, professor, I really do. This has been fascinating and positively frightening. Thank you."

"'Wake up,' that's all I'm saying. Look for the signs while we still can. Because what's coming for us is already here."

Steve took out his earbuds and pushed them into his pants pocket.

"Clark & Division is next," said a recording on the train's loudspeaker. "In the direction of travel, doors open on the left at Clark & Division."

The train slowed, and other standers brushed past Steve as the doors opened. More walked in. In the fleeting stillness, he dried his forehead with both sleeves, then regripped a metal bar for support as the doors closed and the train rambled toward the next stop. His backpack was strapped close to his body, which pressed a sweaty puddle upon his back. Soon, the Red Line subway elevated into daylight, and Steve looked out the window at the passing evening sky. At Berwyn, he walked out the open doors last and let others walk to the exit first. When there was no one left to wave ahead, Steve gripped the hand rail, took the narrow stairs down one at a time, and walked out of the station toward N. Broadway.

After crossing, he walked a few blocks to Wayne Avenue and turned toward Summerdale. On the porch, Steve fumbled for his house key and closed the heavy door softly behind him. He admired the leaded glass, as he had done many times before, and walked to the kitchen. He loosened the straps of his backpack and took it off, resting it on a chair.

"Hello, Steve!" Mr. McGreevy called from the stove. "How was your day?"

"Over! Today is *over*. That's good." He wiped his forehead with both sleeves and shook out his button-down shirt. Two place settings were already on the table, and Steve grabbed his cloth napkin to wipe his face again.

"You know, Steve, you come home every evening and say the same thing. Makes me wonder if you're in the right job." He reached for potholders.

"I'm not. I'm *definitely* not. Umm, over there on the counter..."

"Help yourself! Take two," McGreevy said, turning off the flame.

"Thanks!" His eyes were as wide as the cookies that he began eating. "These are delicious."

"Just baked them this morning. Tonight's going down to the sixties, and it got me thinking that fall's around the corner."

Steve sat down and mumbled, "I hope so. I'm sick of sweating everywhere I go."

McGreevy pulled out a trivet from a drawer and set it down beside the stove. Potholders in hand, he lifted a large pot, set it on the trivet, opened the lid, and inhaled. "Well, this pot roast smells amazing, if I do say so myself!" McGreevy dropped the potholders by the sink and sat down opposite Steve. "Tell me what's going on..."

"I hate my job. That's what's going on. I hate going there every day. I hate my boss. I hate everything about that place."

"So are you looking for something else?"

He swatched his lips to one side. "No."

McGreevy rapped the table. "Well, how are you going to make a change, Steve? Can you move to another department? You said you've been there for what, three years? Isn't that what you told me when you came to see the room a few weeks ago?"

"Yes, sir," he said, looking back at the cookies. "Three years." He got up, which knocked over his bag, and grabbed a handful of cookies. "Thanks for making these."

McGreevy returned to the stove and began stirring the pot. "Take as many as you want, Steve. I'll make more tomorrow."

"Thank you! And that roast smells so good. It's my favorite."

"I remember," he said, grabbing two large bowls and ladling out big chunks of meats and vegetables with dark broth.

"Did I tell you?"

"Of course! How else would I know something like that?"

Steve chewed down another cookie. "Sometimes, I'm just in a haze. You know what would be amazing? Frosting in between two of these!"

McGreevy set down both bowls on the placemats. "I'll remember that."

"This is real nice of you, Mr. McGreevy. Got a house full of tenants, and you're always fixing meals for me," Steve said, wiping his face again and turning toward the kitchen stairs, "but it would be nice to meet someone who lives here. Even to see someone else doing laundry downstairs. I've only been here for a few weeks, but sometimes, it feels like it's just you and me in this big ol' house."

McGreevy picked up his spoon and motioned for Steve to do the same. "I love when your downstate accent sneaks back."

"It does from time to time." Steve blew on his spoon and bit. "Wow." He fanned his mouth and tongue. "Hot, but so good. You know, I don't even remember how I found Summerdale. I just looked up, and there it was. I wasn't even looking for a new place to live."

"Sometimes, this house finds the tenant."

He laughed. "I mean, I've been in Andersonville quite a little bit. Reminds me of Mt. Vernon, how friendly it is. But I've never noticed this street before."

"Strange, isn't it," McGreevy said, blowing on another thick spoonful, "how some things fall apart and others just fall into place?"

He swirled his spoon through the bowl and brought up another bite. "Thanks, Mr. McGreevy. I'm really glad I found Summerdale."

"So are we. Now eat up!"

Upstairs in his room, Steve sat on his bed naked, back to the wall, rubbing his belly with one hand and scrolling an app with the other. He felt full for the moment but knew that he'd be hungry in an hour or two. He'd have to be on the Red Line early the next morning, but he was looking through profiles for a late-night feeding. He replied to a few promising messages from feeders in the Loop or farther south. But after an hour, no connections were made, and the later the hour, the fewer profiles were active. *Not gonna happen tonight,* Steve thought, disappointed.

In the bathroom, he started the water for a shower. Steve looked at himself in the vanity mirror: wide shoulders, big, soft arms, pecs nearly turned over, and long, pink stretch marks on his belly overhang. Steve stepped back and smiled at his reflection. He rubbed his belly again, showered, and went to bed.

"Where are we, Echo Team? It's almost ten. Where are we on outbounds? Emily, where are you?"

A woman in a college sweatshirt turned. "Eleven calls."

"Good. Cassie, where are you?"

"Nine calls and three scheduled after lunch."

"Good. Very good. Tyler?"

"Twelve outgoing. Two on the schedule at noon and three at 1:00."

"Nice. Edgar?"

"Fourteen!"

"Fourteen? Fourteen calls before 10:00? Fantastic, Edgar. Keep it up! And...Steve?"

He turned. "Three."

Michele stepped closer to his cubicle. *"Three?"*

"But I got a sale from one, and..."

"Hey, Cassie, how many *sales?* How many sales this morning?"

Looking up, calculating in her head, she answered with a smile: "Product total is seventeen."

"Seventeen products. Over...what was it, ten calls?"

"Nine," said Cassie, smiling.

One by one, Michele pointed at each person as a number: "Nine, fourteen, seventeen—all these calls with the rest of you. But now we're at Steve's numbers, so pretty insignificant. Cassie is at a strong closing percentage. Edgar, how about you?"

"Twenty products sold over twelve outbounds."

"Twenty sales from twelve calls! Fantastic. See how that works, Steve? More outgoing calls, more incoming sales. Higher calls equals higher sales. Always has, always will. More money for the company and more commissions for you. Get it now? Understand? Because every time I walk the floor and take time out of my schedule to motivate my team, I see you looking at your phone or looking out the window. Maybe start looking at your monitor. Can you do that, Steve?" She glared at him, then began clapping. "OK, everyone on Echo Team, listen. I want you at sixty calls by the end of today with closes at 60 percent. Let's rock this out. You can do it! I'll check back after lunch."

"Thanks, Michele. Great motivation," said Edgar, raising his free hand for her to high-five. After slapping his hand, Michele walked away.

The others in the cubicle row rolled inward and chatted among themselves, excluding Steve. He pulled in toward his monitor and closed his eyes. *I just have to get through three more days, and it's the weekend...*

His phone oinked. A look of surprise came over his face, and his heart immediately began beating faster. He took off his headset and slipped his phone into his pocket and headed for the restroom. In a stall, he flipped down the toilet lid and sat.

The oink was a reply-message. It was interest, and Steve, with shaking hands, opened the envelope icon. He took a breath before reading it: "Hot pig bod. Feed tonight? At hotel on Ontario St. Meet after 6?" And Steve looked at the sender's profile pics: Older, well built, belly. "Sure," Steve replied. "Host?" Send.

As Steve scrolled through other profile updates on his fetish site, he got an instant reply. "Yeah host, my hotel. 7 good? Into funnels?"

Fuck, Steve said, as his penis hardened. "Into funnels. 7 is great." And he sent along his phone number.

Once his penis softened, he walked back to his desk. And his phone vibrated. It was from a number he did not recognize: "Sounds good, pig. I'll send hotel info after I check in."

With a smile, Steve put back on his headset and ran down his call list.

At 6:30 PM, Steve rolled back from his cubicle desk and stretched. The entire row of sales sub-teams, organized by target industry, was nearly empty. Michele's Echo Team rule was that once the daily goal was met, the sales consultant was free to leave. Many, though, chose to stay through the afternoon to crack into the highest commission rates above goal. Steve had other plans.

He swung his backpack over his shoulders and headed to the door. Michele, in a far corner, was still in her office. At the door, he heard her call his name.

"Got a minute, Steve?"

He turned around and walked to her office, holding his breath to slow down his heartbeat. "What were your numbers today?"

"I posted them on the board before I shut off my—"

"I'm *asking* you. What were your numbers today?"

"Sixty-two outbounds."

She opened a desk calendar and began writing. "Sales closes?"

"Fifteen."

"Fifteen?!" She jutted back in her chair. "*Fifteen* sales on sixty-two outbounds?"

He looked at the door. "Yeah, I know. I need to work on those. But I have a couple of follow-ups tomorrow, and I got a few cold-call clients excited about..."

"Follow-up calls from today don't count toward your numbers tomorrow. You know that."

He grimaced. "I understand that, but I want to see if I can close these sales to build future business."

She stood and put her fists on the desk. Her dark blue suit crinkled.

"What's the rule on my team about the daily sales tally?"

Steve nodded. "That a sale has to be opened and closed in the same day or it doesn't count."

"Exactly. Close those sales right the first time..." She leaned back and smoothed her sleeves. "You know what, Steve? We need to go back to basics with you. I want to meet with you tomorrow morning at eight. Bring your book of business, and we'll see where you're missing opportunities that everyone else on my team seems to find."

Steve smiled. "OK. Sounds good."

"You may leave now, Steve."

As he darted out the glass security doors to the elevators, his phone oinked. *Wow*, Steve thought, *Another new message?* An elevator arrived for a small group waiting, but he stepped away as he opened the envelope icon: "Big flight delay, trip cxl. Back in Chi in 2 mths." He took a deep breath and pressed the elevator button. *This guy couldn't text me that? He had to send a profile message, so I'd hunt for my own rejection,* Steve thought as he deleted it in anger.

In the mirrored doors of the elevators, he looked at himself and frowned. His button-down shirt was half-untucked from his shapeless khakis. His shoes were scuffed. The elevator arrived, and the mirrored doors split him in two.

"Mr. McGreevy?" Steve called out the next morning. He walked into the parlor and turned on the light. "Mr. McGreevy?" No sign of him.

Back in the kitchen, Steve stared at the coffeemaker and then to the rear stairs. He wasn't sure where Mr. McGreevy's bedroom was, and even if he knew, he certainly wouldn't knock just to ask him for coffee.

Probably fine to do it myself. Steve pulled out the carafe and poured in water. In the drying rack, he found a mug with the logo of a pork company that shut down after an outbreak.

"Well, good morning, Steve!"

Jolted, Steve turned around. "Good morning, Mr. McGreevy!"

"I'll take over," said McGreevy, pulling a box of filters from a cabinet.

Steve walked to the table with his mug and sat. "Thanks. You make really good coffee."

McGreevy measured in heaping scoops and turned on the coffeemaker. He opened the refrigerator and peeked over the door. "Eggs and bacon?" he asked, pulling out both.

"Sure! I've got time. Meeting with my boss at eight." He rolled his eyes.

McGreevy chuckled as he began cracking eggs into a bowl. "That doesn't sound good..."

"It's not."

He turned on two burners and dropped the eggshells in the garbage beneath the sink. "Then why do you stay?" He set a griddle over each flame—in one he poured the eggs, in the other he stripped down the bacon. After washing his hands, he grabbed a spatula and began pushing around the eggs.

"I don't know, Mr. McGreevy. My stomach turns when I get off the train every morning. And even when it's time to leave, I start panicking because I know I'll have to be back the next day."

The bacon began crackling, and he inhaled. "Mmmm, nothing like the smell *of a stinging hot pig...*"

"Mr. McGreevy! You have a real dark sense of humor, sir."

"*Gallows* is the term, I believe."

"My problems, not yours."

McGreevy reached for plates and set two on the table, followed by napkins and silverware. Once the coffeemaker finished, he pulled a mug from the drying rack for himself and filled Steve's first. "Hang in there, kitten!" McGreevy read aloud and showed Steve the wraparound litter of calicos on his mug. "This one should be yours."

"May I take that to work, please?"

"Sure!" he said, pouring himself a cup and setting it on the table with the carafe. "Get ready for eggs!" he said, returning with the skillet. He rolled scrambled eggs onto Steve's plate, then his own, then returned with tongsful of bacon. Shakers of chives and whole peppercorns, and a bottle of hot sauce, were already on the table.

Steve put his napkin in his lap and began eating. "Thanks! Probably the best my day will get."

"Well, I like to send my boys off with a full stomach. You can't think you're my first tenant who's looking to add a few pounds..."

Steve gulped his eggs. "No?"

McGreevy sat. He sipped his coffee and grinned. "I know exactly what you want, Steve. I just wish you were going off to a job that was a better fit."

"Maybe someday."

"So this meeting with your boss..."

"Just another rundown of what I'm not doing right."

"Can you ask for a transfer to another department?"

He blew on his bacon. "I wish it was that easy. I just feel stuck."

McGreevy leaned back from the table and exhaled. "You're never stuck, Steve, not really. You're just too close to it right now to find the exit. I sure wish I knew how to help."

He lifted his plate. "This is helping."

McGreevy reached for Steve's hand. "Food makes everything better, doesn't it?"

"Morning, Michele," said Steve, knocking on her door promptly at 8:00 a.m. He held a notepad and stapled printouts.

"Close that door." She was tapping on her keyboard and barely looked at him. The glass door was heavy and closed with a loud click.

He pulled a chair out for himself and sat, looking down and holding his breath. He felt sweat gather as he ran an index finger over his forehead. His underarms and underpants were swampy from the train ride and walk to the office; his sweat ring showed through his shirt. When Michele finally looked up, she kept an eye on the office through her window. "I really don't want to keep having these meetings with you. It is absolutely *exhausting* to motivate you, Steve. It really is and I wish you knew how difficult this is for me. No one else I've ever managed has demanded this much of my time, so you need to tell me what I can do to help you stop failing." She rested her elbows on her desk; the ruffles of her white collar rolled over the lapel of her black suit.

"I'm trying, Michele, but..."

She rolled her hands and then her eyes. "Trying, Steve? Come on. Let's see how well you're trying. Let's see your numbers from yesterday. Where are you? Do you have your numbers, Steve? Did you remember to bring them?"

Steve shuffled through the stack and then read scribbled notes from the day before. "I made sixty-two calls yesterday, and I was able to get through but not..."

"You know," Michele started, running her manicured fingers through her dark, bobbed hair. Her tan was even; her makeup perfect, which made Steve hate her even more. "Your pattern is to start off with something a little positive to lessen a big negative. Like, 'Hey, Michele, look at this nice car but not the rusted-out engine beneath the hood.' See what I'm saying? You have nothing but assumptions and excuses. *Every* time."

Steve guffawed. "Well, that sounds like an assumption right there..."

"Excuse me?" She stood up. "When I started here as a sales consultant on the phones, I worked late, I came in on weekends, and I was the first in my onboarding group to make six figures. I did not earn my way into this office by expecting my team to carry me."

"And I'm not either. Can I just talk this out with you, so I can get some direction on my calls?"

She sat. "Fine, Steve. Let's do it your way because you're certainly not open to anything I have to say. Let's go back to kindergarten here. Nuts & Bolts 101. Let's role a call. Go."

He looked down. "Hi, this is Steve Fenwick, and I'm calling for Michele Novotny."

"This is she."

"Good morning, Michele. I'm giving you a call to see if you received an email that I sent you last week—"

"Stop."

Steve furrowed his brows. "I was just getting star..."

"All wrong. You just gave the prospect a reason to say no to you."

"But that script is in our outbound calls guideline book."

"And it sounds like it. I never used those dated scripts, not once. Not *once*, Steve, and I was the first in my onboarding group to make six figures." She rolled her eyes and jammed down on her intercom. "Edgar? Edgar, can you come into my office, please?"

"Sure, Michele," he replied.

Steve wiped his forehead. Michele leaned back, made the slightest head shake side to side, and closed her eyes until there was a knock at the door.

"Come in, Edgar," she said, springing to life. "Here, please have a seat. Steve and I are role-playing outbounds, and I'd like you to show him some better verbiage."

Edgar sat. "Sure, Michele. Hey, Steve," he said, smiling. Edgar never called Steve by his name. And he never smiled. Edgar clasped his hands together and dove in: "Hey there. Good morning! This is Edgar Fontaine, and I'd love to chat with Michele Novotny."

"Right here."

"Great, Michele. I'm so glad I caught you! I've got *the* brand-new CRM interface that'll increase your customer acquisition and retention..."

"Oh, I don't think so. I've heard that before, and we're very happy with our current CRM vendor..."

"I totally hear you, Michele, but this system doesn't replace what you've got; it *enhances* it. No data migration and we've got proven results to back it up. One guy in your industry that switched just one month ago saw a 27 percent increase in conversions. In *one* month!"

Silence. Edgar leaned forward and tapped Steve's arm. He bounced his thick brows and tugged at his rolled-up sleeves. "This is where you shut up and let it sink in. Feed 'em and funnel 'em."

Michele smirked. "I don't know, that just sounds too good to be true."

"And Michele, that's exactly what my client said, but if you've seen your competitor Craven rising up in new conversions in the past few weeks, my contact there says it's all because of this new CRM integration. How about I send over a quick testimonial vid that you can look at and share with your team? Hate for you to lose out on this promotional pricing before it goes away..."

"OK, great, Edgar. Thank you. That was great."

He was all smiles as he turned to Steve. "Say their name, at least, three times and always use odd numbers. And, Michele, that's exactly the script I used to land Craven, which, by the way, is upping their order to fifty units today."

"Fifty?!" Up went Michele with her hands out. "Fan-fucking-tastic, Edgar! Awesome work here," she said, distracted by a new email.

"My pleasure, Michele. And I'll see you out on the phones, Steve." As Edgar opened the door, he turned and shot Steve a middle finger.

"OK," Michele said, looking back across her desk. "So let's role again with Edgar's enthusiasm."

Steve exhaled. "But actually, he said a few things that we really can't back up in an initial call..."

"What I heard, Steve, is a sales consultant who's excited about selling. Look, I know Echo Team used to have this reputation as the dust bin of everyone that couldn't make it to the big leagues on the twenty-second floor where I used to be, but those days are over. I have my marching orders to get Echo in shape. Do you understand what you need to do now?"

He nodded. "I do."

"Good. Now get back on your outbounds, and let's generate some new business today."

Steve stood up. He looked down at the seat and saw wide sweat marks, in the pattern of his wrinkled khakis. Michele had turned back to her monitor, so Steve hoped the print would evaporate before she noticed it.

At his cubicle, Steve pulled out his chair and sat, dropping his notepad and printouts in a hanging basket. He turned on his monitors and took a calming breath. *That sounded so sales-y. So cheesy. But Edgar is cheesy and he gets sales. Maybe I should just try so...*

An oink.

No oinks. Make calls first. Check messages as a reward. Make ten outbounds, and then I can check that message. He signed in his password, and his monitors lit up with new emails and tasks, none of them related to new sales. One was a product return. "OK, I'll check this message and then get to my calls," he said to himself, reaching in his backpack. He kept his phone low and opened the app. The message was a reply to a past chat about a steakhouse meetup. Steve immediately responded yes to the feeder. *If I need to be cheesy, I'll be cheesy. I'll get through these calls.*

By evening, Steve had made sixty-one outbound cold calls and brought in twenty new sales, which elicited backhanded praise from Michele: "It looks like all the time I gave you this morning paid off a little for you."

Steve had messaged back and forth with the feeder, who was in Chicago for a medical convention. Steve checked and rechecked his messages to make sure there wasn't a last-minute cancelation like the day before. When it was time to get off work, he headed out to meet Craig. It was a warm evening, but Steve was nervous and thought an extra few walks around the block would calm him down. It did. He entered the chain steakhouse carrying his backpack and looked for a balding man in a green polo shirt, who had already noticed him. "Steve? You must be Steve," Craig said, extending his hand.

"Hi," Steve said, shaking. "Sorry, I'm a little sweaty from the walk."

"You're very good looking, Steve."

"Thanks, Craig." Steve gave him a warm smile, as he clearly fit one profile of a feeder: a small-framed man who liked pouring food into big men. Professional, sometimes married. An encounter but not always sexual. As the lithe host pulled menus, Craig allowed Steve to walk to their booth first.

"Wow," Craig said, admiring Steve's belly as they sat. "You're barely gonna fit."

"Working on it," he said, smiling sweetly. He flung his backpack onto the seat first.

"We'll fix that tonight. Did you see how many people stared at you as we walked in?" A waitress appeared. "Do you drink, Steve?"

He nodded. "I'll have a beer, ma'am. Any local on tap is fine, but not an IPA."

"Same."

She went through the specials and then left for the bar.

"I can't get over how handsome you are, Steve. Your profile pics were all headless," he said with a laugh. He sipped his ice water.

"Yeah, just feels odd to show my face. I know some guys put face pics up, but..."

"Oh, I hear you. Best to be discreet. Never know where things might wind up."

The waitress returned with their drinks, and they both ordered the full buffet. "And can we get extra dinner plates?" Craig asked her sweetly as she headed for another table.

Steve checked Craig's left hand. No ring. "So you live in Dallas?"

"I have a practice there. When I'm out of town, I cut loose with this a little bit."

"Here you go. The buffet's all yours, gentlemen. Enjoy!" the waitress said, leaving a stack of dinner plates with the chain's logo imprinted on the edge.

"You first," Craig said.

Steve put extra effort into swiveling out of the booth, which he knew would turn on Craig. He loaded up his plate with mashed potatoes, French fries, and his first few thick cuts of steak. Craig had chosen from a plentiful salad bar with a few slender cuts of meat. *Sensible*, Steve thought, as if Craig were his own patient.

"Not into eating yourself?" Steve asked after he swiveled back in.

"No, not for me. But I love loading up big guys like you." Craig raised his beer glass high. "Cheers. To the most handsome gainer I've ever met."

Steve blushed. "Cheers." And he got to work piling it in.

They made small talk, never getting too personal or too political, and by Steve's sixth plate, he was beginning to feel nauseous. "Wow. I think I'm good."

"You're more than good, Steve," Craig said, leaning in close. "You're a fucking PIG." He spoke low, spitting across the table.

Steve patted the top of his belly. "Up to 270. Might be more after this dinner."

"And what are you, about 5'10?"

"Exactly 5'10. With room to grow."

Craig smiled warmly and placed his hand on Steve's for a moment. "Would you like to go back to my hotel? I'd love to load dessert into you."

"I'd like that."

"You like to be fed, Steve?"

"Yeah."

"You gonna let Daddy feed his big boy? Take your shirt off and rub that beautiful belly?"

"Oh, yeah." He was hard.

Craig flagged down their waitress and ordered several oversize desserts to go. And he paid the entire bill.

"So what you're saying, professor, is that food itself is modified to introduce disease?"

"That's common knowledge. Look at the skyrocketing obesity rates, diabetes, in the past few decades, concurrent with chemical additives and diseases that didn't even exist forty years ago. And now, suddenly, there are drugs to treat those diseases by the same conglomerates that introduced those additives?"

"I have to say, this is one discussion we're having here that's occurred to me over the years. What is the relationship between food and disease? Our diet and obesity?"

"Obesity used to be the exception. Look at old photos. Thin was the norm. We didn't have gym memberships and marathon training. We cooked at home. We knew what a portion was. Now, portions are..."

"Portion size is out of control. I was just in Orlando on vacation a few weeks ago, and I was shocked at how overweight everyone was and how big the portions were. The children! That's what stunned me."

"Get 'em early so they're drug-dependent customers for the rest of their lives. And make sure that the foods trigger their cravings and tantrums. It's no coincidence that sugar is in *everything*..."

"We're seeing a lot of research coming out now about the role of sugar, not fat, in our obesity epidemic."

"And those conversations get shut down real quick, don't they? But I'll tell you one thing, and remember this. The worst drug dealers in the U.S. aren't on street corners. They're in grocery aisles."

Steve took out his ear buds and stuck them in his pocket. As he stepped off the train and followed others up the escalator, his stomach growled. He had just eaten breakfast, and he was hungry again.

"Echo, come on in. Everyone in," said Michele, fingers snapping. Workers in the long cubicle aisle removed their headsets and rolled out their chairs. "Come on," she said again, tapping on a few cubicle walls. "Everyone! I have an update regarding Dorton Gregory."

With that name, everyone's ears perked up. Coworkers quieted. "The order of presentation to Dorton is as follows: I go first! I'm first. Then, in order, Thomas, Jared, Cassie, Edgar, and Steve."

Steve shuddered. Cassie looked at him, popped her brows, and gave him a discreet thumbs-up.

"Great work, everyone. I'll be meeting with you individually to go over your slides. We'll all be collating and assembling the presentation packets later this week. All hands on deck. You know Dorton bases his business decisions on what he sees in a team effort. We can win this account. It'll be a very happy holiday for all of us at the end of the year if we do. OK, thank you. Back on the phones now!"

Steve rolled back to his monitors. *I was picked. Michele picked me.* He put on his headset and began his outbounds with genuine excitement.

"Steve! How was your day today?" asked Mr. McGreevy, throwing tomatoes into a steamer.

"Well," he said, dropping his backpack on a chair. "I get to be in the final pitch for a huge new client!" he said with a self-satisfied grin. He patted himself on the shoulder.

McGreevy turned. "That's wonderful, Steve! See, a change of attitude, and now I bet you can't wait. When's the presentation?"

"Later this week. I'm nervous. I mean, I know I'll do a great job. I get to wrap up the whole thing and really go for emotion. I met with my boss to review what I'll say. It's a pretty big deal."

"Well, as it just so happens," McGreevy said, opening a bakery box and setting it on the table. "I picked up these today."

Steve looked inside. "They're too beautiful to eat!"

"Go ahead! I'll be just a little longer with this beef stew."

"Stew again? Thanks!" he said, taking out a glazed donut in the shape of a heart. He bit. "Oh, my God!"

McGreevy frowned. "Indeed."

"Where did you get these?" He walked to the cabinet and pulled out a plate; the donut had sprinkles, and he was sprinkling.

"At that new bakery at Clark & Balmoral."

"There's so much on Clark Street now." And then he put the donut on the plate and thought of the podcast he listened to on the train.

McGreevy noticed. "Don't like it, Steve?"

"No, I do. I just..." He put his elbows on the table. "Sometimes I get myself into a state of panic about everything."

Dropping the lid on the pot, McGreevy poured a cup of coffee for himself, setting it on the counter. "Coffee, Steve?"

"No, just a glass of water I think."

McGreevy reached into a cabinet for a glass and filled it with water from a pitcher in the refrigerator. He handed Steve his water and sat in his usual chair. His coffee mug showed the anatomy of a wasp.

"So there's this podcast I listen to."

"Oh, Steve! A podcast? There's so much nonsense out there in the world." McGreevy sipped, keeping an eye on the stove.

"Yeah, but this one's really good. There's always this anonymous professor on. You never find out his name, but he has all these theories."

"Doesn't *everyone* have theories?"

Steve laughed. "Probably! Sometimes, it's about aliens, and I was listening to one about food, just this morning. Like, how connected food is to disease." His stomach growled, and he rubbed his belly.

"Well, I can understand that. All this used to be farmland up here. In fact, this was a farmhouse at one time."

"Really?"

"Sure was. My family was here long before it was called Swede Town."

Steve drank. "Swede Town? *Andersonville* sounds nicer. And then, I dunno, there was this *other* podcast. Kinda disturbed me. Your mug just reminded me of it."

"Oh?" Standing, McGreevy took a sip before walking to the stove. He set the mug face-out.

"Yessir. It was about insects as weapons." Steve looked at the mug again. "Wasps, actually."

"Awful business, wasps. We've had gigantic nests from time to time, you should know. Bound to happen in a house this old with all these big trees." He turned off the stove and grabbed a trivet. "So what did this professor have to say about wasps?"

Steve took a breath and threw his head back. "Like, basically, remember the Red Line attack? And Union Park?"

"I certainly do. Read all about them." He grabbed potholders and moved the pot to the trivet.

"He was making some connections, saying that wasps were responsible."

McGreevy burst out laughing. "Wasps, Steve? Seriously?"

"Well, yeah, that they can squeeze into small spaces and they can be controlled by the government and kill people..."

As McGreevy rummaged through a drawer, he pulled out a ladle and pointed it at Steve. "You can't believe that?"

"I guess it is silly." He picked up his donut. "I mean," he said, chewing, "even if any of it *were* true, it wouldn't affect someone like me. This professor was implying it was targeting criminals and people like *that*. It was about controlling bad people with Wi-Fi."

McGreevy filled a large bowl and set it before Steve. He returned to the stove and filled a smaller bowl for himself and brought it to the table. "So even if this nonsense were true, Steve, you have nothing to worry about." He snapped open his napkin and set it in his lap as he sat down. "Killer wasps? Wi-Fi signals controlled by the police? "Even if this were real, it has nothing to do with people like *us*."

Steve shrugged. "It is incredible though. I mean, is it possible? Like Wi-Fi, invented for good, right?" he asked, taking another bite. "But how does it get misused?"

McGreevy looked up for a moment. "For sweetest things turn sourest by their deeds."

Steve swallowed hard. "Shakespeare, right?"

"It's just releasing the sweetest things to our corporations and courtrooms for the sourest deeds. Simple as that."

Wiping his mouth of frosting, Steve set his napkin in his lap. He waded his spoon through the stew. "I guess so. It doesn't matter. I'm a good person. And I follow the law. I always do."

"Then none of this should concern you in the least. Now eat up! There's so much more where this came from."

In between calls later that week, Steve worked on his slide. All around him, his coworkers paced the floor on their wireless headsets, talking to customers and organizing, binding, and doing other tasks Michele had assigned to prepare for Dorton Gregory's presentation.

"Steve!"

He popped up. "Yes?"

Michele burst over his cubicle, shaking a crinkled proposal. "Did it *not* occur to you to staple these financials?"

Steve darted his eyes about. "Umm, financials wasn't part of my..."

"I'm sorry, *what?*"

He pointed to the Echo checklist pinned on his corkboard, which showed everyone's name and task. "The financials. I don't know whose task that is, but it wasn't in my..."

"Did it NOT occur to you to check to see if this was going to need a staple?" Others leaned back in their chairs and began looking Steve's way.

Steve shrugged. "It wasn't on my checklist, Michele. I didn't look at the staples because..."

She stepped back and shouted, "'I didn't look at the staples!' Is that what you just said, Steve?" She crumpled up the financials with both hands and threw it on the floor. "I am *so* sick of your excuses, Steve. Why didn't you staple these?"

Steve swung his chair into the aisle. "It wasn't on my checklist! I did everything that..."

"Can you imagine how embarrassing it would have been, Steve, if I hadn't caught your error?"

He stood. "It wasn't my error, Michele! I don't know who had stapling on their checklist..." he said, turning, frantically scanning the list.

She bounced her head side to side and rolled her eyes. "I don't know! Wasn't *my* job!"

He looked past Michele at the long row of cubicles and coworkers. Some laughed. Two, farther down, high-fived each other.

"Michele! I didn't look for it because it wasn't on my..."

She pursed her lips and waved her arms. She kicked the crumpled financials away. "Everyone! Come in, right now, Echo team. I need to have a staff training." She looked up and down the row impatiently. Chairs weren't sweeping into the center fast enough. "Yes, you! And YOU! Everyone!" She pointed back and forth. "Off the phones!

End those calls, everyone. Off the phones NOW! Come on, come onnnnnnnn," she sing-songed, centering herself within the oval of chairs. "Just one time. I'm going to say this *one time.* So everyone gets it. OK? That I even have to say this astonishes me." She pulsed her temples and looked upward, then drew her hands together. "We are a team here. All of us. We work to-ge-ther as a team. Can you say that back?"

"To-ge-ther," the group mumbled, low.

"Not good enough. See? This is our problem. Right here, we are not working together. An agile team would have dropped what they were doing when I asked you the first time. Let's try it again!"

"TO-GE-THER!" everyone shouted.

"There we go! That's it. One more time!"

"TO-GE-THER!" everyone shouted.

Steve reached back to grab the arms of his chair to sit down, and she snapped her fingers. "Oh, no, Steve. *You* stay standing!" The coworkers who had high-fived each other burst out laughing. "Hey, down there? I'm sorry?" She raised a hand high and began snapping. "I'm sorry? Tyler, Ryan, do you not think this applies to you?" Tyler shook his head and waved that he understood. She turned away. "So when we all have a task to do, Steve..." She wagged her fingers at him. "Come up here." He did, and immediately began sweating. "So when we all have a task to do as a team, it's imperative that it be done right. And when one of us fails..." She looked at Steve and then began snapping again. "Where did that financial supplement go? The one that Steve just threw on the floor when I confronted him about his error. Where is it?"

Chairs swiveled and turned until a coworker handed it to her. She grabbed it and held it up high.

"See? See this, everyone?" She waved the financials around and then fluttered the loose upper left corner. "What's missing here? Steve, can you tell everyone on the team what's missing here?"

All eyes were on him. So he closed his. "A staple."

"Very good, Steve. A staple. Can everyone imagine how embarrassing it would have been for us to pitch financials to a prospective client without a staple?"

Much shock and shaking of heads.

Michele circled her arms. "So again, when I say we are a team, that means checking our work to make sure that it's done right the first time. I caught Steve's error in time. Now, Steve, what I want you to do is take every page of these financials, every single one, and I want you to go around and hand one sheet to every one of your coworkers. Go on, hurry up. You've already wasted enough of our time."

She shoved the financials into his hands. As he passed out each page, the sweat dripped down his chin and splashed the crinkled pages. Nearing the end of the oval of chairs, he wiped away sweat with a raised arm, and coworkers began pulling out pages themselves. At the turnaround, a musclebound coworker stuck out his flip-flop and whispered, "Fuck you."

Returning to his chair, Steve raised his sleeves again to dry his forehead and neck. Michele was quiet. Nobody moved.

"Now, I want you to tack this page up in your cubicles, where you can see it. Come on, everyone. Does everyone have a thumbtack?" She swung a hand back and forth. "Who has thumbtacks? Come on. Who needs one?" A coworker handed her a box, and she walked around the oval. Everyone who needed one took one. "Good. Come on. Let's get these pages up on your cubicles where everyone can see them."

She looked back at Steve, who had handed out all the pages of the proposal. "Uh-oh, Steve! You forgot to keep one for yourself."

Coworkers giggled. Cassie bumped Steve's elbow and handed him hers. "Oh, no," Michele said. "No, Cassie, that's *yours*. Steve doesn't feel like he's part of Echo Team, so it's just as well he doesn't have one." He sank into his chair.

Walking to the middle of the narrow oval, she turned around. "Thank you, everyone. Back on the phones!" She clasped her hands and nodded. "Come on, everyone. Back to work. I want big numbers up on my board by eleven, or no one takes a lunch today."

Steve's coworkers stood up one by one and offered their hands to shake Michele's. "Thank you, Michele." "We needed that." A few took selfies with their crumpled pieces of paper; others taped them on their monitors.

Michele walked out of the center aisle and disappeared. Steve gulped, his heart beating fast as he walk-rolled back into his cubicle. As the office returned to noisy-normal, Cassie peeked over. "Hey, are you all right?"

"No," Steve said, tearing up. "I'm not."

Just then, she noticed Edgar listening in. "Good. You shouldn't be," she said loud enough for Edgar to hear and rolled back to her side.

Steve didn't take lunch and didn't eat any snack cakes from his desk. He never stood up, not once. His mouth, like his water bottle, was dry. He sat in his sweaty clothes for so long that the deep hexagonal weave of the chair pad dried into his cotton shirt and pants. When he stood, the heavy chair rose with him and made a ripping sound when it separated.

His coworkers, too, had stayed well past sunset to finish their tasks and outbounds.

Walking down the cubicle row toward the restroom, Steve kept his eyes low and hunched down when he heard Michele screaming in her office. Once inside a locked stall, he laid out even rows of toilet paper, dropped his pants, and sat. He only had to pee, but his legs were shaking so much he thought he might fall over at a urinal. His heart raced, and fresh sweat beaded on his hairline, thinking that he'd have to leave the safety of his stall and return to his desk. And that he'd leave tonight for the safety of Summerdale, but that tomorrow he'd have to return for the pitch. If he had a pen handy, he thought, he'd draw a tiny hash by the toilet paper holder to mark his time.

His urine was dark and pungent. He looked between his legs and saw the hexagonal weave of the chair imprinted through his pants. "Fuck," he whispered to himself, trying to stretch the indents. They wouldn't flatten. Suddenly, his gut gurgled, and he was relieved he had sat down in the stall. After a long while, after his buttocks and thighs began tingling, he reached for the toilet paper. *Here's one good thing about this place: they have good toilet paper. It's lotioned or something. It's probably the best I've ever had in an office. So there's that.*

Walking back to his cubicle, he took a deep breath and took a long drink at a water fountain. He kept his head down as he turned off his monitors, grabbed his bag, and darted to the elevators.

Steve's stomach gurgled for the entire train ride, and after he walked down the stairs at Berwyn, he stopped in a corner café on Broadway and downed two sandwiches and a large soft drink. He immediately felt the euphoria of his dinner with Craig, who hadn't contacted him since their night together.

It was a nice evening, not too humid, so Steve walked to Clark Street to find the donut bakery. He bought three, two of which he ate while waiting to pay; the other he ate on a decorative wrought-iron bench just outside the bakery's windows. But, he thought, he could still easily eat dinner with Mr. McGreevy if he were cooking.

As Steve walked down Clark Street, he turned at Summerdale and saw a woman holding flyers. He adjusted the straps of his backpack, assuming she wanted a donation.

"Please, have you seen my son? Have you?" Steve looked at the flyer: the picture, the name, the description. He shook his head no. The only thing that looked familiar was the address her son was last seen: Clark & Balmoral. "I'm sorry, ma'am. I haven't seen him."

"Do you live up here? In this area?"

"I do now, yes."

"Would you take this flyer to your apartment building? Please? We have them up around the neighborhood, maybe you've seen them? Would you just please post it by your front door?" She stuck a flyer in a woman's hand as she walked by. "Please, have you seen him? This is my son," she called after a woman who turned and shook her head no.

Steve took a flyer. "Yes, ma'am, I'll be happy to post it. Good luck!" he said, walking away. It was only halfway down the block that he realized how cold that sounded. His words *Good luck!* echoed in his mind all the way to Summerdale, where he found Mr. McGreevy at the kitchen table.

"Hi, Steve! How's your day?"

Steve sat down, placing the flyer face-down on the kitchen table. He sighed and hung his backpack over the back of the chair. "Horrible. But this poor mom, over on Clark Street. I just saw her."

McGreevy turned down his lip. "What's wrong?"

"Her son, this woman's son," Steve said, flipping over the flyer. "She's handing out this flyer. Have you seen him? His name is Lucas."

McGreevy looked at the flyer. "No, I sure haven't."

"You haven't?" Steve asked, disappointed. "She's on Clark right now. She seems so lost. I feel bad for her, not knowing. And then..." He shook his head, looked out the greenhouse window. "I said 'Good luck!' when I walked away with her flyer. Like, *Oh good luck finding your son!* I mean, how cold could that have sounded?"

McGreevy reached for Steve's hand. "She knows what you meant and that you meant well. Don't think twice about it."

"I sure hope so." He pulled back his hands and threw his head back. "I always say the wrong..."

"Let me take a closer look..." said McGreevy, pulling glasses from his shirt pocket. "Oh, yes." He dipped the flyer to look in Steve's eyes. "I really should wear my glasses. Lucas is my tenant."

"At Summerdale? Is he here now?"

"Down in the basement, the last time I saw him."

Spinning the kitchen chair around, Steve flew open the basement door and ran down, gripping the handrail. "Lucas!" he yelled into the dark. He turned on a lightswitch. "Lucas? Are you down here?"

And out of the dark, Lucas appeared. "Hey! What's up?"

"Hi, Lucas. It's your mom! She's on Clark Street right now with these." He looked down at his empty hands. "Well, she has flyers with your picture on them. She's so worried about you. She's out there right now!"

"My mom is? Where?"

"Out on Clark."

Lucas shook his head and laughed. "What's your name?" Steve felt relief and a chance to redeem himself from the sting of *Good luck!*

"I'm Steve. We both live here. You're actually the first tenant I've met."

"So you're at Summerdale, too?"

Steve nodded and turned toward the stairs. "Yeah, can we just go? Sorry, but she's so worried about you. She's barely holding it together. She hasn't heard from you in..."

Lucas held out his hands to quiet him. "Look, Steve, was it? She's my mom and I love her and everything, but she forgets things. I just talked to her this weekend."

"You did?"

"Yeah. I was just home in Indy. And we've talked since then. She just doesn't remember it."

"So she knows you're OK?"

"Totally. Would you like me to go out there with you, to see her?"

He smiled. "Would you?"

"Sure." Lucas led the way upstairs.

"Mr. McGreevy!" Steve yelled out as they walked into the kitchen. "Mr. McGreevy!"

But he was gone, and so was the flyer. Steve made sure he had his house keys, but left his backpack.

Running behind Lucas, Steve closed the front door and struggled to keep up. Outside, the trees rustled.

"She's going to be *so* happy to see you."

Lucas said nothing, as if Steve wasn't there. They just walked together, passing children on bicycles, a muscled runner in tight gear who bolted around them, and an older lady carrying a grocery bag. And then Lucas stopped. He grabbed Steve's hand, looking back toward Summerdale House.

"Steve, I want you to know that your heart's in the right place."

Steve smiled. Tingles sudsed up his arm, his hand still in Lucas's. "Thanks. Your mom's just going to be so happy to see you."

Lucas gripped tighter and looked back at the house again. He peered into Steve's eyes. "Remember what I'm about to say. Promise me?"

Steve smiled and shrugged. "Sure."

Lucas looked back at the house a third time. "Mr. McGreevy is not your friend."

"I don't understand."

"You will."

They unclasped and continued walking, saying nothing else to each other. Steve felt a pit in his stomach as he saw Lucas's mom just ahead. "There! Do you see her?"

"I see her."

"Hey!" Steve called out, "Mrs..." He turned to Lucas.

"Call her Nora."

"Nora! I found Lucas!" Steve looked at Lucas, who smiled back at him and whispered, “Don’t forget what I told you.”

Nora turned, still holding flyers. Surrounded by sympathetic passersby, she shouted, “Yes, I’m Nora! You must know Luke, then! Where is he?”

Steve and Lucas stopped, inches away from her. “Right here!” Steve said, throwing his arm behind her son.

“Where?” she asked.

The others stopped handing out flyers and glared at Steve.

“Here!” Steve looked directly at Lucas, tapping his shoulder. “He lives in my house just down the street.”

“I don’t understand,” Nora said, shaking her head. “Where’s Luke?”

“He’s right here!” Steve said again. “Lucas, say something! Tell your mom you’re OK. Tell her what you told me, that you were just at home in Indianapolis...”

Said Lucas, “At our house, at Guilford and 57th.”

Said Steve, “At your house, at Guilford and 57th.”

“Yes, that’s where we live,” Nora said, nodding. “That’s where Luke grew up. Where is my son?”

But Lucas just stood there. Steve stomped his feet. “Lucas!”

“Who are you talking to?” she asked. “You said you found him. Where is he?”

Steve looked at Lucas. “Right! Here!”

“Oh, my God,” said one of the women in the circle, who put her arm around Nora as she began to cry.

Another woman stood with her mouth open, staring down Steve.

"Lucas!" Steve yelled. "Say something!"

A man in the circle stepped toward Steve. "You need to get outta here," he yelled, stepping in front of Nora. "Right now."

Steve looked at Lucas again, poking him. "Why aren't you saying anything? Lucas!" he shouted. "Talk to your mom! Hug her! Tell her you're OK!" But Lucas stood in silence, grinning at Steve.

Nora rubbed her eyes. "My son has been missing for three weeks. I have not heard my son's voice for three weeks! He was last seen a block away. I have put up flyers everywhere! He was out with friends, friends of his that I can't seem to find!" She put her hands over her eyes.

"But, ma'am, he said he just visited you!" Steve shouted, looking again at Lucas.

"Jesus Christ!" said the woman with her arm around Nora. "Get outta here! Whoever you are! Go away, right now!"

Steve began shaking. "Lucas!" he yelled again, looking straight at him. "Why aren't you saying anything?"

The man grabbed Steve's collar. "Get outta here before I knock you out..."

Steve's heart raced. Once in the man's grip, Lucas disappeared.

Nora wailed. Her flyers blew into the air until there were none left in her hands. The women around her gathered closer, holding her, whispering comforting words. One of them took a threatening step toward Steve. "Go!" she shouted.

The flyers floated in the air as Steve broke from the man holding him.

Steve started walking away, but the man grabbed the back of his shirt, forced Steve around, and punched him in the mouth. "Go to hell for doing that to her!"

Knocked over, Steve landed on his side.

"Shhhhh..." said a woman holding Nora. "He's gone. Whoever that was, he's gone now."

As Steve got up, one of the flyers scooped high through the air and landed face-up in his hand.

But the flyer didn't show Lucas.

The missing person, who hadn't been seen for weeks, was Steve.

He crumpled the flyer and ran, block after block, back to Summerdale.

"Mr. McGreevy!" he shouted once inside. "Mr. McGreevy?"

The house was empty. He ran through the parlor and into the kitchen where he drank glass after glass of water. His body shook; his blood was racing so fast that he felt dizzy standing. He dropped the glass in the sink and looked at the basement door. He opened it.

"Lucas?" he called down the stairs. "Mr. McGreevy? Is anyone down there?"

No answer. But as he backed away, he heard a voice from the darkness below: "Steve?" He turned on the light and walked, one step at a time, into the basement. "Lucas! Are you down here?" In the large, cold room, he saw stone walls, heavy wooden rafters, and several doors, some of which were nailed shut. A washer and dryer, a treadmill. A cheval mirror, covered with cobwebs and turned to the wall. Crates on pallets. But no Lucas.

He put his hand on the railing and walked upstairs to the kitchen, closing the basement door behind him. In the kitchen, he opened the refrigerator. Empty. He looked through the cabinets. Empty, every one. He sat at the table and shook his head. "I'm seeing things that aren't real," he told himself. But as his heartbeat dropped, he felt his lower lip throb. He checked his mouth for blood—his fingers showed none—but he opened a few drawers and found a plastic bag and dropped ice cubes into it. He twisted the bag closed and held it to his lower lip, picked his backpack off the chair, and walked upstairs.

On the second floor, Steve stopped. "Mr. McGreevy?" he called from the landing. There was no response. He walked down the hallway of dark paneling and antique wallpaper. A paisley runner covered the hardwood floor. At the end of the hallway was a fern on an ornate wooden stand, soaking up the fading evening light through lace curtains, and, just to his right, the wide staircase to the parlor. On the second floor were many doors, all closed, all locked. Keeping the ice to his lips, he walked back to the rear stairs and walked up another flight. There were more doors on the third floor that, Steve assumed, also belonged to tenants. None of whom, except for Lucas, he had ever met. No numbers, no names, no sounds, no voices. Steve felt completely alone in the house as he closed his bedroom door and locked it.

The room was nearly dark, so he turned on the lights, and in the bathroom mirror, he looked at his swollen lip. *Damn*, he said aloud, knowing he had to present to an important client in the morning. *Maybe it will go down overnight?*

He twisted the bag again—the ice was melting—and dropped his backpack on the bed. Drowsy, and wishing this day had never happened, he sat on the edge of the bed and rolled backward. He closed his eyes and rubbed his belly, which, even on his back, was fully round. Moments later, with the ice bag on his mouth, he fell asleep.

At midnight, he jolted awake. He turned on his side, set a knee to the floor, swung his arms forward, and lunged up to stand. His head throbbed. The bag had poured out on the mattress. After checking the time on his cellphone, he turned on the shower and breathed in hot steam. As he took off his clothes, he thought, *I need a CPAP. I can't put the sleep study off anymore.*

The hot shower relaxed him. Afterward, he walked nude through his room, lowering the window blinds one at a time, and organized everything for that morning: wallet with transit card in backpack, keys out of the pants he was wearing, cellphone charging, alarm reset, earbuds in their case, notes for his presentation. A pressed shirt and dress pants with the belt already looped through.

He resigned himself to presenting with a fat lip as he turned off the lights. *I'll shave when I wake up and do the best I can with it. Put all of this out of my mind. I need sleep. It's a big day ahead, and I'm going to impress everyone, especially Mr. Gregory.*

In bed, he noticed a new, oblong outline in the window shade closest to his bed. Through the moonlight, the craggy oval curved against the hard, forty-five degree outline of the dormer window frame. He watched little dark blots bouncing up to the window and back: *thud, thud-thud, thud.* Their wing spans were magnified by the incoming light. Steve convinced himself that he was imagining things again, rolled over on his pillow, and fell asleep.

The next morning, just as his alarm went off, he awoke and went to the bathroom. He felt his lip; it had swollen even more. "Fuck," he said, looking at himself in the mirror. After washing his hands, he shaved, maneuvering around his mouth as best he could. He threw everything he needed into his backpack and put on his dress clothes; he wore no tie but carried a dark sport coat over his arm. He locked his bedroom door and walked downstairs.

"Morning, Mr. Mc..." Steve said, but the kitchen was dark. He turned on the lights and set his backpack and sport coat on a chair. There was still no food in the refrigerator and no sweets left out. And his stomach was gurgling. So he picked up his things and walked out the door to the train.

The Red Line came, and there were no empty seats, so he stood with his back to the emergency evacuation instructions. He decided not to listen to his podcast, thinking back to his conversation with Mr. McGreevy: *I'm a good person. And I follow the laws. So that has nothing to do with me.* At his stop in the Loop, he walked off the train with dozens of others onto the escalator and made his way in to work, stopping for fast food breakfast on the way.

At his desk, Steve found new notes on his slide, already dropped into the conference room queue, and studied the changes Michele had made. There were only a few coworkers in the cubicle aisle, and the few who were there were dressed better than usual. As Steve studied his new notes, Michele walked past. "Hey. I found a..." She stared at him as he looked up. "What happened to you?"

"Oh," he said, covering his mouth, "I fell." He slurred.

She threw out her hands, which flipped the lapels of her blouse from her suit. "I don't understand how you can be so careless before a presentation like this. I really don't, Steve."

He shrugged. "It just happened."

"At least, put some ice on it. Hopefully, that occurred to you. I really don't need you to be a distraction this morning." And she walked away.

Steve laughed. *It's never going to be right for me here.* But she did give him an idea, so he walked to the break room to find anything he could use from the freezer. Someone had left a pillow-pack from a cooler, so Steve rinsed it off in the sink and held it to his mouth. And the cold felt good.

Steve heard Michele's voice just outside the break room. "There's a comic from a magazine I was reading. I put it on your desk. Drop it in the last slide of the deck after yours."

"Sure," Steve said before he walked to his cubicle with the pack. He put on his sport coat and dropped his wallet, keys, and cellphone, on silent, into the pockets.

Steve found the folder on his keyboard and opened it. The comic showed a man hiding under an office desk, bullets flying overhead, and a snarky caption. "This is disgusting," Steve said under his breath. *But still,* he thought, *do it. Just keep everything OK with her. Do what I'm told and everything will be fine.* So Steve walked to the media room, opened the heavy lid of the scanner, sent the image to himself, and dropped it in the presentation in the conference room queue.

The large room was warm, and in his sport coat, Steve began sweating. He rolled back from the table and quietly removed it, maneuvering it over the back of his chair. Slide after slide, presenter after presenter, and then, on cue, Steve stood up and took the remote and moved confidently onto his summary slide, driving their message home. Michele looked happy. Dorton Gregory looked happy.

And then, the final slide, that he had just added. Steve's heartbeat picked up. "Oh, wait, sir, there seems to be one more slide here! Just a little humor to end our presentation with you, Mr. Gregory."

"Sure!" he chirped.

The cartoon went up.

Mouths dropped.

Dorton's eyes scanned the cartoon back and forth, and he looked down, exhaled loudly, as if running a race, and brought his hands to his face. The room was quiet. Steve's smile faded. The only light was coming from the slide, and Michele walked quickly to the wall control and shut it off. She raised the shades.

Michele spoke first. "Mr. Gr—"

With both fists, Dorton pounded the table. "I was in a shooting. Did you know that? In California, two years ago. *Steve*, was it? Is that your name?"

He looked down and gulped. "Yes."

"I lost two colleagues that day, Steve. They were my friends. We founded this company together. Our initials make up our company's name. They had wives, these childhood friends of mine. They had children, both of them. Do you want to know their names, Steve?"

He nodded. He began sweating.

"Their names were Gary and Edward II. They both left wives and five children among them."

Michele turned. She cleared her throat and started, "Mr. Gr—"

"Don't!" He flung out a hand and turned to her, then back to Steve. "But you don't care about any of that, do you, Steve?"

The room was quiet. No one moved. And no one spoke.

"My loss. Your joke." He heaved and drew the back of his hands to his eyes. "That *anyone* could think that was...could be funny..." He stood and grabbed his jacket from a hook on the wall. He glanced around the room and settled his eyes on the thick proposal with the picture of his California headquarters on it. He shoved the proposal across the table, and on the other side, Steve's coworkers let it fly to the floor. Dorton opened the door and turned. "If you didn't already have a fat lip, Steve, I'd give you one now." And he left, raising his sleeves to his eyes. "Fuck you all."

After a long moment, Michele closed the conference room door and grabbed the back of an empty chair. "Who added that slide?" She shook her head gently side to side. "WHO?"

No one spoke. So she did. "That last slide was not in the final deck that I approved last night. So I'm asking again. *Who* added that slide?"

Steve looked down.

She held up her copy of the proposal. "Someone added it last minute because it wasn't in here..."

Suddenly, shouting. "Not me!" "It wasn't me!" "I would *never!*" said one coworker after another and another and yet another. Then as the chatter built up around the table, only Steve, looking away, stood apart by his silence.

Michele noticed. She swung out her arms. "Steve? Was it you?"

The room quieted.

"You told me to..."

Everyone began shouting at him. She swung out her arms again to force silence and pressed a red button on the intercom. "Michele Novotny in the main conference room! Security, immediately!"

As every colleague stared at him, Steve broke down. "You told me to add it! I did what you told me!" he screamed.

He stepped forward, and she held her hands out. "Stay right there." He didn't move until two security guards opened the door. She pointed at Steve. "He's fired. Get him out of here. Right now, you're fired. Get him out! Take him down to security immediately. Do NOT stop at his desk."

The guards patted him down and grabbed his arms, forcing him outside. When he resisted, they bent his arms backward. After he left, Michele closed the door, and the conference room erupted.

Outside, every colleague in every cubicle row was already standing and staring. Somehow, row after row, they already knew. Phones rang, and went unanswered, but cellphones were held high, trailing Steve as the guards walked him down the long row of cubicles. Approaching his desk, he slowed and began turning, wriggling for his backpack, but the guards quickened their pace. Tears streamed down Steve's cheeks, and he dipped his eyes into his shoulders one at a time, as far as the grip of the guards would allow. At the glass doors, with his back to the cubicle rows, someone shouted, "Get out of here, you fat fuck..." As a guard closed the doors, everyone inside cheered.

His daze wore off long enough to realize that his keys and wallet and cellphone were still in his jacket, still in the conference room, and he slurred it through tears. "They'll be returned to you before you're released," one guard said quietly, pressing the elevator button with his free hand. As the doors opened, two more guards alighted and asked for directions to Steve's cubicle. Inside, once the elevator doors closed, Steve slumped over and sobbed. The guards, who guided him out, were now holding him up.

The elevator descended and opened to a brightly lit floor with unfinished concrete. Flimsy gray lockers lined both sides of the hallway, and every gap had graffiti etched into the cheap drywall. After a short walk, one guard opened a door and turned on the light. Steve was guided to a chair beside a card table. "Where am I?" Steve asked, taking a seat. "I need my wallet and phone..."

"Wait in here," one of the guards grunted, locking the door behind her.

The room had a water cooler, but no cups, a dented tissue box with none inside. So he sat in the cleanest-looking chair in a line of broken chairs pushed against the wall. Testing it, the legs of the chair splayed, but held him. He leaned into the torn-up back pad and stared straight ahead, letting his mind wander to the early morning, to Michele, and the direct order she had given. *Every fucking day*, he thought, *it's damned if I do, damned if I don't*. So Steve sat quietly and waited, wiping away his tears, then his sweat. His eyes burned, but he tried not to rub and redden them. Though he sat still, his heart beat fast and his forehead stayed wet. His underarms and underwear felt clammy. And he could smell the artificial sea breeze of his deodorant.

After half an hour passed, he exhaled loudly, put his hands on his knees, and stood. *Are they looking through my wallet, my phone, my photos, my texts? My web activity on my desktop?* The bones in his lower back popped. *There's a camera on me, somewhere in here; I can feel it.* Becoming inquisitive, like a lab rat, he explored the room's dented boundaries and looked for a camera, finding one cut into an acoustic tile, aimed at the door. As he twisted the doorknob, he turned so his hand would be absent from the camera's red-blinking eye. But the doorknob spun and spun, and after a few more tries, he sat down again.

More minutes. More sweat.

Outside, Steve heard voices approaching, with the clanking of locker doors opening and slamming shut. A few voices were close by, so Steve pressed his ear to the door. He began tapping. "Hello?" he said, softly, trying the doorknob again. When the voices didn't respond, he pounded on the door.

The voices stopped; a woman, speaking Spanish, sounded surprised. Then another went, "Oh!" a verbal curlicue that needed no translation: *This is the room for bad people. And someone's inside.* "Hello?" Steve asked again, louder.

No response. No voices. Just a careful, quiet retreat from the door.

Just then Steve realized that the anonymous people he walked past every day, the maintenance crews in drab uniforms, save for the name patches he could never be bothered to read, were now walking past him free on the other side. For if he was locked in the bad room, he imagined them thinking, then he must have done something to deserve it. *But I did what I was told*, he repeated over and over.

So he sat. He tried the doorknob again. It spun.

The shift workers had gone away, and it was quiet again. Until something crawled out of an acoustic tile and dropped from the ceiling to the floor.

It was a wasp.

And another.

And another.

And another.

And another.

And another.

CHAPTER FOUR

DAVID

He stepped into the lobby elevator and looked down, making eye contact with no one. The car glided up to a floor and stopped and people alighted; another glide, another floor, another deload, until finally, it was his floor. David stepped sideways to ease his way out. His shoes clicked loudly on the polished marble floor, and he opened the glass door of his law firm with heft.

"Morning!" he called to a woman whose back was turned to him. She didn't respond, so he walked down the dark hallway to his office, one of dozens, and left his glass door open. He put down his book bag, took off his coat, and sat in his leather swivel chair, a deep-seated luxury he ordered himself on his first day at the firm, seven years ago. *If I'm going to sit on my ass for fourteen hours a day, I may as well do it in style.*

He rolled his mouse and slowly the large monitor came on: calendar first, then email, then desktop shortcuts, and wallpaper of the Breckenridge mountains at dusk, a place he and Ben loved. A raft of Word document drafts opened in quick succession, the topmost landing a cursor on the last word he typed two weeks prior: Beholden. He stared at the word, the cursor flashing just behind it, waiting for

David to move from two weeks ago into the present. To update his document, his life, his past to his present. But he couldn't. It was time-stamped, that last word, beholden, and to change it, alter it, amend it, would be to pick up from the moment his life changed forever. He began tearing up.

But suddenly, he had company.

"Hi, David," the woman said as she came into his office and closed the door behind her. She sat in a plush chair opposite David. "I just wanted to say again that I'm so sorry about Ben. I truly am."

David put his hands on his desk and looked her in the eye. "Thank you, Kate. I really appreciate that."

"Almost a year now with George. Hurts every day." She reached for David's hand. "I think the worst part was, when I came back here, no one wanted to talk about him. Acknowledge him. Remember that he had a name. Everyone thought not talking about him was the kindest thing they could do. But hearing George's name spoken by the people who worked with him was what I needed most."

David smiled. "He was an incredible judge, Kate. He changed so many people's lives."

"He did." She looked out the window at the rising sun. "And so will you."

David withdrew his hands and put them under his eyes. "Thank you," he said, nodding. "This is just so..."

"I know," she said, leaning back. "This is just your first day. I don't remember how many times I had to run to the ladies' room and cry that first week. If you need to talk, David..." She fluttered her hands. "I mean, we're all just *people* here. Fuck this attorney and legal secretary shit..."

David clasped his hands together and laughed. He wiped his eyes.

"And between us," she started, looking into the hallway, "I'm glad you're back. They *really* need you on the Union Park case. You're the only moderating voice on our team. I know we're not representing the side you want, but..."

"You know what, though? I spent time with it last week, trying to get my mind off things. I reread the statements from the witnesses on the train, the police, the families, the paramedics. All 598 pages of it. We missed some details. And I'm coming around..."

"I'm glad." And then she smiled warmly. "You were missed around here. So if you want to talk over lunch or a get a drink after work, just let me know. OK?"

He sniffled as she stood up and patted down her skirt. "I will, Kate. Thank you."

She smiled again warmly and walked away quickly. David stood for a moment but then ducked out to catch her, hug her, thank her, but she was gone. He walked down the dark hallway after her, and found her in a quiet row of cabinets, leaning over herself, crying. He walked backward slowly, carefully, quietly, and returned to his desk.

"Hey, hey, hey!" yelled an older man in a fine tailored suit, tapping on his window glass.

David looked up from the monitor and smiled. "Ira!"

"How are you, buddy?" Ira asked, shaking his head side to side and sitting down.

"How about your ol' mentor takes you out for some lunch?"

David looked at the clock: 12:12 PM. “I dunno, I have so much work to catch up on...”

Ira clicked his mouth like a ventriloquist’s dummy: “Why can’t David go out for lunch today, MR. HAMMOND?”

David rounded the desk and shushed him. “Ira!”

“Mr. Hammond works David TOO DAMN HARD.”

He swatted Ira’s arm. “Shh! Stop that. Someone’s gonna hear you!”

“Mr. Hammond, can David go to lunch today?”

“Stop! I’ll go! Jesus. Just let me send this one last email. You really know how to get your way.”

Ira sat forward and deepened his voice. “Top litigator in the firm. No one brings in new business like me, kid. No one.”

David sat down and laughed as he stared into the screen. “And you never let me forget it.”

“Hey, I’m just setting the example, so you get a piece in *Crain’s* about your work.”

David was half-listening as he scanned his missive and hit send. “Don’t I need a big house like yours in Wilmette first?”

“Dawwwww...” Ira stood, shaking out the wrinkles in his suit. “What’s with you, Davy? Always loving everyone but yourself?”

“Old habit. C’mon. Let’s go.”

It was late afternoon, and he hadn't stood up from his swivel chair since he'd returned from lunch with Ira. In his doorway stood someone David didn't recognize, knocking gently on his glass door.

"Hi?" David asked.

"Sorry to bother you. I'm Alexa. I'll be interning here."

David stood and extended his hand. They shook, and he turned his open palm to the chair. "Please."

Alexa sat and smiled; she swiveled her toned legs to the side and placed her hands upon her plaid skirt.

To David, she seemed a bit uncomfortable. "So this is your first day here?" he asked.

She smiled. "I feel so lucky to have been chosen for your intern program."

"Where're you in law school, Alexa?"

She smiled wider. "Northwestern."

He smiled back. "Very nice. My alma mater."

"I know. I wanted to seek you out."

"Seek *me* out?" David turned down his mouth. "I haven't done much to speak of yet."

"That's not true, David. You've done so much. More than you know. You have no idea how much you've done." She held the compliment, not extending it, not explaining it, just letting it sit for a moment so long that David ended the silence.

"Well, thank you, Alexa," he said, dipping his forehead. "It's nice my work is known somewhere."

"It is." She stood and took a step toward his desk. "A lot of things are good in your life, David. But you don't realize that, do you?"

He shook his head. "I'm sorry? That's an odd thing to say to someone you just met."

Another step forward. She leaned down to meet David's eyes and whispered, "Ben still loves you. And he always will."

David gulped. He shot backward in the chair. "Look, I don't know if someone down the hall put you up to this on your first day, but I just lost my husband two weeks ago and..."

She took another step. "He's with you, David. He's with you right now. He watches over you every day."

He teared up. "I think you should leave, Alexa."

"And the answer is yes, David. He hears everything you say to him at night before you fall asleep. And that picture you keep looking at, the one of you and him with the mountains behind you..."

David pointed to the door. "Leave! Alexa, leave my office, right now!" He stood and smashed his hands down on the desk.

But she shook her head, for she had more to say. "But, David, he wants you to know these things..."

"ENOUGH!"

Retreating to the door, she tilted her head. "OK. I understand. You're not ready." And another step into the hallway. "Ben still loves you, D.J.J.D."

As this stranger turned out of his office, David raised his hands to his mouth and dropped to his chair. He turned to the window, overlooking the Loop in the late afternoon sun. His lips quivered, and the tears came hard. He leaned upon his knees and howled and didn't care who heard him. He stared out the window at the people and cars so far below and lost track of time. In silence, he wiped his eyes and turned to face the empty, open doorway, where Alexa had stood.

From his left hand, he removed his wedding ring. In the iridescence of his monitor, the only light left in his office, he maneuvered the ring to read its inscription: WALK THIS WORLD WITH ME, D.J.J.D.

He blew his nose and cleared his throat before pressing the intercom. "Hi, Kate? Can you get me the HR file on a new intern named Alexa? No, I don't have a last name, but she's at NU Law. Oh, no, I didn't look at the time. Of course, tomorrow morning's fine. Thanks, Kate. Have a good night."

Before putting his ring back on, he kissed it and held it to his heart.

David walked outside his glassy, glossy skyscraper and made his way to the Red Line. On the subway, he jostled and turned and made his way and breathed easier the farther north the train journeyed. At the Berwyn stop, David walked onto the wooden platform and lined up with other commuters to walk downstairs and out to N. Broadway. Catching the green, he crossed the noisy street and then, just off Broadway, the trees rustled and birds sang and children played. Peace.

David turned onto Wayne Avenue and walked up a block of wide homes of many styles and manicured lawns with colorful flowers in the ground and in the air. Hanging baskets swung in the breeze in the archways of every front porch.

And there was Summerdale, his new street and new home, upon a little hill on the corner, with purple phlox overtaking a big round rock at the sidewalk and new plantings by the lattice beneath the porch. Mr. McGreevy sat on a chair and looked up from his paper. "Hi there! How was your first day back?"

David sauntered up the stairs and leaned against a column. "It was good. Weird, but good."

"Weird? How so?"

David shook his head, dropped his bag. "Just a lot of people trying to cheer me up, I guess."

"Well, tell me about it. Come ye apart and rest a while! Have some lemonade with me. I made it fresh this morning."

"No, I'm good," he said, pursing his lips.

"Oh, come on, one glass! Enjoy the evening light with me."

"Thanks, Mr. McGreevy. I think I just need to bring up a sandwich and have a good, long sit in my room, as my grandmother used to say. You know, just be alone in my thoughts."

McGreevy laughed and swatted David's arm. "Whatever you need."

Inside the house, David headed to the kitchen, but once there, standing before the open refrigerator, he didn't feel hungry, so he walked up the rear stairs and unlocked his bedroom door. After dropping his bag on his desk, he unbuttoned his Oxford, then unbuckled his belt, took off his pants, his shoes, his socks, and in his underwear and undershirt, he sat upon the bed. The setting sun sprayed gauzy, crawling squares upon the hardwood floor, through the dormer window. He watched the squares glide farther away, minute by minute, until they were slender rectangles, then thin lines, and then gone.

He began to cry. "Why, Ben?" he whispered into the warm air of his bedroom. "Why did you leave? I don't...I still don't understand why! It wasn't your time. We had so much to do together, so much planned." He wiped his eyes and stared at the ceiling, imagining a silvery reflection wasn't from a passing car but a sign from Ben. "Are you here? Are you really with me? Do you hear me talking to you right now?" Hugging himself, David rolled onto his pillow and pulled it up to his chest. "I miss you, Ben. I miss you so much." Again, he turned. "If you're with me? If that was you today, or a messenger? If that was you, speaking through her, I wasn't ready. But I need to know you haven't left me."

He sat up and walked to his bag and pulled out his phone. He opened Photos and scrolled to Favorites and tapped on one, expanding it. The photo was of him and Ben in Breckenridge, in ski gear, holding mugs of beer with the sunset over the mountains just behind them. David stared at the screen and pulled the desk chair out, wailing. He clicked the phone off, then swung out and knocked his bag to the floor; he stomped his feet again and again until he calmed down. Sitting forward in the chair, he pressed his palms into his eyes and let the tears roll off his nose and into the cloth of his rumpled undershirt. "I miss you, Ben," he whispered. "I don't know how to do this without you." He sat up, looked up. "I know you're here. I know you're with me, and I believe that you can hear me. But help me when a message comes from you. Help me just...accept it."

Reaching into his shirt, he pulled out a cross necklace. He held it tightly with both hands. "I want you to be at peace, Ben. But I want you to be with me."

He leaned back in the chair and took deep breaths in and out. Shaking his head, he stood up, dried his eyes, and walked to the bathroom. He ran cold water and looked at his red eyes in the mirror, tucking the cross back into his shirt. "God," he said aloud, noticing how tired he looked.

When the water was cold enough, he ran his hands and forearms beneath it, enjoying the numbing sensation upon his skin.

Off came his undershirt, then his underwear. Leaning forward, he gave himself a playful belly rub and his cross dangled free. He scooped up his clothes scattered about and tossed them into a hamper in the closet; his bag, reshuffled and returned to the desk.

Into the cool bed sheets, he sent himself, stretching out his legs first and his arms last. He pulled the covers up to his face and sighed. It was a new bed, a new bedroom, a new address. *Would Ben follow me here? Is that what happens?* David asked himself. *Walk This World With Me.* The room darkened quickly, and he drifted off to sleep.

The next morning, David stepped off the elevator and walked down the dark corridor to his office. He opened the door and set his bag upon the chair. As he turned on the lights, a manila folder on his keyboard caught his eye. "Kate's in already?" he asked himself as he picked it up: *Foresman, Alexa,* followed by a long employee number. But the folder was empty.

Soon, Kate walked by. "Morning, David. You get that folder?" she asked with a laugh.

"Yeah," David said, opening it and turning it upside down. "Where's the rest of it?"

"We don't have anything up from HR yet. Alexa starts *today*."

"Knock, knock, knock!"

David looked up from a stack of file folders later that morning. It was Ira.

"Aww! C'mon, Davy. Don't give me that look. I've got a big surprise for you!" Ira said, blinking an eye and flipping up his palms—*stand up, stand up!*

Ira ushered someone into his doorway. "Hi, David. I'm Alexa Foresman," she said, stepping into his office to shake hands.

"Hi?" David said, stunned. It was the same young woman. The same handshake. Wearing the same clothes. David looked at Ira. "Can I talk to you outside, Ira?"

"Nah, I gotta run, but since this is Alexa's first day, I thought you'd be a natural to take her out to lunch. You're both Northwestern Law grads. Did you know that?"

Alexa turned to Ira and giggled, "Well, not yet! I still have one more year..."

Ira smacked David's glass door. "How many times do I have to tell you, Alexa? At our firm, we're all..."

"Ira!" David interrupted. "Now?"

"Aww, ya got this, buddy," he said, turning down the hallway. "Oh, and, Alexa, if this guy doesn't take you to Henrici's for lunch, you let me know. It's the least he can do since you'll be interning for him all summer."

David's eyes widened. "Excuse me, Alexa," he said as he bounded past her. "Ira! IRA!" David shouted down the hallway.

They caught up at the elevators. "What, David? What's wrong?"

"I can't take her to lunch. She was in my office yesterday."

Ira guffawed. "*Today's* her first day!" He pressed the elevator button and held it. "She just got her card from security this morning." He swung his head around. "You know how tight they control this building. It's a fucking fortr..."

David shook his head side to side. "Can't do it, Ira. Nope. Can't. Sorry. Get someone else. Assign her to someone else."

"What's the problem? She's attractive and you're gay. It's the perfect lunch date."

"She was here yesterday, Ira. She said things, things about Ben."

The elevator doors opened, and Ira stepped in. "Alexa started today. She's never been on this floor before, and you've been begging me for an intern for over a year. She's into the Union Park case, David, you've got a real advocate with her." Ira threw a hand to the elevator door and poked his head out. He reached out for David's shoulder. "Look, buddy, I know you've gone through the biggest shock of your life, of *anyone's* life. And I'm so sorry. Everyone here loved Ben. But I can't give you any more time off to figure this out. You want her to jump ship? Every peer firm in Chicago wanted this girl, David, and she chose us. Look at her resume. It's *insane* for a first-year. Working on Union Park was her deciding factor, so don't fuck this up."

Ira stepped in. The doors slammed shut, and David leaned against the wall. He ran his fingers over the engraved brass plate of the elevator buttons.

"David?" Alexa asked, peeking around the corner. "If today's bad for you, we can..."

David shook his head. "No, no. It's good. We're good. I had some deposition questions for Ira. Could you wait in my office? I'll be there in five. Please?"

She forced a smile and walked away. David darted into the nearest restroom, slammed shut a stall door, and banged a palm onto the marble wall. He kicked the toilet handle repeatedly so the sound of flushing water would muffle his crying. But suddenly water sloshed over the rim and soaked his shoes and pant cuffs. "Fuck!" he shouted, shaking his legs, one after the other.

He walked to a long wall of sculptural marble sinks and antique mirrors tilted outward on old-fashioned hinges. "Pull it together. Pull it together. I must have imagined that she was here," he told himself as he wiggled his toes and realized his shoes were soaked through. A final look at himself before walking back to his office: *Could today get any worse?*

"Hi, Alexa. I am so sorry for the delay. So, first day, huh?"

She sat primly on the chair, legs crossed to the side, and held a small purse.

"Yes, that's right, first day."

"And never, *ever* been on this floor before, right?"

She laughed. "I haven't. In fact, all three of my interviews were downstairs at human res..." She stopped, noticing the sloshing sound coming from his shoes as he paced. "What happened to you?" David's pants were dripping.

He closed his eyes and grabbed the sides of his head. "Umm. I was at the urinal and after I flushed, the damn thing overflowed on me."

Her mouth dropped. “Oh, my God!” She stood and swung out her arms. “OK! Here we go. Around the corner for new pants and shoes and take-out for the walk back? Back within the hour and Ira won’t suspect a thing.”

David opened his eyes and exhaled. He immediately liked her. “Perfect.”

“Great. Just be sure to tell me what I had at Henrici’s.”

“David!” said Mr. McGreevy, looking up from his newspaper. He sprang off his chair on the porch. “How was your day?” he asked, folding his paper over.

“Interesting.” David took each step slowly. “It was interesting.”

“Well, then,” McGreevy said, sitting back down. “Why don’t you pour yourself a glass of lemonade and tell me about it?” he said, pointing to a chair. Several empty glasses encircled the pitcher on the wicker table. “I noticed you’re not much of a coffee drinker...”

David almost begged off, but then dropped his bag, pulled another chair closer, and poured himself a glass. “Thanks.” He chugged it as he sat. “Oh, wow. That is refreshing. You made it?”

“Old family recipe. You’ll never guess what’s in it.”

“Huh. So, yeah, weird day,” he said, refilling his glass from a large pitcher. “We have this new intern. She’s brilliant. And my boss asked me to take her to lunch ’cause today was her first day, and that’s something we do at my firm, and I run to the bathroom and...” He took a long swig.

McGreevy looked enraptured.

"...and the urinal splashed all over my pants and shoes!"

McGreevy looked horrified. "The *urinal*, huh?"

"Yeah," David continued. "Right before I'm supposed to take this star intern out to lunch at Henrici's. But she quick-changes plans and suggests we go to this really nice clothing store I've shopped at only once, when I needed a killer suit for court, but wouldn't you know they remembered me? Me! A one-time shopper, and this salesman sees I'm with a sharp intern and acts like I'm their best client." David finished off his glass. "I can't exactly afford what I bought, carrying a mortgage plus the rent here, but damn, I look good!"

McGreevy's mouth went to the side. "You certainly do."

"OK! I gotta get upstairs, more work to do tonight. Thanks for the lemonade, Mr. McGreevy. It's got this taste, almost..." He squinted and took another swig. "Not exactly earthy, but thick. It tastes like sweet iron. It's even kinda reddish." He swirled the ice in his glass.

McGreevy cocked his head. "I'm so glad you like it," he said, lifting the pitcher. "Have some more..."

"I gotta get upstairs. Thanks, Mr. McGreevy!"

David walked into the house and set his glass in the kitchen sink. He opened his cabinet and grabbed a high-calorie protein bar. Up in his room, he locked the door and put down his bag on the chair. Off came his Oxford and he walked to the window and let the afternoon light shine on his purchases: black silk-blend flat-front trousers ($198) and new black wingtips ($450). He pulled up a pant leg and showed himself his argyle socks, black with red and yellow crisscrosses and intersecting diamonds ($19). Out of his pocket, he pulled a claim ticket for dry cleaning and shoe repair ($52). And then he thought,

The most embarrassing straight-gay meet-cute ever? Priceless.

He went back to his bag and pulled out a small piece of paper from an inside pocket and opened up the laptop on his desk. He sat down and unfolded the paper. It was a phone number with a 773 area code, and nothing else.

As he held the paper, David thought back to the words that were whispered to him: *She's very gifted. She'll be able to communicate with Ben.* And David shook his head and folded it back up and stuck it in a desk drawer. He closed his laptop and leaned backward in the chair and took a deep breath quickly and let it out slowly. "Are you here, Ben?"

David swung his arms out to stretch and yawn and then snapped back to sit upright. He opened the laptop again and signed in and entered the phone number in Google.

"Your search did not match any documents," Google said. And a few related search suggestions followed. He looked again at the scrap of paper, and reentered the numbers one by one, this time without the dashes. "Your search did not match any documents," his laptop said again.

Now he was intrigued. He entered his office phone, and Google returned his law firm's name and address. Two entries down, his name appeared and on another two entries farther down. He cleared the field and entered his cellphone and Google listed options for reverse phone lookup and lists of many numbers just one or two digits away from his. And then, he entered random numbers after 773. Someone's name and address popped up. Again, 773 with seven random numbers after. Another name and business listing. And another seven random numbers after 773, which showed a name and home address. For good measure he repeated with 312, 847, and 630. All the same result.

He closed the Google window. He swung the mouse arrow up to the top menu: Safari-History-Clear History. "Are you sure, David?" his laptop asked as a warning box reminded him that all cookies and history would be permanently deleted. "Yes," he said to his laptop. "History cleared," his laptop said in a soothing voice of confirmation.

"Restart," David said.

"Restarting," his laptop said back.

As his screen went dark, David got up and walked to the toilet to pee. *It's a mistake,* he thought. *Every number in the world is in Google.*

He flushed and washed his hands with a big green bar of soap with little flecks of broken rice that tickled his palms. He pulled a fluffy white hand towel from a metal ring by the sink and patted his forehead. McGreevy's lemonade had left a bitter taste in his mouth, and he smacked his lips.

"I'm back, David!" said his laptop.

Sitting, leaning forward, clearing his throat, David said slowly the phone number to search.

"That number does not exist. No information can be found on..."

"What the..." David mouthed.

He opened another window and typed the number anew, using only his index finger for the numbers and dashes.

"Your search did not match any documents," Google said.

David opened a new search window and retyped the number without the dashes.

"Your search did not match any documents," Google said again.

Every other search portal he could think of all returned the same answer: Not Found.

He held the number up to eye level, looking at the seemingly normal assembly of an area code, a prefix, and a line number. The late afternoon sun made the paper glow from behind.

"Who are you?"

Looking at his bag on the chair, his heartbeat picked up. The curiosity of an attorney who graduated at the top of his class simply could not let a mystery like this go on.

Out of his bag came his phone. Into the phone went the numbers. Onto his ear went the phone.

The number connected. He began sweating.

The phone rang once. Twice. And the landline phone, obvious by the clink it made coming off the cradle, was answered by a woman. "Hello, David."

Stunned, he dropped the phone onto the desk and pressed the red hang-up button so many times the phone jammed and shut itself off. For security reasons, his cellphone was unlisted.

He bolted off the chair, knocking it over, and fell back onto the wall. He grabbed the top of his dresser to steady himself. The woman's voice repeated in his mind over and over until his vision blurred. Shaking his head, wiping his forehead with his forearm, he took deep breaths and closed his eyes until his heartbeat slowed down.

I will never call that number again.

The next day, at his desk, when he could no longer preoccupy his mind with an affidavit, he looked at his cellphone. He hadn't deleted the number for the great fear of accidentally redialing it. So there it sat in his call history, waiting, taunting.

His intercom buzzed. "David, your two o'clock conference call just cancelled."

Rising, he yelled at Kate. "Again?"

"Sorry," she replied, and the top button on his desk set went dark.

Suddenly, a free hour. "Not so bad," he told himself. *Time to work on tomorrow's case for the Cook County Forest Preserve.* But he looked again at his cellphone and noticed a little smudge across its screen.

Should I? David knew himself and that he'd never settle. He had cried again last night, spoke again to Ben last night, and asked God to simply help him get through last night.

The cellphone, sitting there. He got up and closed the door. Then a colleague came by and looked through the glass, tapping his left wrist furiously. He shrugged his shoulders. *I forgot to tell Brian!* David made an apologetic face and drew an index finger across his throat. Brian pressed his middle finger to the glass and walked away.

"Not my fault!" David shouted, smacking his desk.

Looking at his cellphone for a moment, he thought of calling from his office line. *No, then she'll have my office number, too.* And then he remembered an old pay phone in the concourse, the underground commercial hallways connecting buildings in the Loop. He grabbed his phone, his wallet, and darted to the elevators. *No caller ID, no tricks, no knowing it's me.*

At the elevator, he stopped. He walked over to Kate's desk.

"Got any quarters?"

She looked up from a tall stack of papers. "Doing laundry?"

He gave her a look.

"All right. Let me see." She pulled her purse from a desk drawer and opened her wallet. She handed him six quarters, and he ran off. "Hey, what about my laundry?" she yelled after him, laughing.

Down the elevator sank, floor after floor, and the button he had pressed, Concourse Level, opened to the maze-like, interconnected, underground Chicago Pedway. He alighted and walked into an artificial, over air-conditioned, marble-walled circuit of hallways and blind corners. Registers from countless tiny shops rang the smallest items of fast commerce. A woman in a drab maid's uniform vacuumed the thick-carpeted entrance of a five-star hotel. A shoe-shiner sat up high on a wooden podium with little iron stands for men and women to raise up their shoes one at a time.

David walked down the hallway where he remembered it, remembered making fun of it, remembered asking himself, *Who would ever need that relic?* And then realized that who was he.

As he approached it, he looked over each shoulder, self-consciously, thoroughly, for he hoped no one from his firm or any other firm would see him, and brought out his cellphone. He picked up the receiver and dialed the number. *Or do I put the money in first, because I don't remember.* "Deposit fifty cents, please," said a recording. He dropped two quarters into the slot and waited. Up went his heartbeat.

The phone rang once. Twice. And it was answered.

"Hello, David."

He flipped back to the wall and gulped. "Hi. I got your number and..."

"He's with you, David. Ben is with you right now."

Stunned, David looked about the concourse: the light marble walls, the scuffed middle path of an otherwise shiny floor; a square, stone-covered garbage can with a red *No Smoking* symbol; two crumpled coffee cups. Everything appeared normal to David but their conversation.

"I guess I have questions about..." He began tearing up and turned to the wall. With his free hand, he wiped both eyes. "...about him. Us. Why did he..."

"Won't you come see me, David? He desperately wants to talk to you."

David grabbed the phone box and steadied himself. "I...what do I do without him?" He flipped the receiver outward, far from his mouth, so she wouldn't hear his sobbing.

"I can help answer those questions and bring some comfort."

David dropped the phone, letting it swing on its metal-coil cord. His hands covered his face, and he wailed, not caring who saw him. After a few deep breaths, he picked up the phone again. "Sorry," he said, hoping she was still on the line. "OK. Where am I going?" He wiped his face dry.

"I'm in Rogers Park. My studio is 1101 W. Greenleaf. That's off Sheridan."

"That's not far from our condo," he mouthed. David repeated her words in his mind, a trick he used often in the courtroom. "When?"

"In one week."

He threw his head back. "I have to wait a week?"

"New bookings with me have a two-year wait, David. Your friend there moved you into my awareness."

A few more words and David had the day and time set. He hung up the receiver, and his quarters dropped into the cache.

"God," he said under his breath, wiping his fingers once more across his eyes, "what the fuck am I doing?"

"Well, you're up early, David!" McGreevy said, pulling the carafe from the coffeemaker. "Here, come join me for a cup."

"No, thanks, Mr. McGreevy. I'm good," David said as he tapped his pockets to check for his wallet, cellphone, and keys. He looked toward the front door.

McGreevy dropped his voice and furrowed his brows. "Come on, now. *One* cup. You're always in a rush." He looked at the chair opposite his, an invitation to be seated.

David checked his cellphone: twenty-five minutes before the appointment. "I guess I can have one cup." He pulled out a chair and sat. "I didn't get any sleep last night. I could use a pick-me-up."

Out of the drying rack, McGreevy pulled a mug with *ESPERANZA* spelled in white lilies and set it before David. "I just knew I'd make you a disciple," he said as he poured. He stopped just shy of the rim. "Black?"

"Black."

McGreevy let out a few more splashes. "So tell me, why no sleep?" He returned the carafe to the coffeemaker and sat opposite David. He sipped from his half-empty mug, which showed a trail of ants with dollar signs for legs.

"Oh, just..." David began, but he was no good at the game of hemming and hawing. "Ben. It's Ben." Wrapping his hands around the hot mug brought a smile to his face. "This heat feels good. I don't know why."

"Warmth in hand always does. Just a human thing..." McGreevy stopped mid-sentence and watched something behind David move through the kitchen to the back stairs.

David turned. "Is someone here? I don't see anything." he said, sipping.

McGreevy took his mug to the carafe and refilled it. "So what's going on, David?" he asked with his back turned. "I haven't seen you very much this past week." he said, returning with a steaming mug.

David sipped. "Just busy with work, I guess."

"I see. So why're you up so early on a Saturday? Doesn't look like you're dressed to go running."

A laugh. "No." He sipped again. "Just me and some friends getting together to...watch the sunrise at Foster Beach."

"A beautiful sight, isn't it, the lake at sunrise?" He breathed in deeply and smiled. "A new day of fresh possibilities."

"Living here, you just take all of it for granted. It's going to be winter before you know it. So better enjoy the summer now, right?" David took another sip and looked away. "You know, can I ask you something, Mr. McGreevy?" Another sip.

McGreevy nodded his head and raised an eyebrow, inviting his question.

"Were you ever married? Or have anyone special? I haven't seen any old photos on the walls downstairs or anywhere else. A house this old in the same family usually has old photos around."

McGreevy twitched his mouth and dipped his head. After a moment of thought, he smiled. "Oh, yes. I had someone very special. Someone I miss very much, as a matter of fact."

"Was..." David paused, not wanting to assume the next word, a gendered pronoun. David had assumed his landlord was a kindly, elderly gay man but as an attorney he knew to assume nothing. "Well, I'm very sorry to hear that, Mr. McGreevy."

"It hurts like hell to lose someone you love with all your heart, doesn't it? You'd do anything to see him again, wouldn't you?"

David read his coffee mug and then closed his eyes. "Yes, I would. Because it hurts like hell that I can't. Actually, I'm..." he started.

"What?"

With his eyes closed, David almost told the truth. "I just miss him so much, you know?" He looked McGreevy in the eye and smiled. "I would do anything to have him back, to be with him again."

"I know you would." Across the table, McGreevy reached out and tapped David's arm. It shook the mugs and a little spilled. "It's the hardest thing to hear right now, I know. But you can't live in the past. And that's where your heart is right now—in the past. That's the thing with the human heart, David. Beats fast. Runs slow. It takes time for faithful hearts to separate..."

David looked down.

"So give yourself that time."

Leaning forward, David nodded. "Thanks, Mr. McGreevy. Ben died so suddenly. No one was expecting it, least of all him. And then I just couldn't stay in our condo anymore. The next day, I woke up and I had to get out of there. Everywhere I go, there's memories of him."

He shook out his hands. "No need, David. I understand." When David looked away, McGreevy shot him a dirty look. "I knew you were mourning Ben when you showed up at my door."

"You did?" As he stretched, his belly fell out. "I don't remember, but I must have shown it. I don't remember anything about that morning. I'm an attorney, and I barely looked at what I signed. That's how messed up I was. But I'm really glad I found Summerdale. I've needed this place. It's exactly what I wanted." David tucked himself back in.

"I hear that *all* the time. Although it surprises me that you've kept your condo and haven't fully moved in to Summerdale. All my other tenants do."

"Well, I only got a room here because I couldn't go home and see everything of Ben's. His clothes, his books. You know, his toothbrush is still on the bathroom sink. I can't get rid of stuff like that. Not yet. So that little room upstairs is all mine, like I'm at an offsite work assignment, and nothing at home has changed. Keeping the condo keeps time frozen, in a way."

Sipping, McGreevy nodded and stared at the far wall. "I understand,

David. It does create a bit of a challenge for me, though..." He snapped back. "For you, I mean. A challenge for *you*." McGreevy pushed out from the table. "Well! I have a yard to water. We haven't had any rain, and the watering ban starts soon. Have a good day, and, David..."

"Yes?" he asked, putting his hands around his cooling mug.

McGreevy smirked. "You go and enjoy that sunrise with your friends." He walked out with his mug and closed the kitchen door behind him.

David checked the time again. "Time to go," he told himself as he took one last swig and put the coffee mug in the sink.

A short cab ride brought him to the lakeside, dead-end Greenleaf Street—so close to the water that the waves drowned out early-morning traffic on Sheridan Road. David was back in the heart of Rogers Park and two blocks from their condo on Glenwood. He checked and checked again that he was at the right address and was about to press the right buzzer. He fretted, for it would be horrible to ring the wrong apartment before dawn.

With his triple-checked assurance, he rang the buzzer, and the front door clicked open. He walked up three flights of creaky, carpeted stairs and into a long hallway that smelled like old books, dark but for a single light at the far end.

The door, as he approached it, opened. "Hello?" he asked softly, poking his head inside. "It's David." His body was tense through and through.

"Come in," a soft voice spoke, the same voice David recognized from the phone call. "Close the door behind you."

The room was dark, but a large picture window revealed the slightest light rising over Lake Michigan—a sliver of color that barely separated water from sky, earth from air. David looked out this window, mesmerized.

"Come here. Come here, or we'll miss it," called the voice again, and David stepped into the darkness.

On the other side of the room, a short woman turned on an old-fashioned floor lamp. She stood up straight and smiled. She walked to him and held out her hands.

"Welcome, David James." The woman had a kind smile and a warm touch. He immediately relaxed, exhaled.

"Thank you."

"Come by the window." She waved at him as she walked to a settee. "I want to see you by the sunrise."

The woman wore a shawl, and by the light of the lamp, David noticed that she was handsome, not a witchy hunchback like in the movies. He sat down. She sat down. David gave her a nervous smile as she stared into his eyes. "There's no need to be afraid here, David."

"I barely slept last night." A cool rush came over David's body, as if he had entered a walk-in freezer. He got goosebumps and a chill ran down his spine. His arms tingled.

She tilted her head and smiled, drawing wrinkles around her eyes. "He's with us. Tell me, David. What do you see out the window? Right now, what?"

He looked out. The sliver was wider, brighter. "The sun's coming up. It's beautiful." David turned to look at her, but her eyes were closed. Her hands were tightly clasped, and her white brows twitched.

"Keep talking..." she whispered, nodding.

"My landlord. He was up early, just like me. We talked, but I didn't tell him I was coming here. I didn't tell anyone."

"Your landlord of the place you now call home?" Tipping her head forward, she exhaled loudly. She grabbed her chest and popped her eyes wide. "It was sudden! It was sudden, David. He was not in pain for long. He was aware of what was happening, and before anything else, he wants you to know that there was nothing you could have done for him. Nothing!"

He sat straight up and nodded. She looked behind him, following something as it moved behind David. "Ben hears everything you say to him at night. Every word, David. Every, every, every, every word you say to him, he hears. You must believe this."

"OK," he said, softly, again and again. He began tearing up. *This is real. Ben is here.*

"He wants you to know that he's at peace. He feels no pain. And there was absolutely nothing you could have done for him. He wants you to stop thinking that. He knows you are blaming yourself. You must accept that there was nothing you could've done."

"It was a blood clot," David said. "That's what the examiner said." He looked out the window. The slightest sliver of the sun shone on David's face, and he began to cry. "Why did this happen? Why did you leave me?"

She shook her head and joined him looking out the window. "God needed him. It was his time."

"Of all the people, why him? Why Ben? Of all the people to take, why him? He was the kindest...he never hurt anyone!"

She laid out her hands and stopped him. "It was his time, David."

David shook his head. "I don't understand what that means! Why does everyone say that?"

"He wants you to accept it."

David screamed to the ceiling. "I can't accept it! Don't you understand that?"

"Shh...Shh..."

"Sorry. But how do I do this without him?" he asked, rubbing his hands over his arms, quieting himself. He wiped his eyes. "Why? Why meet someone like Ben, why bring us together, at the end of his life? We had plans together. It makes no sense!"

"But he's with you, David. He hasn't left you. He's here right now. He visits you every day."

"Every day?"

"Yes!" Again, she looked past him. A look of surprise came over her face, and she giggled like a schoolgirl. "Well! He says your ass looks good in the pants you just bought, but the shoes are too lawyer-ly."

David laughed out loud and wiped his eyes. "Ben saw that?"

"He sees everything. He wants you to know...he wants me to tell you that he *walks with you,* David."

At that, David began crying. He took off his ring and held it between his right thumb and index finger. "God," he cried to the ceiling, "I wanted you to! You're the only one I've ever loved! Does he know how much I loved him?"

She looked at him cold. "He loved you even more, David."

It was sunrise. Rays of reds and oranges encircled a bright yellow circle rising, dancing upon the calm lake. On the horizon, a dark sky faded away. Details of the room around him slowly appeared.

Paintings. Furniture. Books.

"Do you understand, David? He has *not* left you."

He dried his eyes with his hands, and she offered him a nearby box of tissues. "What does he want me to know? I want to hear from him."

"He wants you to donate his clothes to the Brown Elephant and stop being silly about the toothbrush. He's upset that the coroner listed his body as 'overweight' and not 'beefy'."

David laughed and clasped his hands. "That sounds like Ben."

"He wants you to know that he's proud of you and that your grandmother watches over you, too."

"Yes," he said, his voice trailing. "I've always felt that."

She paused, looked out the window. "A promotion is coming. Immediately. Someone you're close to in your office. A female who is feeling a loss as deep as yours, but it's not as recent."

"Kate," he sniffled. "Her husband died a year ago. Her husband was a judge, a fine judge."

"She's put this in motion. She's worked her connections for you. She has a lot more influence there than you realize."

He clasped his hands and said a short prayer silently. "Kate? That's amazing. But even after all the time I've taken off? I've been off for weeks."

She threw out her hands. "Why do you reject this, David? Why do you question your worth? Others have moved ahead of you, others with less instinct, less passion. That passion you have for your clients—why don't you have it for yourself?"

"I, I don't know." He looked at the floor, for he had no answer.

A serious look. "Why haven't you called Ben's parents since the funeral?"

Stunned, David looked up and struggled to respond. "I don't know. I guess I haven't but..."

Again, she threw out her hands. "Tell Ben why. Right now. In your own words, tell him why you have not called his parents."

He laughed. "I feel like I'm being scolded."

"You are. Tell him."

Looking down, he popped a shoulder. "I guess I've never felt at home with them, even after we were married." He looked at the ceiling and raised his voice. "I always felt that they thought I wasn't good enough for you. We talked about that. They were a little cold to me at the funeral."

"Reach out to them, David. They're hurting terribly. This has devastated them. His father, especially, but he isn't showing it. Ben wants you to reach out to them and start a new relationship with them. Visit them. They need you."

"They do?"

"He wants you to do this for him, even if it doesn't make sense to you."

"OK. I'll call them today and fly out to Columbus."

"There's a box, David."

"A box?" He looked to the ceiling, the walls, noticing more of the room in the soft, diffused light of dawn.

"The one you keep closed but look at often. And, David..." she raised her voice and waited for his eyes to meet hers. "He knows what you kept from him."

David returned a quizzical look.

At that, she held up an index finger. "He *knows*, David."

And at that, he dropped his head into his hands and sobbed. "I'm sorry..."

"It makes no difference. He loves you just the same. He forgives you. You must remember this for what's ahead."

Tilting his head back, he brought his index fingers to his eyes and wiped. "God..."

"Now he's asking me about that box again."

"It's Ben's things, things I wanted near me, but not out in the open yet."

"He understands why you keep them hidden. But don't keep them hidden any longer. He misses seeing you holding...a teddy bear?"

David rolled his lips inward and nodded. He reached for a tissue and blew his nose. "It was his childhood teddy bear, his favorite. The first time I went over to his apartment, I picked it up off a shelf. He had it on a shelf with all these trophies and medals, awards from work. I just took that teddy bear off the shelf, and I sat on his bed, and as I held it, he took a picture of me." And his voice trailed off.

"What was so special about that moment, David?"

Another tissue. "That was just our third date, the first time I saw his apartment. He said that was the moment he knew. He *knew* I was the one. Everything clicked, right then, and he wanted a picture to remember that moment forever. But he didn't tell me any of that. He never told me until I heard his vows." He wiped his eyes. "And that's why I can't look at it anymore."

She reached for his hands. "Bring it out. Bring all of it out. Soon, these things will be a source of comfort to you."

David rolled his eyes. "I can't imagine how."

"Do these things, David. Do them now. Do what he's asking." She closed her eyes and put together her fingertips and rolled her hands one over the other. "And now he's calling you by...by letters. Not your name, just letters."

David dropped his face into his hands again and nodded.

She opened her eyes and squinted at the ceiling. "Is it D.J.J.D.? Is that right?"

He rolled his fingers in and set them beneath his eyes, drying them. "Yes. That was his nickname for me. It's on my ring. On the inside."

"Tell me about D.J.J.D. He wants to hear the story. He wants to hear you tell me the story."

David looked down and smiled. He grabbed another tissue. "We were drunk," he laughed and wiped his eyes again. "We just got back from some fundraiser, I don't even remember what for. We were still just dating, and we weren't exclusive, but I didn't let myself think I could ever have someone like Ben—someone that driven, that good looking. So we got back to my apartment and we took off our bow ties and took off our jackets, and we leaned back on my couch, and he started calling me D.J., like it was his new nickname for David James."

She motioned for David to take his time; he was running out of breath.

"So, he's slurring it, slurring 'D.J.' and he starts calling me J.D. and..." David started crying. "And he said, 'You're a lawyer. Your initials should be J.D. not D.J.' and he started mixing them up, back and forth. We were so drunk, and it was the funniest thing to me, and we both started laughing, and then we stopped talking and just held each other for a really long time. Really tightly, like I didn't want to let go of him at that moment, and I felt through my heart that he didn't want to let go of me. We didn't say anything. Not a word. We just held each other, and after a long time in his arms, I started crying because that's when *I* knew."

"You and Ben are soulmates."

"Then why did he leave? I don't understand why he's gone!" He held in a breath. "I miss him! Every..." His voice trailed off, and he dropped his head. "When he held me, I felt like nothing could hurt me. I haven't felt that way since I was a child."

She pointed, directed him to the window. "Look up, David. Look up and tell me what you see."

Air blew out from his pursed lips, and he shook his head. "The sun? A new day? Morning. God."

"Yes. All those things. Night has gone. He's here, David, but he's here with you in a different way. Ben has not left you."

Another tissue. "I believe that. I do."

"Good. Our time is ending. Go back to bed and you will sleep better than you have since Ben was called home. And when you wake up, you will find a new peace around you. Will you do that for him?"

"Yes, I will. Thank you." To the ceiling, he whispered, "I love you, Ben."

She stood. And he stood. "Thank you," he said, reaching around for his wallet. "Well, I guess I should have asked before I walked in..."

She put her hand on his. "It's been taken care of."

David cocked his head. "How? I should pay you something."

"It's taken care of."

Ira even paid? "Thank you. I feel so much better," said David, sucking in air through his nose to clear it. "I didn't sleep at all last night. I was so nervous."

She smiled. "Go get some rest. And do what Ben asked."

He walked toward the door. "I will. Thank you so much."

"Be safe, David. At all times, be safe. Good-bye."

He closed the door behind him and walked back through the musty hallway and downstairs. Outside, he stopped to look at the sunrise halfway over the water. He walked down concrete steps onto the beach and watched a young man playing fetch with his dog, a fit woman in shorts and a sports bra stretching her legs at the lakefront trail, and gulls gathered, pecking the sand for food. Life was around him. Light was around him, and he closed his eyes, breathing in the sudden peace he felt. "Good morning, Ben," he said under his breath, opening his eyes to the fast-rising sun. He put his hands over his heart. "You're here with me now. I know that you're with me, Ben."

Up to street level, David walked, and at Sheridan Road, he stopped. After a short wait, he flagged a cab home and went directly to bed.

David awoke at sunset. He roused himself from bed, for the evening light felt as warm on his face as morning light. At his nearby phone, he looked at the time and added an hour. *Still early enough to call Ohio.* He sat up and scrolled and pressed a number.

"Hello?"

"Hi, Arlene. It's David."

"David!" she exclaimed. Then, she spoke away from the phone and said, "Paul, it's David."

"How are you?" he asked, but then winced, for he hated when people asked that of him.

"Day by day. Hour by hour, some days. David, we were actually just on our way out..."

David shifted on the bed. "I can call you back tomorrow. But really quick, I'd like to fly out to Columbus and spend some time with you and Paul."

A sigh, a pause. "We'd love that. I think it would be good for all of us. We hardly had any time to talk, the three of us, when we were in Chicago."

"We didn't." He started sniffling. "I'll call you tomorrow, maybe in the evening?"

"That sounds fine, David. It's so good to hear your voice."

"Same. Take care, Arlene."

"Good-bye."

David ended the call and walked to his closet, still holding the phone. From a high shelf, he pulled down a box to the floor and opened the crossed flaps with one hand. He felt for Ben's teddy bear and lay back on his bed. With the teddy bear in one hand and his phone in the other, he excitedly scrolled for a not-so-recent number and pressed Call.

"Hello?"

"Hi, Mom! It's David."

On the train Monday morning, David thought of different ways to approach Ira, to thank him, to tell his mentor how grateful he was for helping him with something so personal. That after years under his guidance, he finally understood what the partners meant when they spoke of their firm as a family. *What do I say to Ira? How do I thank him? I have to say something.*

Upstairs from the subway he walked, across the busy Loop streets and into his building, up the elevator, and onto his floor. And still no words came to him.

Just out of the elevator, David found Ira.

"How was your weekend?" he said, throwing an arm around David.

"Great!" he said, joining him for a fast walk down the hall. He motioned David to his office and closed the door.

"I'm glad, David. Have a seat."

As David sat in a plush chair, Ira sat behind his desk and leaned back. He sprang forward and threw his elbows onto the desk. "I've got news."

"Really?"

"Big news, David!" Ira turned down the sides of his mouth and raised his eyebrows, a look of compete self-satisfaction. "I nominated you for partner, and you can't say anything yet..." Ira cocked his head and held a smile. "But you GOT IT!"

"I did? And *you* did?" David tried to look surprised. "You're kidding. Wow. I mean, wow." He tried, but he couldn't sell it. "You nominated me?"

Ira sat back and squinted. "You knew about this, David?"

"No! Not at all."

Shaking his head, Ira looked down and spread out his fingers on the desk. "Don't bullshit a bullshitter."

"Ira! I haven't heard anything about this. We've talked about becoming partner for a while but..."

Ira smacked his hands together and jutted his jaw side to side. "I know you, Davy. I know what you look like when you're excited, and this isn't it."

David licked his lips. "I am very excited, Ira..."

"But you knew it was coming now?"

"Look, I was going to tell you this..."

"Jesus fucking Christ!" Ira shot up from the chair and leaned on his fists. "You're not leaving us, are you, David? Are you leaving us? Is that what this about?"

David's eyes widened, and he held out his hands. "No! Ira! I would never think of leaving. You've been *family* to me."

Another shift in his jaw. "Really, David? Because before Ben's passing, I know you had a few meetings over at Riggs."

David looked down.

"Yeah, that's right. Look away from me, buddy. I know *everything* here." He tucked his hands in his pocket and clicked his tongue. "Everything! All right. Tell me what's going on. How did you find out? Because I'm going to fucking fire whoever told you."

David gulped. He stood, met Ira in the eye. "It's not anyone here. Ira. It's not." David said, holding Ira's gaze, outstretching his hand toward his chair. "Please?"

Ira sat first, then David.

"Nobody here told me anything. No one. No need to fire anyone. OK?"

"Who, then?"

David leaned forward and rested his elbows on his knees. He clasped his hands and let out a nervous laugh. "I went to see that medium you recommended. She's the one who..."

Ira bolted up. "A medium? What are you talking about?"

David sat up. "That phone number you gave me."

"I never gave you a phone number! For a medium?"

"Yeah, you did, Ira. On my first day back."

"You mean a psychic? A fucking *psychic?* Have you told anyone about this?" Ira began pacing behind his desk and grabbed a football from a high shelf. He blew off the dust and squeezed it hard.

Shaking his head, David whispered, "No, I haven't."

"Then DON'T!" Ira shouted, and then caught himself. He clawed his fingers into the football and dropped his voice. "Don't."

"I won't. I just remember you gave me..."

Ira threw the football into the corner. He brought his hands to his temples and sat, closed his eyes, and drew in short breaths. "Look, look, look, look, look..."

David teared up. "I'm sorry, Ira, I..."

Bolting forward, he slashed his hands through the air. "Stop it, David. I never gave you a number. To a fucking psychic, are you kidding me with this?" He stared down David. "Share this with anyone?"

"No."

"You sure? Because I never gave you any number, David. OK? And whatever you just told me, you never went to a psychic. Because if anyone hears that, you're finished here. And that will reflect on me. Understand?"

David shook his head. "I never went."

His voice deepened. "You *never* went." He reached over his desk and pulled David's collar and stared into his eyes. "I nominated you for partner. If anyone finds out that you went to some..."

"Ira, I got it!" David pulled himself free. "I won't say anything."

Poking his desk with his middle finger, he spoke softly, "This is my reputation, too. We all feel for your loss, David. Everyone loved Ben. And you know that you can be completely out here. That's not something you can count on at Riggs. But I think you know that. Or, at least, you should."

"I know that, Ira. I appreciate that I don't have to hide anything here. Thank you for your nomination." David stood up and reached for the door.

"Get outta here. One more thing, David," Ira said, running his fingers down the sides of his mouth.

David turned, still holding the doorknob. "Anything."

"The announcement is going out to the firm mid-morning, and seventeen is taking you to lunch at noon. Hammond and the rest. Your afternoon has been cleared and Kate is setting up calls with Northwestern Law and *Crain's*."

"Great."

"David, you're going to be a partner here." Ira stood and gently put his arm around David. He spoke low. "But right now, I want you to go in the bathroom. And I want you to walk in, and I want you to look at yourself in the mirror." Ira smacked David's hand off the doorknob and opened the door himself. "And I want you to practice looking FUCKING surprised!"

Once David was in the hallway, Ira slammed his door. David began sweating and leaned against the wall. In the distance, he saw Kate, who stopped to give him a discreet thumbs-up. He forced a smile and gave her a thumbs-up back.

David walked to the bathroom and made sure nobody was in the stalls. At a mirror on a long wall of sinks, David looked at himself.

Smiling. Wide eyes with smile. Open mouth with wide eyes. Hands to the sides of his face, open mouth look of shock. A step back, shoulders back. Hands to the heart rehearsing, *Me, partner?* Head dipped, eyebrows raised, and a fresh smile.

But none of it made him feel happy. Not because of Ira, but because of Ben. Because Ben wasn't there, wouldn't be there, couldn't be there.

"Ben?" David asked the mirror. "Can you see all this happening?" He looked at the ceiling. "It's the promotion I've been waiting for, the one we always talked about." He began tearing up. "Partner, Ben. Me! A partner at a top Chicago law firm. This is the promotion you always said was just on the horizon."

He grabbed the sink. He turned on the cold and ran his hands under the faucet, one, then the other, and again, and again, until his hands throbbed. "Why aren't you here for this, Ben? Why can't I share this with you?" He smacked the side of the sink. Another glance in the mirror, and he splashed his face with cold water. "OK. Time to look happy."

"You look horrible! What happened?" McGreevy asked David as he walked into the kitchen.

"I got promoted."

"At a title fight?"

David pulled out a chair and dropped his bag down. He laughed. "To partner. Do I look that bad? It smells so good in here!"

McGreevy motioned for him to sit. "I guess you went out and... celebrated?"

"That we did!" David sat and put his elbows on the table and his face in his hands. "The partners took me out, and there were a *few* drinks. I sobered up in the cab. I had him drop me on Clark, so I could down a sandwich, but I'm still so hungry."

Rounding the table, McGreevy put a hand on David's arm. "I can do better than that! I'm just taking a roast out of the oven. Why don't you join me?"

Demurring, David held out his hands and looked away. “Naaaah, I don’t want to eat your dinner!”

“You’d be helping *me*. Truly, you would.” He smirked just as David looked away. “Besides, it would be nice to celebrate this very sudden news with you.”

“Well, if you really do have enough for two...”

“More than two.” McGreevy got up to pull plates and wine glasses from a cabinet. He nodded behind David. “Why don’t you choose a bottle...”

David turned and noticed a tall wine rack built into the wall. “How did I miss this?” he asked as he popped up to examine the labels. “Has this always been here, this wine rack?”

“Pick your favorite. I’m just sure it’s there...” McGreevy shined up two glasses. “And sometimes, David, exactly what you need appears exactly when you need it...”

He pulled a bottle. “You have a ’73 Chateau Margaux?”

McGreevy shrugged. “Let’s see if it lives up to the hype.”

“How do you have all this wine?” he asked, pulling out another vintage, then another.

McGreevy walked to the table and put the glasses down. “I just collect things over the years...here and there and everywhere.”

David admired the old label and wiped off the dust. “Well, it’s a helluva wine collection...”

McGreevy took the bottle and gave it a prideful look. David sat as McGreevy walked to the sink and opened drawers. “I’ve got a corkscrew here somewhere.”

Sitting sideways, David hung his arm over the back of the chair and sighed. “You know what, Mr. McGreevy? This is really special. Thank you.”

“Now, now, now, David, the pleasure will be *all* mine.” He found the corkscrew and fussed with the bottle for a moment. And then, a soft, elegant pop. He took a whiff. “There we are. Hello, grapes!”

David laughed. McGreevy began setting the table, and David half-stood to help, but McGreevy shook out his free hand. “No, no. This is your dinner. You’re the guest of honor.” With the flair of a fine-dining waiter, McGreevy filled both high-stemmed wine glasses and set down two dinner plates piled high.

The fragrance of the wine intertwined with the roast was intoxicating to David: the sweet smell of summer vegetables, his favorites, contrasted with the deep soul of butter melting inside a steaming potato, cracked open in foil. David closed his eyes and thought of the many pleasures of life and said a thankful prayer for this one.

“Cheers,” McGreevy said, holding up a wine glass as David opened his eyes.

David smiled and clinked. “Cheers, Mr. McGreevy. Thank you.”

They both drank and fell silent. “Mon Dieu!” exclaimed David.

“Wow,” McGreevy whispered and then laughed. “That’s quite something.”

After the first few bites, David would have stayed quiet, absorbing the pleasure of the meal, but that he had a dining companion who had cooked it. “So I know I asked if you had...someone special in your life, but what about your family? Did you grow up here in Summerdale House?”

Putting down his knife, McGreevy considered the question. "My family and I have lived here a very long time, yes. And this house is all ours."

The answer struck David as odd. Perhaps, he thought, he had crossed a line, so he changed the subject; he was not in court pressing a witness. "Well, Mr. McGreevy, this dinner is much better than the fancy lunch we had today."

"I'm glad."

David cut into the roast and watched the blood drain and pool. "Lucky for me that you were cooking such a big meal tonight! I mean, what are the odds?"

"Indeed." McGreevy smiled as he chewed. A little blood escaped his mouth, and he collected it on his finger and licked. "No, David, it's *me* who's lucky."

"This has such a unique flavor, this roast. Not like anything I've ever had. It's not gamey, exactly, but it's..." David offered, as he smacked his lips and tried to find the right words to describe it.

As he looked down at the meat on his plate, McGreevy made an *Awww, shucks* expression and raised his shoulders. "Just something I had lying around. Polish, with some German..."

A smile passed quickly, and David looked away. "Ben was Polish and German."

McGreevy smirked. "You're kidding!"

"Well," David said, looking up. "Anyway. This is delicious, Mr. McGreevy. It really is."

"It warms my heart that you think so, David."

After small talk over seconds, McGreevy cleared the plates. “Can I help?” David offered, half-standing.

“No, no, no,” he said, waving him down. “You enjoy the rest of the wine. Finish him off.”

David poured out the last few drops. “This wine is hearty. *Heavy?* I don’t think heavy is a wine word, but I can’t think of anything better. And you know, I’m not even buzzed. I just feel so...nourished.”

“As any good wine should,” McGreevy said as he returned to the table with two small plates. A circular shot of chocolate was upon each. “Enjoy!”

“You make chocolates, too?”

“These two are from that fancy new bakery at Clark & Balmoral.”

David wiped his mouth with his napkin and put the chocolate to his lips and bit. “Oh, wow! What...are they?”

“Both from France.”

“They’re delicious! Or however you say ‘delicious’ in French.”

McGreevy looked up and squinted. “*Délicieux*. I’m glad you like it, David. Here, have mine. At my age, I should watch the sweets. Would you like more roast? There’s a little more left...”

As David reached for the second chocolate, he widened his eyes. “Yes, please!”

“You know,” McGreevy started as he walked to the oven. “This roast has a really surprising flavor, doesn’t it?”

He drank. “I’ve never tasted anything quite like this.”

“It’s the funniest thing, David,” McGreevy said, opening the oven door and taking out the roast, giggling. "It's human."

David choked up a chocolate. He sipped his wine and started laughing. "Oh, OK! Sure. Give me some more human. You have such a warped sense of humor, Mr. McGreevy!"

He closed the oven door and placed the roast on a small plate soaked with dark red juices, beside David's dinner plate. David looked down, cut into the roast, and ate it with a smile.

"Now that's a beautiful sight." McGreevy settled back in his chair, watching David eat and swallow and then made a fist, bringing it gently to his forehead. "Oh, David! It completely slipped my mind. I hope you won't be angry."

David sliced another piece. "About what?" He chewed and cut yet another.

McGreevy smirked. "Someone's waiting for you."

"For *me?* Where? I didn't see anyone when I came in." He washed down the last of the wine. "Is he in the parlor?"

"No, he's not down here," McGreevy said, nodding his head toward the rear stairwell. "Upstairs. In your bedroom."

David stood. "There's someone in my bedroom? What do you mean? I have the only key. That's what you told me!"

"Someone's waiting for you in your room. He's going through your things. Right now."

David's heart started pounding. "Who!"

McGreevy stood and began clearing the plates. He winked. "Just go up. Don't keep him waiting. He doesn't like to be kept waiting." He started the faucet and dropped the plates in the sink.

"Look, Mr. McGreevy, I appreciate this dinner, but I have a real problem with you letting people into my room."

"Oh, David," McGreevy said, dipping at his knees like a jester before a king. "I'm just the messenger around here. Go on up. Go on, go, go, go!" he said, shooing him upstairs with the whisk of a hand.

Angrily, David grabbed his bag and headed up through the rear stairwell. On the third floor, he walked to his door. He tried the knob. It was locked. *McGreevy's fooling with me.*

The hall lights brightened, then dimmed, then went dark.

David grabbed his room key and opened the door. He paused, then walked in and turned on the light. But the light didn't come on. He closed the door and tried the switchplate by the bathroom. No light. And in the dark room, in the light from the window upon the floor, he saw shoes and dark pant legs, standing, shifting.

The pants moved at the knee, as if walking forward. But all else was darkness.

"Who is it?" David yelled, backing up to the wall behind him. "Who are you?"

No more movement.

David began sweating. He wiped his forehead. "Look, whoever it is..."

Into the light from the window dipped a hand, fingers curling, beckoning him close.

David stepped past the bathroom door and reached again for the light switch. On, off, on, off, but no light came. He reached in his bag for his phone, but it wouldn't activate. Click, click, click, but no light came.

Now from the shadow both hands were outstretched in the light. Palms out, for an embrace. The shoes stepped into the moonlight upon the floor. Left, then right, and then the legs disappeared as they walked toward David.

With his back at the wall, David reached for the door and tried the knob. It spun in his hand. He turned the knob the other way, and it locked up. He pulled at the doorknob, the jamb, the hinges, but nothing would move.

Running a hand out to the wall behind him, staring at the dim light from the window, he retreated to a corner where he felt safe. But his eyes couldn't adjust to the darkness around him.

And then, a voice, from across the room.

"David?"

"Ira!" David yelled. "Ira, what are you doing here?"

Behind him, a hand touched David's arm, but he turned and saw only the geometric shadows of a shawl. And he breathed in a musty smell.

"Hello, David," said a woman's voice in the darkness, touching him again.

It was Alexa.

David yanked away her hand and ran to the other side of the door. He flicked the light switch on and off and off and on, but the light didn't come. The woman followed him.

Running into the moonlight on the floor, David stood with his back to the window.

"Who are you?"

Before him, at the edge of the shadow on the floor, the shoes appeared again and moved. Left, right. David looked up but saw no body, no face, only darkness.

Two hands popped into the light, palms out again for an embrace. There was a break at the knee, a step forward and into the light appeared a face.

It was Ira.

David backed up against the window glass and screamed. Ira took another step forward. David closed his eyes and wrapped his arms around himself.

And then, a click. A click of the lights. The lights were on.

Shaking, David opened one eye and then the other and saw no one in his room.

He unwrapped his arms and walked to his door. It opened. He looked out the hallway, fully lighted.

"Mr. McGreevy?" David shouted down the hall.

Sweat ran down his face, so he walked into the bathroom to grab a hand towel. *I was just imagining things. That's all it is. Too much stress with Ben and work and I'm imagining things.* As he wiped the towel over his forehead and through his hair, he heard footsteps behind him.

Turning quickly, he saw nothing. He gulped and kept his eyes open as he dabbed his sweaty face and neck. The footsteps continued.

"Who is it?" he asked, his voice high and cracking.

"Have a seat, David," said a familiar voice. The door slammed shut and locked.

David walked out of the bathroom and looked around his room. "I can't see you. Where are you?"

"Sit. Down."

The chair pulled away from the desk and stopped in the middle of the room. And David sat.

"David," said the voice again, from the left and again from the right.

At the ceiling, at the window, at the door, at the bed—everywhere David looked he saw nothing. But the voice he heard clearly.

"David James?"

"I can hear you!" David shouted.

A loud thud behind him. David looked up at the ceiling and saw Mr. McGreevy curled up in a corner, like a spider. He rolled down the wall.

Jumping up, David grabbed the chair and held it in front of himself. McGreevy hunched and twitched, each lurch revealing a less solid form; he floated and David held the chair high. McGreevy laughed and pulled the chair from his grip, throwing it to the far wall. The lights went out.

Shutting his eyes, David held his hands over his face. Through his fingers he spied the darkness but saw nothing before him. Looking up and down and left and right, he reached out around furniture, walking carefully toward the door, and felt for the switchplate. No light came. Again the doorknob spun in his hand.

He uprighted the chair and sat, thinking of a thousand questions to ask the empty room, but he found no voice to ask them. He cleared his throat again and again until he began coughing up. The room grew cold. He reached into his shirt and held his cross tightly between his fingers.

McGreevy appeared and sat on the bed, across the room. “That won’t help you, David.” He smiled slightly. Slowly, the room illuminated, but not from the light above.

Again he cleared his throat. “What is all this? Who are you?”

“You have a choice, David James. A choice to make right now. And once you’ve made it, there’s no returning...” McGreevy stopped and guffawed. “For fuck’s sake, David, let go of that stupid cross. Only three of us are in this room, and God isn’t one.”

David stood, held the back of the chair tightly. “What are you talking about?” He looked to the window. He closed his eyes and began reciting the Lord’s Prayer.

McGreevy passed the window and sealed it with a wall. “Stop praying, David. God isn’t here.”

David began coughing up, crying. “I don’t understand this!”

McGreevy grinned. He stopped before David, and a shadow appeared beside him, with his head bowed. “You have a choice. Make it quickly or I will make it for you.”

The shadow raised his head.

“Ben?” David shouted. He reached, but his hand sailed through.

“Look at me, David. Look here, in my eyes. Look at me! You can be reunited with Ben forever, right now.”

David gasped, looking at the shadow. He gripped the chair tighter. “What do you mean?”

“Forever!” McGreevy said, petting the shadow. “In death.”

“What!” David shouted.

"Or you can walk out of Summerdale alive and enjoy all the money, all the rewards of being partner and everything after in a career more successful than you can imagine. You'll change federal law. You'll argue successfully before the Supreme Court. Twice. And you'll retire a wealthy man with The Honorable before your name. You will live another forty years, very comfortably."

David shrugged his shoulders. "That's my future?"

"All of it. You won't remember any of this, of course. No, you won't remember this little trade, so you can look genuinely surprised and not have to rehearse it in a bathroom mirror..." McGreevy paused and reveled in his shock. "Now *that's* the look, David! That's the look Ira wanted. See, it will be so important when these things happen that you actually look surprised. So you can hold that fucking cross and thank God for all the gifts THAT I GAVE YOU..." McGreevy tapped his fingers beneath David's chin, bending his neck back. "...or forego all of it to be with your heart's true love. Partner with Law. Or partner with Ben."

David's heart raced.

"But if you choose to live..." McGreevy said, smiling.

"Yes?" asked David.

"If you choose all these gifts I'm offering...you'll never see him again."

"Well, not until I'm in heaven..." David said, wiping his forehead, entirely self-assured. He patted the back of the chair.

McGreevy sneered. "No heaven. No husband. You'll belong to me, just like every other tenant who said yes." He dipped his head low and raised his eyes beyond their sockets. "Your love or your life, David James!"

David fell into the chair and cried. "What are you saying? I don't understand this."

"Yes, you do. You understand this very well, my *Christian* son." McGreevy stepped away. "This is the same choice I've given thousands and thousands and THOUSANDS before you! After they're found."

"I am found!" he shouted, nodding his head. "I am saved!" He ripped out his necklace and dangled the cross before McGreevy. "See this? He is my Lord and Savior! Not you. Nothing in my life is from you!"

McGreevy laughed and pointed to the bed. "Nothing from me, David?"

At that, still seated, David looked upon his body upon the bed, splayed out, lifeless.

"That, David, that is how you'll be found if you choose Ben."

David shot up from the chair, backed up to the wall, huddled over himself, but he couldn't take his eyes off his own lifeless body upon his old bed, their bed, the one he shared with Ben, a four-poster still in their condo.

David shouted, "That's not me! That's not how God..."

"It is you, David. Don't you see that? God isn't there, and God isn't here. Never was."

"I didn't want to be here!" Just then, the body on the bed moved. It flipped over, and David recognized himself. From the bed, his hand reached out, and David felt his arm forced toward the bed. He dug his feet into the floor to stop the pull, like a magnet, until he heard a scream. On the bed, David had shot himself.

David turned and began choking.

"Wouldn't you give ANYTHING to be with your love again?"

The shadow raised his head.

"I don't understand this!"

"David?" asked Ben softly as he held out his hand.

"Answer him, D.J.J.D." McGreevy said even softer.

David turned away and closed his eyes. He heard a distant siren and voices around his bed. The first: "I, I don't know! I heard a gunshot, and he was right here! It's David. He's my neighbor. We have each other's keys! His husband just died and I...please, just help him!"

And another voice, shouting: "OK! Clear away, clear away! Over here now! NOW!"

The voices faded. David doubled over, thinking, thinking, thinking. "No! I can't do this. I can't choose. How do I choose this?" he shouted. "My parents? I'd never see them again? Tell them I love them, tell them good-bye? This would destroy them. They're still mourning Ben! I can't leave my mom and dad!"

"You already have," McGreevy whispered, pointing at the bed. "It's done, David. You just shot yourself. Unless you choose to live for me. Time's running out..."

As David looked up, Ben walked closer and held out both hands. Around the bed, emergency techs cradled his bleeding skull.

"Your life or your love. Free yourself, David. Join us and free yourself of the worst addiction there is." McGreevy turned down his mouth and shouted at the ceiling, "For the greatest of these is *love*." He spit each word with disgust. He turned to David. "You came to me BROKEN! More broken than any addict I've ever seen."

"He just died! Ben just died! I lost the love of my life!" David felt lightheaded and began to see his own breath curling in the chilly air. Ben reached out to help David, but he backed off, staring through the shadow that looked like Ben and spoke like Ben, low and soft. The touch of his hand was like Ben's. And just at that moment, David noticed Ben wore the same shirt he had put on the morning he died. David began crying, for this was not an illusion. None of this was an illusion.

This was real.

This was Ben.

David grabbed at his ring finger. *Walk This World With Me.*

The bed rolled closer, and David looked upon his body, bleeding, motionless. Ben stood beside it. David's head began pounding and his eyesight faded.

"Quickly, David." McGreevy laughed. "Your love or your life? You can't have both. Few ever do."

David looked again at his own body. And then he looked at Ben, handsome Ben, holding out his hands, still wearing his ring.

But McGreevy grew impatient. "Stand up, David. Fall into your body on the bed and bring yourself back to life or take Ben's hand." McGreevy stepped closer, shouting, "Fall into your body, David, and the gunshot goes away!" He smirked and blinked his eyes fast. "For richer or poorer, in sickness and in health, 'til death do you part..."

David nodded, for he understood he had no more time. He inhaled all the air he could and made his choice. Closing his eyes, David stood tall and fell into Ben's waiting arms.

As they rose to the ceiling together, they both looked down over their bed, over David's body, over the medics around him. "OK. That's it. Time of death 11:59 p.m. Gunshot to the head. Zip him up for the coroner. Bus is waiting outside."

But at the ceiling, David stalled as Ben ascended. Ben knelt down, reached out both hands frantically, but he couldn't hold David with him. David stretched his arms into the ceiling rafters; his legs kicked wildly in the air, but his hands couldn't hold on. Ben disappeared, and as he disappeared, David descended into the cold air of the bedroom and slowly floated down to Mr. McGreevy.

He was smiling, McGreevy was, and he broke off David's necklace. He slipped David's wedding band from his ring finger and put it on his own, then bent David's cross in half. He threw the necklace across the room. "Do you think I'd lose a legal mind like yours to my enemy?"

Standing upright, David looked at his body, hollow but feeling, conscious but invisible. He looked at the ceiling for Ben.

McGreevy laughed. "He's gone, David. Ben is gone. Gone from your life. Forever."

"I chose him! I gave up my life for him. I did what you asked!"

McGreevy threw his head back and laughed. "Love or money, David? Always take the *money*. It lasts longer." He circled David, whose feet sank into the hardwood floor. "You could have had all the success in life that I promised you, but noooooooo," McGreevy sing-songed. "You had to choose love. Love! You gave up your life for it, just like any addict," he shouted to the ceiling, where Ben ascended. "Who cares about your parents, your family? Who cares about Ben's parents, who have to grieve your death right after their own son's? Who cares about your colleagues, your clients, all of them finding out you shot yourself? Who cares about your parents having to identify half your face in a morgue? Who cares about anyone you left behind? Not you!"

David shook his head. "No! That's not..."

"Don't be too disappointed. I tried to corrupt that good heart of yours, but I had my doubts you'd choose the money." He smirked. "So I took out a little insurance on you."

The floor was in David's knees.

"Insurance?"

"Ha, insurance!" McGreevy snapped. "Now *there's* an industry I know well."

"What do you mean?" he screamed to the ceiling, waving his arms.

"You ate a human, David. The flesh of three, actually. One to honor the Father, one for the Son, and one especially for the Holy Ghost."

He shook his head from side to side and put out his arms to prop himself on the floor. "No. No, I didn't!"

"Yes. Yes, you did, or you wouldn't be sent down. No, I just couldn't allow..." He cocked his mouth open to the side, like a ventriloquist's dummy. "For you to go up to heaven and be with the love of your life!"

David began spitting up, then knocked his own stomach to force open his throat. He vomited across the floor.

He pulled at his tongue, widened his mouth, and coughed out something spongy that rolled from his lips across the floor.

It was a finger. As David looked closer, ants dropped out of a tendon and crawled around the floor, pulling trails of blood with their legs. They crawled onto the discolored skin and rounded the base, forming a ring. Becoming a ring. A wedding ring.

Ben's.

David threw up again.

"Poor Ben!" McGreevy frowned. "It hurt me to show him what you and Eric did together..."

David shook his head, still coughing. "You're lying!"

"When Ben was here...."

"You're LYING!"

"At Summerdale House. Just before you. And he was so angry with you, David. So *angry* that he led you right here himself. To this very room. Where he died, what is it now, three weeks ago? Four? Oh, who's counting?"

"You're LYING!" David screamed again.

"So when you ask yourself, What could I have done to save the love of my life? *Not* fucking Eric would have been a good place to start. You remember, don't you, David? Ben suspected something right away, and you lied to him, right to his face. And when you lied to him, he withdrew from you, and he showed up at my door and poured out his little broken heart. To me. Which you just ate."

"You're a LIAR! Ben would never hurt me!"

"Just like you would *never* hurt him, right? That's the thing about love. You think they'll never hurt you back. And they always do. But he kept a secret from you, too, David. His little addiction. When he knew you weren't being faithful. And that's when he came to find solace with me. When he was *found*."

"You're lying!" David looked up at McGreevy with disgust. "You're a liar! What *are* you?"

"Not what, David. *Who*." McGreevy swung his arms in fast circles, like propellers, to chill the air. The timbre of his voice dropped so low that the floorboards wobbled: "I'm beneath a body, a human, David, that looks and speaks to you in a way that you understand. Nine, eight, seven hundred years ago, I looked and spoke differently than I will seven, eight, nine hundred years from now." McGreevy turned his back and raised his hands high, adjoining them finger to finger, palm to palm. He pulled in his thumbs, tipping up his fingers into a steeple. "Who am I, David? This is a church." McGreevy turned slightly and smiled. "Here's the steeple. Open the doors..." And McGreevy's hands blew apart. The red gush from his wrists dried midair into razor-winged locusts that tumbled to the floor by the hundreds and scurried upon David. After chewing away his clothes, they latched upon his naked body, biting holes into his sweaty skin to inject larva into his rich, sweet marrow. And he couldn't push them off, not one. Then at once, they burrowed out and returned to the air. The wail of whipping wings faded as the locusts returned to their nest, regenerating McGreevy's aging body with David's siphoned blood. "Who am I?" McGreevy asked again, smirking. "I think you know."

David sank lower into the floor. He kicked his legs through the ceiling below but that pulled him in deeper, like quicksand. The taste of varnish coated his throat, and he began coughing up sawdust. The locusts had bit into him so deeply that they exposed his tendons.

Plinking together his healed fingers, McGreevy looked down at David. "Your legal mind under my control will be very useful. I can feel the Union Park case turning my way already. With so many more to come. So many rights to reverse. That sweet, maple-paneled Wisconsin veneer of yours with pure Hell beneath it. Think of the votes you'll get when you run for judge! You will do great things, David. For *me*."

David's arms dipped into the hardwood as he tried to prop himself up. "For you? *How?*" David looked at the rising floorboards surrounding him, nearly at his shoulders. Deeper into the floorboards David fell until his entire body disappeared, and the screams of his soft, deep voice with it.

Energized by his blood meal, McGreevy stomped down hard, and again, at the floorboards David had fallen through. Then he noticed that he had left a scuff. He knelt down and spit on the floor, then smoothed it dry with the side of a hand. McGreevy stood and took off David's ring, dropping it into his shirt pocket. He patted his chest, satisfied.

As McGreevy closed his eyes to disappear, he felt a quiver beneath his feet. The twisting grain of the wooden floorboards whirled and turned, reversed, unwound. The floor softened and dissolved—only McGreevy's weightlessness kept him from falling through. Low beneath him, he looked directly into the basement at thousands of arms twisting and legs kicking, reaching for anything to hoist themselves up, out, away, free: a swarm of bodies wading within a pool of red, but one body—only one—began floating upward.

The hands of the others in the pool grabbed at the body ascending. But their every lunge, every grasp, every swing at freedom failed, for they could not hold what they could not have. Rising through the empty first floor, then the second, blood from the pool below slid off the ascending body and filled and fed every floorboard crack and crevice, every grain and split, restoring the wooden floors of Summerdale House until, in the third-floor bedroom, the body stalled eye-level with McGreevy. And then David awoke, floating.

McGreevy dropped a fist hard into David's neck, but stumbled through and knocked himself into a far wall. Turning, McGreevy's eyes widened and reddened as he screamed at the ceiling in a language David didn't understand. The ceiling opened to the light of a morning sky, and David reached up for Ben's waiting hands. "You're safe with me now. He lied to you about everything. I love you, David, and I forgive you," Ben said.

"I love you, too, Ben, and I'm sorry," David said. They held each other as they ascended, and the ceiling closed beneath them.

David's bedroom slowly faded. David's Summerdale slowly faded. McGreevy reordered the bedroom as if David had never lived there. Because the next tenant was waiting outside.

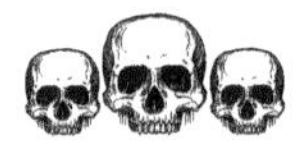

There was a knock at the front door of Summerdale House. McGreevy opened it with one hand; in the other, he held the FOR RENT sign.

"Hi," said a good-looking young man. Despite the heat, he wore sweats and a long-sleeve T-shirt. Despite his youth, dark circles ringed both eyes. "Sorry," he said as he scratched his right forearm. "I was just wondering if you had a room open."

"Come on in," McGreevy said, fluttering the FOR RENT sign. "Today's your lucky day!"

"Thank you, mister..."

"McGreevy. Name's McGreevy. I'm the landlord." He smiled and extended his hand. "Nice to meet you, Mark."

A look of surprise. "How'd you know my name?"

McGreevy pulled up Mark's sleeve and examined the swollen scabs. "Looks like you've been waiting outside about a year."

Mark dropped his sleeve and shook his head. "I've never been here before. I've never seen this house before."

McGreevy scrunched up his nose. "Why don't you go have a seat in the kitchen, right back there? I just put on some coffee. Grab a mug from the rack. Make yourself at home." McGreevy shooed him along,

"Go on, go on! Go, go, go!"

As Mark sauntered into the kitchen, McGreevy looked outside, beyond his front porch, onto Summerdale & Wayne. Hundreds of stone-faced souls were lined up, as far as he could see. Smiling, McGreevy whispered to himself, "Of all the houses of all my siblings around the world, these souls wait at Summerdale House."

All souls stood quietly, unaware that they were queued up together in the same long line. But none stepped forward after Mark, so McGreevy nodded. "Take your time, everyone. I'll be with you soon enough..." As he closed the door, he looked at the sign before tucking it in a drawer in the hall tree. "This old FOR RENT sign doesn't last five minutes anymore."

"This coffee's dope, Mr. McGreevy!" Mark called from the kitchen. "Hey, that room—the one for rent? Is it available now?"

"It sure is, Mark," McGreevy called back. "My last tenant left Summerdale just this morning. Give some thought to what you want your room to look like." McGreevy turned toward the kitchen but stopped. He stepped back from the hall tree and stared at himself.

In the mirror, he admired his pocked, mottled skin and looked deep into the swirling red pools of his eyes as dismembered arms and heads splashed within them. Thick, veiny wings unfurled and settled out beyond his wide, muscled shoulders.

McGreevy walked into the kitchen and turned on a smile. "Welcome home, Mark. We're ready for you. Now let's go upstairs and look at your bedroom..."

SUMMERDALE II

October 2020

ABOUT THE AUTHOR

David Jay Collins lives in Chicago. Summerdale is the beginning of his horror novel series. Gaybash is his first novel.

Follow David at davidjaycollins.com

ABOUT THE ARTIST

Thom Collins (AKA tdcollins) is an award-winning artist and designer from Hermosa Beach, California, currently living in Pleasant View, Tennessee. Thom now focuses on writing and illustrating graphic novels.

View his work at tdcollins.com and 5ive9ine2wo.com

CPSIA information can be obtained
at www.ICGtesting.com
Printed in the USA
FSHW010335030619
58661FS